OCT 2022

THE PLOT AND THE PENDULUM

THE PLOT AND
THE PENDULUM

Jenn McKinlay

BERKLEY PRIME CRIME
New York

BERKLEY PRIME CRIME
Published by Berkley
An imprint of Penguin Random House LLC
penguinrandomhouse.com

Library of Congress Cataloging-in-Publication Data

Names: McKinlay, Jenn, author.
Title: The plot and the pendulum / Jenn McKinlay.
Description: New York: Berkley Prime Crime, [2022] |
Series: A library lover's mystery Identifiers: LCCN 2022016727 (print) |
LCCN 2022016728 (ebook) | ISBN 9780593101803 (hardcover) |
ISBN 9780593101827 (ebook)
Subjects: LCGFT: Detective and mystery fiction. | Novels.
Classification: LCC PS3612.A948 P58 2022 (print) |
LCC PS3612.A948 (ebook) | DDC 813/.6—dc23/eng/20220407
LC record available at https://lccn.loc.gov/2022016727
LC ebook record available at https://lccn.loc.gov/2022016728

Printed in the United States of America
1st Printing

Book design by Laura K. Corless

For Christina Hogrebe, agent extraordinaire, who crafted the brilliant title for this book. I could not ask for a smarter, savvier, more professional representative, and I am ever grateful that you're mine.

THE PLOT AND THE PENDULUM

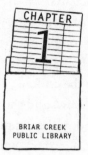

CHAPTER
1

BRIAR CREEK
PUBLIC LIBRARY

Lindsey Norris, director of the Briar Creek Public Library, was seated at the reference desk gazing out the window overlooking the bay and the archipelago called the Thumb Islands. The large maple tree on the front lawn of the library was in its final stages of autumn vibrancy, and the leaves were dropping like colorful confetti every time the breeze coming in from the ocean stirred the tree's limbs.

October was here, which indicated that shorter days were coming and winter would follow soon with fires in the fireplace and days spent reading while the snow piled up outside. Lindsey was more than ready for some quality binge reading. Bring it on.

She glanced around the library, watching the comings and goings of the patrons and staff. She liked to pause every now and then and try to see the library from a visitor's per-

spective. Was the interior engaging? Did it invite people to
linger? Were there plenty of the most in-demand items? How
comfortable were the chairs? Lindsey considered all of it.

Colorful displays of books greeted patrons when they
first arrived, and seasonal ephemera decorated the windows. The library staff changed them out regularly to keep
them interesting. Was the building clean? Yes, the town had
an amazing cleaning crew, and the staff made it a practice
to sweep through and gather materials left on the study
tables several times per day. Was it friendly? Lindsey
glanced at the first point of contact for patrons. The circulation desk.

Ms. Cole, the head of circulation, was stationed at the
desk. She was wearing a white blouse with navy slacks,
which was a shocking departure from her usual monochro-
matic style consisting only of shades of blue, whether they
were complementary or not. Formerly, Ms. Cole had been
nicknamed "the lemon" for her puckered personality, but
she'd mellowed over the past few years and was presently
running unopposed in next month's mayoral election.

Lindsey was resigned to losing Ms. Cole to her govern-
mental duties, and despite the many ups and downs their
relationship had endured since Lindsey's arrival, she knew
she would miss Ms. Cole and her pragmatic ways. There
was a steadfastness about her that was rare in employees
these days. Still, as a lifelong resident of the town, with an
unparalleled institutional memory, Eugenia Cole was going
to make a fantastic mayor.

Before Lindsey could get too maudlin, a scarecrow wandered past her desk, leaving a trail of paper leaves in his wake as a pack of children followed, collecting the maple, oak, and birch leaves with the excitement only a group of toddlers could bring to such an activity. Lindsey met the scarecrow's gaze, and he winked at her over the heads of the children.

Aidan Barker, the library's temporary story time person, was dressed in patched overalls that sported big, brightly colored felt pockets sewn over the knees and bib, a flannel shirt, and a straw hat that perched on his head just off center enough to make him look friendly. The kids gathered the leaves and raced back to him, stuffing his felt pockets until they were bursting.

A young boy who looked to be about three shoved a handful of leaves into one of the pockets on Aidan's knees, patted the flannel and said, "Here's your insides, Mr. Scarecrow."

"Thank you, young man," Aidan replied. Then he did a little jig as if adjusting his leaves. The boy laughed and scampered off to find more.

The child's mother smiled, carrying a sleeping baby in her arms, and said, "This is brilliant. Maybe I can get him to do some leaf pickup in our yard when we get home."

The scarecrow tipped his hat to her as she chased after her son.

Lindsey smiled and said, "Wild guess here. You're reading about scarecrows in story time?"

Aidan said, "Correct. We're reading *The Scarecrow's Hat, Scaredycrow* and *Barn Dance!*"

"The kids will love it," she said. She gestured to the big maple outside the window. "Perfect timing, really."

"I hope so," he said. "My wife is a tough act to follow."

Aidan was the husband of Beth Barker, the library's regular children's librarian who was out on an extended maternity leave with their newborn daughter Beverly, named for the beloved children's book author Beverly Cleary, who had recently passed. During Beth's final stages of delivery, there had been some labor-induced talk of naming the baby Ramona or Beezus, but Aidan had prevailed and Beverly won out.

"How are Beth and baby Bee today?" Lindsey asked. In addition to being her children's librarian, Beth was also Lindsey's best friend, and while they talked often, Lindsey had been giving the new mother some space, mostly to rest around the rigorous nursing and diaper-changing schedule she'd been maintaining for the past few months.

"Amazing," he said. "They're both just amazing." His voice held a note of awe. "But Beth is ready to get back to the library. I think she needs to talk to some grown-ups, use her creativity, and get away from the constant cycle of nurse, nap, poop, rinse, repeat."

"We can't wait to have her back," Lindsey said. "Not that you haven't been wonderful, but . . ."

"No, I understand completely," he said. "This is definitely Beth's space, and I am just a placeholder. Thank you for arranging a job share so she can come back part-time. I don't think she'd be willing to leave Bee otherwise, and this will give me a chance to be home with the baby while she works. I expect to level up my bottle-feeding and rocking-to-sleep skills."

"I'm glad it worked out. And thank you for filling in for her story times. I don't think she'd trust anyone else," Lindsey said.

"It helped that my library director is a new parent, too," Aidan said. "She gets it."

Aidan was a children's librarian in a neighboring town, and he and Beth had met while performing dueling story times. When Beth went on maternity leave, Aidan's library director agreed to lend him out for the story times in Briar Creek until Beth was ready to come back.

"Is there any chance we'll see Beth today for crafternoon?" Lindsey asked.

"I know she read this week's book *The Code of the Woosters* by P. G. Wodehouse," he said. "So, she's planning to attend, but it's really up to baby Bee and the sort of day she's having."

Lindsey nodded. "Understood."

"Mr. Scarecrow, can we have stories now?" a little girl asked. Her hair was twisted into tight spirals on top of her head and held in place by hairbands sporting brightly colored flowers. She was trailing a very grubby and clearly well-loved blanket behind her. Lindsey squinted at it. She thought it might have been a nice shade of lavender at one time, but now it was a tired hue of pale gray. The girl's father followed her, carrying a bag that was already full to bursting with picture books.

"Of course, let's go get started," Aidan said.

Lindsey didn't think she imagined the relieved look on the father's face. He barely suppressed a grunt when he picked up the bag of books and hurried after his daughter, who was skipping toward the story time room.

Aidan clapped his hands in a short pattern, and the children stopped what they were doing and clapped back. And just like that, they had gathered the last of the leaves and exited the main area of the library, leaving sweet silence in their wake.

The quiet that followed their departure was short lived.

"Hot dish. Hot dish. Coming through," a voice announced to no one in particular.

Lindsey swiveled on her chair and saw Paula Turner walking through the main room of the library. She had two oven mitts on her hands and was cradling a casserole dish that was giving off steam. She was headed toward the meeting room where they held their weekly crafternoon sessions.

"Go ahead, boss," Ann Marie Martin said as she joined Lindsey behind the desk. A former library assistant, Ann Marie had been promoted to the position of adult services librarian when she graduated from library school last spring. As the mother to two rambunctious tween boys, she considered this job her oasis from the chaos. "I've got the desk."

"Thanks. I don't have any questions to turn over to you. Other than a visit from a scarecrow, it's been very uneventful."

"I'll take that as a good omen for getting my adult programming calendar done, then." Ann Marie smiled. Quiet moments in the library, which was the center of their small community, were rare.

Lindsey hopped up from her seat and hurried after Paula. She wanted to make certain the meeting room door was open for her since Paula appeared to have her hands full.

"What's in the hot dish?" Lindsey asked as she caught up to Paula. "It smells amazing."

"Sweet potato casserole with a crunchy pecan streusel." Paula glanced at her. "And that's just to start."

Lindsey opened the door, and Paula entered the room. The table where the crafternoon members gathered to discuss a book, work on a craft and eat was fully loaded with food. It looked like a whole feast had been prepared.

"You've been busy," Lindsey said.

"Don't tell the others, but you are my test subjects," Paula said. She put the casserole dish on a trivet in the center of the table and tossed her vibrant orange braid over her shoulder. Paula dyed her hair with the seasons or her mood, whichever motivated her the most when she was getting it done. It had been a pumpkin shade of orange for the past month.

"Test subjects?" Lindsey asked. She wasn't sure she liked the sound of that.

"My parents are coming for Thanksgiving, and my dad is a meat-and-potatoes guy," Paula explained. "Honestly, if there isn't a slab of dead animal in the center of the feast, he feels deprived. I'm hoping I can serve a fully vegetarian meal, and he won't be disappointed. Thus we have the sweet potato casserole, figs in a blanket, salt-and-pepper radish chips and cornbread, because cornbread goes with everything."

"Agreed." Lindsey nodded. "You're a braver woman than me. I would never subject anyone to my cooking by hosting a holiday meal."

Paula laughed. "Good thing your sister-in-law owns the Blue Anchor restaurant so you don't have to."

"I married up," Lindsey agreed.

She glanced out the window at the town pier, hoping to catch a glimpse of her husband, Mike Sullivan, known as Sully to his family and friends. In addition to piloting the local water taxi that serviced the residents of the Thumb Islands, he also ran a seasonal tour boat. The pier was empty, so she assumed he was out on the water. That was another reason she enjoyed winter, more time with her husband at home as his tour schedule diminished.

"Are we late?" Violet La Rue asked as she and Nancy Peyton appeared in the doorway.

As the retired Broadway actress she was, Violet entered the room dramatically in her usual flowing caftan with her silver hair held back in a bun at the nape of her neck. With her deep brown skin, large dark eyes and prominent cheekbones, she was a strikingly handsome woman, and people always turned to watch her when she crossed a room. Violet made every entrance look like a jaunt on the red carpet.

"We can't be. We're never late," Nancy Peyton said. Short in height with wavy hair that was slowly turning from silver to pure white and sparkling blue eyes, Nancy was a "Creeker," meaning she'd been born and raised in Briar Creek and had never left. Widowed young, she owned an old captain's house on the water, which she'd converted into three apartments, one of which Lindsey had lived in when she first arrived in town to work as the library director.

While technically senior citizens, both Nancy and Violet were incredibly active in the community. Best friends, they represented what Lindsey hoped she and Beth would be one day, growing old together and still getting up to shenanigans. They were also two of Lindsey's favorite residents and had been with the crafternoon club since the very beginning.

Lindsey noticed that they both carried their tote bags with their latest craft project, which was crochet. She sighed. The only part of crafternoon that Lindsey didn't care for was the craft part. She was equally awful at all handicrafts, and no matter how hard she tried, she couldn't craft to save her life. The crocheted bucket hats they were working on were an exercise in torture.

"Where's your project?" Paula asked, looking pointedly at Lindsey's empty hands.

"Did you know Sir Pelham Grenville Wodehouse was called Plum by his friends and family?" Lindsey asked.

"She's changing the subject," Nancy said to the others. "That means she's made a muddle of her crochet."

"Who made a muddle of their crochet?" a voice asked. They all turned to the door to see Beth arrive, pushing a stroller.

"Baby Bee is here," Nancy cried, keeping her voice soft in case the baby was sleeping.

Any talk of crochet was forgotten as they all gathered round to admire the baby, for which Lindsey was grateful. She really didn't want to trot out the tangle of butternut squash—colored yarn in front of her friends. It was supposed to be a hat but looked more like an angry mitten. She joined the group as they gazed in wonder at Beth's little girl.

At five months old, Bee was a pudgy butterball of unparalleled cuteness. She had her mother's dark hair and pert nose and her father's dimpled chin and pretty eyes. She blinked at them, not at all alarmed to have so many faces peering down at her.

Beth unfastened the strap that secured Bee and hefted her out of the stroller. Nancy was there with her arms outstretched, and Beth handed her over, clearly happy to share. Bee gurgled at Nancy, who looked enchanted.

Beth stretched her arms over her head and then sat on one of the sofas, looking content to rest for a minute. Nancy walked the baby about the room with Violet by her side, reciting sweet baby rhymes that had Bee mesmerized.

"I knew it was a genius idea to read this week's book," Beth said. She watched Nancy and Violet and then wagged her eyebrows at Paula and Lindsey. "Now I can sit here and eat lunch without interruption for the first time in months."

"I hope you like sweet potatoes," Paula said.

"Love them," Beth assured her.

"Lindsey, there's a man waiting for you out in the

lobby," Ms. Cole said as she entered the room, clutching her crochet bag and a copy of this week's book.

"Oh?" Lindsey asked. Ms. Cole appeared agitated, which was unusual for the normally unflappable librarian.

"I would have sent him away, but I believe he's *William Dorchester*," Ms. Cole explained in a hushed tone.

Nancy gasped. Her eyes were wide, and Nancy stared over the baby's head at Ms. Cole, as if she couldn't believe what she'd just heard. The rest of the crafternooners glanced between the two women, trying to figure out why this name made them so disconcerted. Violet took the opportunity to lift the baby from Nancy's arms, and Nancy didn't object, showing how distracted she was.

"William Dorchester? Are you sure?" Nancy asked Ms. Cole.

"Not one hundred percent," Ms. Cole admitted. "It's been years since I've seen him, after all, but he does have the Dorchester high forehead just like his father and grandfather, assuming he is William the Third. I tried to get his name, but he said he preferred not to give it."

"That's weird," Paula said. "If he wants to talk to Lindsey, he should give his name."

Lindsey silently agreed.

"Oh, dear," Nancy said. "If it is William, why do you suppose he's here?"

"No idea," Ms. Cole said. "He was very circumspect about his business."

The group was silent while taking this in, and Lindsey wondered if she was about to deal with an overly aggressive salesman or an aggrieved patron. Neither one of which would be good for her digestion.

"Not to make it all about me, but I have a casserole here that's getting cold," Paula said.

At the mention of food, the ladies adjusted their priorities accordingly and moved to take their seats at the table.

"Before I go out there, can I ask why the arrival of William Dorchester, if that's who this man is, is so shocking?" Lindsey asked.

Nancy looked at Ms. Cole, who nodded while spooning some of Paula's casserole onto her plate.

"Because he's the son of Marion Dorchester," Nancy said. "You know, the old lady who lives in the neglected old mansion on the edge of town. As far as I know, he hasn't been back here since . . ."

"The runaway bride went missing," Ms. Cole said.

"I was going to say nineteen eight-nine," Nancy said. She looked annoyed to have her thunder stolen.

"Runaway bride?" Beth asked. She was munching on a fig in a blanket. "Tell us more."

Lindsey glanced at the clock, aware that she was keeping the man waiting. "Abridged version, please."

"William Dorchester was in love with Grace Hartwell, but his mother, Marion, refused to let him marry Grace as she deemed her unsuitable or, more accurately, too poor," Nancy said. "Grace married Timothy Little instead—"

"The Little League coach?" Paula asked. "The one who's married to Barbara and has the twin grandsons that he brings into the library all the time?"

"Yes, that's Tim," Nancy said. "He was married to Grace, but she went missing six weeks after their wedding. He and William Dorchester had a terrible fight as William accused Tim of murdering Grace. Tim denied it, naturally."

"Tim Little was accused of murder? How have I never heard of this?" Beth asked. "I've known Tim and Barbara for years. I didn't even know that he'd been married before."

"It was thirty-three years ago, and there was never any proof of foul play," Ms. Cole said. "They never found a body, and Tim had an alibi. William left town after Grace disappeared, swearing to his mother that he would never marry—to spite her—and he hasn't been seen since."

"He never returned, not once, in all these years," Nancy said. She frowned. "I wonder what brings him here now?"

Lindsey blew out a breath. "Well, I suppose I'll go find out."

CHAPTER

2

BRIAR CREEK
PUBLIC LIBRARY

L indsey had been gone for only a little while, but the library had entered its second phase of the day. After the children in the morning, the library became a hive of early afternoon activity. Milton Duffy was setting up for his chess club in one of the study rooms. Mary Ellen Denton was prepping a section of the children's area for her granddaughter's Girl Scout troop. She'd told Lindsey yesterday that they were coming by to work on building bat houses, which was their badge project. Meanwhile, in the corner of the library by the large window with the comfy armchairs, the local investment club was gathered to debate their latest investments. Lindsey heard someone say, "Bitcoin," which was received with many groans, and she made a mental note to check on their resources for investing in cryptocurrency, because she'd bet dollars to donuts—breakfast being much more reliable than digital money in her opinion— that someone in the investment club was going to ask.

Lindsey approached the front desk, where Sue Gideon, one of their new part-time circulation attendants, was checking in materials. Sue smiled at Lindsey. Her brown hair was trimmed in a low-maintenance pixie cut, and she wore enormous earrings as if to compensate for the lack of hair. Today's were overly large beaded hoops, very festive. Sue was a retired schoolteacher who loved books and people, so she was perfect for the library.

"Hi, Sue," Lindsey said. "I was told there is someone waiting to speak to me?"

"He's right there." Sue tipped her head toward the end of the desk.

Lindsey glanced past Sue and noticed a middle-aged man standing off to the side who had a brown leather backpack hanging off one shoulder and looked as if he was waiting for someone. Presumably her.

"Thanks," she said. She took a moment to study him as she approached.

He appeared to be in his mid to late fifties with fine wrinkles in his deeply tanned skin. His hair was silver and receding from his large forehead, just as Ms. Cole had said. He was dressed well but not appropriately for the season given that he was wearing expensive sneakers and khaki shorts with a red polo shirt. His only concession to the cooler temperatures was the heavy navy blue windbreaker he had on.

"Hi, I'm Lindsey Norris," she said. She extended her hand. "The library director."

"William Dorchester," he said. "Thanks for meeting with me on such short notice."

Mr. Dorchester shook her hand in a firm grip. She noted he had deep brown eyes and a nose that was slightly crooked, as if it had been broken. He didn't smile when he greeted her. Instead, the tight set to his lips was grim as if he wasn't happy to be here.

Lindsey kept her face blank as if she'd never heard the name before. Weren't Ms. Cole and Nancy going to be surprised to discover they'd been right?

"No problem," Lindsey said. She tried not to think about the sweet potato casserole and figs in a blanket she'd left behind. "Would you like to speak in my office?"

Mr. Dorchester glanced around the library as if checking to see if anyone was listening. He nodded and said, "That might be for the best."

"This way." Lindsey led him behind the circulation desk and through the workroom where the book trucks with the returns were parked.

She kept the door to her office open and gestured for him to take the seat across from her desk. He sat and unzipped his jacket, making himself more comfortable.

"Can I get you anything? Coffee? Water?" she asked.

"No, thank you," he said. "I only have a few minutes, and then I have to get back to my mother."

"How can I help you?" she asked.

"My mother is Marion Dorchester," he said. "I'm sure

you've heard of the Dorchester mansion on the outskirts of town." Lindsey nodded. Everyone knew of the Dorchester mansion. It was one of the oldest homes in Briar Creek and was a favorite stop on the historic homes tour, although no one had ever been allowed on the premises, and it could be viewed only from the street. "She's no longer able to care for herself, so I'm here to sell her home and use the money to put her in an assisted-living facility."

"I'm sorry to hear that," Lindsey said. "I imagine it's a very difficult task."

"Thank you, but it's fine," he said. "My mother and I aren't close. In fact, we haven't seen each other in over thirty years. The past few days have been difficult, to say the least."

Lindsey nodded. This made sense. She hadn't lived in Briar Creek long, but it wasn't a big community, and if William Dorchester had ever come to town, she was certain she would have heard about it, especially given the dramatic events leading to his departure.

"What can I do to help you?" she asked. "We have a wide variety of resources available for dealing with eldercare, and I can get you in touch with some of the local support groups as well."

"Thank you." William looked momentarily nonplussed. "But that's not why I'm here."

"Oh?"

"No, you see, I find I am in the position of clearing out several generations of Dorchester possessions," he said. "One of which is the family library."

"Oh, I see," Lindsey said. "Do you know what you want to do with the books?"

She'd had this conversation before with people clearing out their parents' or their own houses. It was a conversation she dreaded. Yes, she considered books sacred, and she was not the world's greatest weeder when it came to the collection, but when patrons came to her with water-stained, tobacco-infused, moldy books that were of no value—none—it was frequently difficult to get them to see that the book had ceased to be worth keeping when half of its pages were missing. In fact, people generally believed that if the book was old, it must be worth something. Nope. That just wasn't how it worked. She braced herself.

"I want them gone," he said. "I'd like to donate them to the library, and if you want to throw them out, sell them in a book sale, or add them to the collection, that's fine with me."

Lindsey felt her spine relax. Mr. Dorchester was being very realistic about the situation. Excellent. The Friends of the Library regularly sorted through donated boxes of books, and they were very discerning about what made it into their book sale. This would be no problem.

"Would you like us to come and pick up the books?" she asked. "Or do you have them with you?"

He smiled at her humorlessly. "This collection is more than a few boxes, I'm afraid."

"Oh." Lindsey pursed her lips and then asked, "Any idea how many volumes are in the collection?"

"Twelve thousand, give or take a few," he said.

Lindsey blinked. That was a considerable collection.

"They have been well kept and for the most part are in mint condition," he said. "Here, I brought one with me."

He opened the backpack he'd put on the floor at his feet. Inside was an archival box, which she recognized from her days working in rare books. He placed it on Lindsey's desk and lifted the lid. Lindsey gasped when she saw the distinctive bright blue cover with four gilt stars.

"Is that a first edition of *The Adventures of Tom Sawyer*?" she asked. She could feel her archivist fingers itching to touch the book.

"Here." Mr. Dorchester reached into his backpack and retrieved a pair of white cotton gloves. He held them out to her with a smile as if he understood her excitement. It was the first genuine moment of good humor Lindsey had seen from him.

She pulled on the gloves and very gently opened the cover. Inside it read, "1876. Published by the American Publishing Company in Hartford, Connecticut." There was some wear on the gilt title on the spine, and the woven cloth cover was worn on the corners, but it was in excellent condition.

"This book is worth thousands of dollars," she said. "Are you sure you want to donate it to us?"

"Yes," he said. "I don't need the money. The sale of the house will more than cover my mother's needs, and I have no interest in trying to sell the books or find someone to sell them for me. I am trying to make this entire transaction as quick and as painless as possible for everyone involved."

Lindsey didn't know what to say. Never had a patron come to her with something old that had actually proved to have value. She wasn't sure the library was the appropriate place to maintain such items.

"I'm happy to donate the cabinetry, too," he said. "Part of the reason the rare books are in such good shape is because they've been kept in glass cases. Not all of the books are first editions. There are many that I'm sure have no value, and of course you can do with them as you will."

Lindsey pondered the book on her desk. This was a quite a gift he was offering the library, and she was grateful, but something also felt off about the situation.

"This is incredibly generous of you, Mr. Dorchester," she said.

"Please call me William."

"All right, and I'm Lindsey," she said. She glanced back down at the book. "I know that you said you didn't care, but even if you just have a few volumes like this, that's a tremendous amount of money. Are you quite sure you don't want to have them appraised or donate them to a much worthier institution? I think there's quite a profit to be made if you have more books of this caliber."

"I'm not interested in profit. I'd like them to go to the library," he said. "My family has never contributed to the well-being of the community, so this is my way of making amends."

"All right," Lindsey said. "Perhaps we can install a plaque and call it the Dorchester Collection."

He shook his head. "That's not necessary, although I

appreciate the thought. I don't want to rush you, but I'm hoping to put the house on the market as swiftly as possible. Once my mother is settled in an assisted-living facility, I'll be going back to my home in Florida."

"Oh, yes, of course," Lindsey said. "I'm certain I can get a group of volunteers together, and we should be able to box up the books and put them in our storage room, where they'll be safe. It might take us a few weekends to get it done."

"That would be fine," he said. "I imagine it will take at least a month to make the house presentable for selling."

Lindsey thought about her crafternoon group. She knew she could count on them to chip in. Her friend Carrie Rushton, who ran the Friends of the Library, would help them, too. She hoped she wasn't overpromising, but even if she was, it couldn't be helped. Until she saw the extent of the collection, she had no idea how hard it would be to move all of the materials.

"Would it be possible to stop by this weekend and assess the collection?" she asked. "I can be more accurate in estimating how long it will take after I see it."

"Absolutely," he said. "Saturday morning at ten?"

"Perfect," she said. She couldn't believe she was going to enter the Dorchester mansion. Milton Duffy, the president of the historical society, was going to be beyond jealous.

William rose to his feet and Lindsey did the same. He shook her hand one more time and said, "This is a huge help to me. Thank you."

"You're very welcome," she said. "If you change your mind and want a plaque on the door, I'll make it happen."

He laughed, and there was genuine mirth in the sound. "No, thank you, my family doesn't deserve that sort of recognition. Frankly, breaking up the library is going to kill my mother . . . or at least I can hope it will."

Lindsey felt her mouth form the shape of an O. She had no idea what to say to that. She opened the top drawer of her desk and selected a business card. She handed it to him and said, "In case you need to get in touch with me, this has my office number and my cell phone."

"Thank you," he said. "I'll leave that volume with you, if that's all right."

"Sure," she said. She had wanted to examine it more closely, but now it felt tainted by the spite that William had displayed for his mother.

"If there's any conflict with Saturday, I'll let you know. Otherwise, I'll see you then."

She walked him back through the workroom to the lobby.

"Have a good day, Mr. Dor . . . er . . . William," she said.

"You, too, Lindsey," he said. He headed toward the front door and waved at her on his way out.

Lindsey waited until he was out of sight and then hurried back to the office, boxed up the first edition and put it in the library safe for security purposes. She then strode back to the crafternoon room, eager to enlist the help of her squad in Saturday's project.

There was a lively discussion happening when she opened the door, and no one noticed her return.

"Bertie is my favorite character," Nancy said. "He drives the entire narrative with his shenanigans."

"I'm partial to Jeeves," Ms. Cole said. "He is a gentleman's gentleman, and it's his ingenuity that saves the day."

"He is a perfect foil," Paula agreed. "You can't have Bertie without Jeeves and vice versa."

Lindsey shut the door behind her and made her way to the food table. She was starving.

"Well?" Nancy asked.

Lindsey grabbed a plate and loaded up on casserole, figs in a blanket and radish chips. "Well what?"

"Is he William Dorchester?" Ms. Cole demanded.

Lindsey glanced at the table. In addition to the others, Charlene La Rue, Violet's daughter, and Mary Murphy, Sully's sister, had joined them. All eyes were on Lindsey, but she took her seat at the table before she answered.

"I think Jeeves is my favorite as well," she said. There was a collective groan, and she smiled. "All right, all right, yes. It was William Dorchester."

Nancy gasped and Ms. Cole nodded as if unsurprised to have her suspicions confirmed.

"What did he say? Why is he here? What did he want to talk to you about?" Nancy's rapid-fire questions gave Lindsey no chance to answer.

She took a bite of the casserole while Nancy caught her breath. It was delicious. "This is excellent, Paula."

"Thank you," Paula said. She tossed her orange braid over her back. "So, what did Mr. Dorchester want?"

Lindsey chomped on a fig in a blanket. "This is also really good."

Paula made a circular gesture with her hand as if to say, *Keep going.*

"Shouldn't we explain who William Dorchester is to Mary and Charlene?" Lindsey asked.

"They did while you were gone," Charlene said. "Quite the mystery about the runaway bride. I might have to do a follow-up story on it for the news."

Charlene, just as beautiful as her mother, was a broadcast journalist in New Haven.

"They didn't have to tell me," Mary said. "I grew up listening to the story of the runaway bride. She became a cautionary tale to all of us girls not to marry a man we don't love."

"Do you really think she ran away because she didn't love Tim?" Beth asked. "He's such a nice man. He's always laughing and joking, and he's so great with the kids. His Little League teams adore him. Plus, he and his wife, Barbara, do so much for the community."

The table was quiet. Lindsey wondered if they were all thinking the same thing she was. That if you wanted to live in the town where everyone suspects you murdered your wife, you'd spend the rest of your days proving what a great guy you were. The thought made her a bit queasy, although that could have been the radish chip. She had gotten to know both Tim and Barbara Little over the years, and the thought of Tim being a murderer, well, it just felt completely wrong.

"You don't think . . . ?" Beth's voice trailed off.

"That Tim Little murdered his new bride?" Lindsey asked.

"They never found Grace's body. Divers even searched the bay," Ms. Cole said. "It was as if she simply disappeared."

"Statistically, assuming something bad did happen to her, it's usually the spouse," Violet said, though she didn't sound convinced. "But Tim helps build sets for our theater productions, he and his wife are active in the church, he volunteers at a shelter in New Haven, and she teaches adult literacy. They are amazing people, and I know it sounds ridiculous, but I've never gotten a murderer vibe off Tim."

"What's a murderer vibe?" Nancy asked. "Do they have to try to kill you or someone you care about, or do they just need to look like they could?"

"I can't explain it," Violet said. "But you know how some people make the hair on the back of your neck stand up? Well, Tim doesn't do that. I have a really hard time believing he's a killer."

"Maybe he did kill her, but it was an accident, and he's spent his life trying to make amends," Paula said. "He would have been very young in nineteen eighty-nine."

"Twenty-four," Ms. Cole said. "They both were just twenty-four, and the rumors around town at the time were that she disappeared after they had a heated argument outside the Dockside Café, which is what the Blue Anchor used to be called."

"We're jumping ahead here," Lindsey said. "By leaps

and bounds. No body was ever found. There's nothing to indicate that Grace Little was murdered. I'm assuming if the police had had any suspicions at the time, then Tim or somebody would have been arrested."

"Things were different in the eighties," Ms. Cole said. "Domestic violence was still the dirty little secret that no one really talked about, DNA testing wasn't really all that, and you still had a very strong good old boys network. Men tended to look the other way if a man treated his wife poorly."

"It's true," Charlene said. She glanced at her mother. "Do you remember the Rudolf family in the Hamptons?"

Violet's face tightened. "Oscar Rudolf, that bas—"

"Every summer, at some point, there'd be a blowup at the Rudolf house," Charlene explained to the group. "And the next day the wife, Lily Rudolf, would appear with a black eye or a fat lip. Apparently, she had a knack for walking into doors."

"Doors with knuckles, it sounds like," Beth said. She hugged baby Bee, who was fast asleep on her chest, close.

"One year Charlene was over there playing with the Rudolf children, even though I usually insisted they play at our house—"

"They'd just gotten the new PlayStation," Charlene said.

"Right, you were over there playing, and then the storm, a.k.a. Oscar Rudolf, blew in," Violet said. "The entire neighborhood could hear him yelling. I've never been so scared. I had to call the police to help me get my baby out of there." She patted Charlene's hand. "The police arrived just in time. The kids were trapped in the backyard, too afraid to go near the house."

"It was terrifying," Charlene agreed. Her eyes were wide with the memory, and she shivered.

"When the police knocked on the door and no one answered, they went inside and found Oscar holding Lily by the throat. I genuinely thought he was going to kill her." Violet shook her head. "I ran past them and out to the backyard to grab Charlene. As we were leaving their house, I passed the officer talking to Lily. He handed her a tissue, she had a bloody nose, and the man actually asked her what she'd done to make Oscar so mad that he punched her."

As one, the crafternooners gasped in outrage.

"Like it's her fault he used her as a punching bag?" Paula said. "I don't care what another person does, it's never okay to punch them unless you're defending yourself."

"Agreed," Mary said. "And if you are defending yourself, make sure when you punch them, they stay down."

Lindsey met her gaze and nodded. She knew Mary had some experience with defending herself, and while she hated that it had happened, she was glad her sister-in-law had been trained well by her older brother Sully.

"What happened to the Rudolfs?" Lindsey asked.

"We stopped going to the Hamptons after that, but I ran into Lily a few years later. She was working as a personal shopper at Saks. Shortly after that summer episode, Oscar turned her out for a younger woman," Violet said. "Lily looked happier than I'd ever seen her."

"I'm glad she got away," Nancy said. "So few wives do."

The table went silent, the women acknowledging this harsh reality.

Lindsey knew the statistics on domestic violence were grim. The latest data indicated that one in four women and one in six men would suffer physical violence at the hands of a partner in their lifetime. She knew this because she'd helped a few patrons when they needed to get out of a bad situation by connecting them with outreach centers, support groups and shelters. It was one of the more rewarding parts of the job, getting people the information they needed to really change their lives and, in some cases, keep them alive.

"I don't like thinking of Grace as a victim," Mary said. She pushed her thick reddish brown hair away from her face. "Maybe she just woke up one day and decided she didn't want to be married. I mean, she was so young. Perhaps she realized she wasn't ready and just left. It wasn't nice of her, clearly, but that's the story we always believed about the runaway bride when we were kids, and I prefer it."

"I do like that narrative better than thinking she was murdered," Beth said.

"I do, too," Ms. Cole said. "It's much more satisfactory to think she took off and is saving penguins in Antarctica or something. In any event, what did William Dorchester want?"

"Oh, right," Lindsey said. "I'm glad you reminded me. I'm going to need everyone's help with this project." They gave her their full attention. "It seems he wants to donate the entirety of the Dorchester library to us."

"The Dorchester library," Ms. Cole said. She looked surprised. "I've only heard about it from others, having never been in the mansion myself, but isn't it a large collection?"

"Very," Lindsey said. "Which is why I need all the help I can get. What is everyone doing on Saturday?"

"Wild guess here," Violet said. "Packing books?"

Lindsey laughed. "I was hoping you'd say that."

"Not to be a buzzkill," Nancy said, "but did William mention how his mother felt about him donating the family's library?"

Lindsey sighed. "He didn't, but I got the feeling she might not be happy about it."

Both Ms. Cole and Nancy looked at her with their eyebrows raised.

"It'll be fine," Lindsey said. "I'm sure of it."

She was sure of no such thing, and judging by the dubious expressions on the crafternooners' faces, she wasn't fooling anyone.

CHAPTER
3

BRIAR CREEK
PUBLIC LIBRARY

S ully and Lindsey arrived at the Dorchester mansion at ten
minutes before ten o'clock. The house was set back from
the road and was surrounded by a small forest of maple, oak
and hickory trees that were in full color and looked aflame in
shades of red, orange and yellow. When the breeze ruffled the
tree limbs, the leaves dropped as if released by giant fists.

Lindsey studied the enormous Victorian with the ginger-
bread eaves. It had a neglected air about it, with peeling
paint and crooked shutters, and a yard that had the bones
of a well-designed landscape but had become overgrown
and wild over the past few years.

The three-story house with the turret was at the end of
a long cul-de-sac, which it had all to itself. There were no
other houses on the street. The nearest neighbor was on the
next street over, making this road unusually quiet for the
active village of Briar Creek.

"If I didn't know for a fact that Marion Dorchester still lived here, I'd think the place was abandoned," Sully said.

"It does feel that way, doesn't it?" Lindsey agreed. "But according to her son, she does live here, and I got the feeling she isn't happy about him giving away the library. I have no idea how she's going to react to us. I hope it doesn't get messy."

"Only one way to find out," Sully said. He opened the car door and climbed out of his old pickup truck. Lindsey did the same on her side.

They walked down the gravel driveway that was littered with fallen leaves. Lindsey saw an ancient Volvo and a Mercedes parked in front of the detached garage. Unlike the Volvo, the Mercedes was shiny and new looking. It had a Florida license plate, so she assumed it belonged to William.

They had just made it to the bottom step of the porch when the front door opened and William came out to greet them.

"Good morning," he said.

"Hi, William, this is my husband, Sully," Lindsey introduced them, and they shook hands.

William's smile looked forced, and Lindsey wondered if he'd changed his mind about making the donation to the library. Just then the sound of something smashing came from the house, punctuated by a yell.

"Is everything all right?" she asked.

"Mother is a bit resistant to the idea of parting with the library," he said. "Her cook-slash-housekeeper Mrs. Sutcliff is trying to get her to eat some breakfast and get dressed; however, my mother is not feeling cooperative."

"Did you want us to come back another time?" Sully asked.

"No." William shook his head. "I'm on a tight schedule. Mother will just have to come to terms with the reality of her situation. Mrs. Sutcliff is retiring, and no one is willing to take her place. My mother has no choice but to reside in an assisted-living facility."

There was another crash, followed by a screech. Then a door slammed. It sounded as if someone was having one heck of a tantrum.

"If you'll follow me, I'll show you the way to the library," William said. He turned and went back into the house.

Lindsey exchanged a look with Sully. She wasn't sure what her look said, but she hoped it showed how grateful she was to have him here. Family drama was more than she'd bargained for when she agreed to take the Dorchesters' library.

"We can always leave," Sully said under his breath.

Lindsey grabbed his hand and gave it a quick squeeze. She glanced over his shoulder at the street. The others hadn't arrived as yet, which was good. It would give her a chance to assess the situation. If it got ugly, she didn't want to subject her people to that.

She stepped into the dim interior of the house to find it surprisingly clean and tidy. The parquet wood floors of the foyer gleamed, and the faint scent of lemon furniture polish perfumed the air. A wooden staircase off to the side led upstairs, while the foyer opened up to a large living area.

It was there that William stood beside a frail-looking woman seated in an armchair. Lindsey assumed she was his mother, Marion Dorchester. She was wearing navy slacks and a white turtleneck sweater with a charcoal gray cardigan over it. The large sweater swallowed up her shrunken figure. She wore stylish navy flats on her feet. Her hair was dyed jet black, but the age spots on her hands and face, and the wrinkles that creased her brow, eyes and lips gave away her age. At a guess, Lindsey would put her just over eighty.

Another woman, wearing a white dress shirt and black pants, stood behind Mrs. Dorchester. She had curly silver hair, a round face and soft brown eyes. Lindsey assumed she was Mrs. Sutcliff. Despite the yelling and smashing noises from a few minutes ago, Mrs. Sutcliff's gaze was full of gentle concern.

"William, no! You can't do this! This is my house! My home!" Mrs. Dorchester cried.

It was a pitiful wail of anger and despair, and Lindsey felt her heart clutch in her chest.

"Mother, stop it," William said. His voice was stern. "You're making a scene and we have guests."

"Not my guests!" she snapped. Her head swiveled in Lindsey's and Sully's direction. Her eyes narrowed and she spat, "Get out!"

Lindsey took a step back into Sully.

"Stop it, Mother," William said. He turned to Mrs. Sutcliff. "Please take her back to the kitchen and try to get her to eat something."

"I'm not hungry!" Mrs. Dorchester puckered up her mouth, as if she were a little kid, and shook her head from side to side.

"How about some cinnamon sugar toast?" Mrs. Sutcliff asked. "You like that."

Mrs. Dorchester stopped shaking her head. She gave Mrs. Sutcliff side-eye. Her voice when she spoke sounded younger and softer. "With butter?"

"Of course," Mrs. Sutcliff said. She nodded to Lindsey and Sully and then helped Mrs. Dorchester to stand and led her toward the kitchen, which Lindsey could just see through an open door at the back of the room.

Mrs. Sutcliff kept talking as she escorted the elderly woman. "We'll toast the bread until it's golden brown, melt the butter on it just so, and then sprinkle sugar and cinnamon on it just the way you like it."

"I want three pieces," Mrs. Dorchester declared as if she expected a fight.

"You can have as much as you want," Mrs. Sutcliff said.

"With tea?" Mrs. Dorchester asked.

"Of course." Mrs. Sutcliff nodded at Mr. Dorchester when she shut the door behind them.

As soon as they left the room, William's shoulders dropped and the tension in his face visibly eased. "As you can see, she needs more care than one person can provide. Mrs. Sutcliff has been amazing over the years, but I can't ask her to put off her own retirement for us. My mother has been diagnosed with dementia, and it will only get worse. Thankfully, she gave me power of attorney over her and the Dorchester estate, making the entire process of liquidating the house and its contents easier."

"Still, I imagine it's difficult," Lindsey said. "I'm sorry you have to go through this."

William turned and met her gaze. His eyes held the first

spark of warmth she'd seen in them. "Thank you. I appreciate that." He gestured to a closed door at the end of the room. "Shall we take a look at the library? You can get an idea of what you'll be dealing with. I apologize in advance for the mustiness of the room. We keep the windows latched and the door shut to try and preserve the books."

"Sounds great," Lindsey said. "We have volunteers coming to help us start packing."

They crossed the room, working their way around the ornate exposed wood-frame sofa with its two matching armchairs. The wood was dark brown and the upholstery an embroidered beige. It looked like something that would have been popular at the turn of the last century. Lindsey supposed that was possible, given how long the Dorchesters had resided in Briar Creek.

"It's right through here," William said. He grasped the old crystal doorknob and tried to turn it. It wouldn't budge. "Well, that's weird."

"Is something wrong?" Lindsey asked.

William jiggled the doorknob. It didn't turn in either direction. He frowned. He glanced at them and said, "I think it's locked."

Sully crouched down and glanced at the doorknob. "But it doesn't have a lock."

William let go of the knob and stepped back as if he'd been shocked. "But then how could it be . . . ?"

Sully tried turning the knob. It wouldn't turn. "It must be broken. I have some tools in my truck. I'll go grab them."

Lindsey watched him depart. There was a crash from

the kitchen followed by a shout that was definitely Mrs. Dorchester. With a put-upon sigh, William said, "Please excuse me. I'll be right back."

"Absolutely," Lindsey said. "No problem."

She waited until the door shut behind him, and then she tried the doorknob. Not surprisingly, it didn't turn. She crouched down like Sully had and examined the hardware. It was as old as the furniture, with no visible sign of a lock, which she supposed might have been normal for back in the day. She tried the handle again. Still stuck. She jiggled it, wiggled it, tried to push the door and turn the knob and then pull the door. No luck.

"I've brought reinforcements," Sully called to her.

He reentered the house, carrying his toolbox, and behind him were the crafternooners Nancy, Violet and Paula. Ms. Cole was working at the library, Mary was at her restaurant, Charlene was filming a story for the news in New Haven, and Beth was home with the baby. It was a small crew today, but Lindsey figured they were just doing recon to assess how much work moving the library was going to require. Assuming they could ever get into the room.

"Where's William?" Sully asked.

"He was needed in the kitchen," Lindsey said.

Paula stepped right up and tried the handle. "It feels locked." She studied the crystal knob. "But there's no lock. Usually, there's one of those old locks with the fancy key, like something you'd see in steampunk fashion."

"I'm assuming the knob is broken," Sully said. He took some tools out of his toolbox and crouched down beside

Paula. "If we can slide something thin between the latch and the strike plate, maybe we can get the door to open."

Paula looked at his toolbox. "Good idea. What do you have in there?"

Sully popped the lid and the two of them started to forage, looking for items that might work.

"Have you tried asking nicely?" Violet asked. "It's an old house, maybe it's feeling violated by so many new visitors."

They all turned to look at her.

"What?" she asked. "Houses have feelings."

"She's right," Nancy said. "You can feel all of the energy in this house from the lives that have resided within these walls."

"So, we should say, 'Please'?" Paula asked. "Or 'Open sesame'?"

Sully grinned. "Worth a shot."

Paula turned to the door. "May we please enter the library?" She tried the knob. No luck. She looked at Lindsey. "Maybe it needs to be you since you're the head librarian and all."

Lindsey blinked. "Okay." She looked at the door. "May we please enter the library? We want to take care of the books."

Violet nodded at her as if to say, *Well done*.

Paula reached out to try the doorknob, but Nancy said, "No, it should be Lindsey."

Lindsey reached out and grabbed the crystal doorknob. It felt warm to the touch—not enough to burn but just enough to be noticeable. Huh. She tightened her fingers around it, and with a click, the knob turned and the latch slid back, allowing her to open the door.

"Okay, that was creepy," Sully said.

"What do you think—" Paula began, but William returned, interrupting her.

"Oh, I see you got the door open," he said. "Excellent."

Lindsey glanced at the others. They all wore matching expressions of *What the heck?* But no one seemed inclined to explain that they asked the house for permission to enter the library, so they didn't.

They all stepped back, allowing William through. He pushed the door wider, and Lindsey rose up on her tiptoes to peer over his shoulder. Her curiosity felt like an itch she couldn't quite reach.

The room was dark, with the drapes drawn and lights off. She tried not to think of this as another warning, assuming the locked doorknob had been the first. A warning of what? She shook her head. She was being ridiculous.

William snapped on the lights, and the room came to life. Short shelves of books filled the space, while floor-to-ceiling bookcases lined the walls. Like the rest of the house, the library was immaculate.

"My mother always kept the drapes drawn so that sunlight wouldn't damage the books," William said. He moved from window to window and pulled the heavy fabric aside. "I don't suppose it could hurt to let some light in now that they're moving to a new home."

Lindsey noted that one wall of bookcases had glass doors. She assumed these were the rare books that William had mentioned. The lighting was gentle, the carpet soft, and the furniture—two armchairs in front of the fireplace—

looked well worn. There was a restfulness about the room that she found calming. She figured it had to be the books because it definitely wasn't the mysteriously locked door.

"All right," she said. "Let's each pick a section of the room and start examining the books. Anything that is in bad condition, we'll have to weed out."

She glanced at William. He nodded, indicating that whatever she decided was fine.

"I've got some flattened boxes in the truck," Sully said. He glanced around the room, taking in the shelves and shelves of books. "I'll bring them in, and we can try and get an idea of how many more we're going to need."

Just then, Marion appeared in the doorway. She had a bit of cinnamon sugar on her chin, and she was carrying a piece of toast. "Out! Get out! No one is supposed to be in here!"

For such a petite woman, she had a booming voice. Her short black hair stood up in wild spikes as if she'd been clawing at it.

William stepped forward. "Mother, stop."

She hissed at him, sounding like a feral cat. Then she scurried behind a short shelf. She draped herself across the top and said, "You can't take my books, not my precious books."

Lindsey felt the plaintive cry in her soul. She would be devastated if someone came to take away her personal library. She glanced at Violet, Nancy and Paula and knew from their pained expressions that they felt the same way.

"Mother!" William snapped.

Lindsey held up her hand in a *stop* gesture.

She turned and approached Mrs. Dorchester. "Hi, Mrs.

Dorchester, we haven't met properly. I'm Lindsey Norris, the director of the town library."

Mrs. Dorchester didn't move. She stared at Lindsey as if trying to decide if she was friend or foe.

"Do you want to show me your favorite books?"

Mrs. Sutcliff appeared in the doorway. She looked winded. She whispered to William, "I just stepped out of the room for a moment."

"It's all right," he said. "I knew this was going to be difficult for her."

"Mrs. Dorchester?" Lindsey brought the woman's attention back to her. "Which book is your favorite?"

"Marion," she said. "My name is Marion."

"All right, Marion," Lindsey said. "My favorite book of all time is *Anne of Green Gables*."

Marion stared at Lindsey with an intensity that made the hair on the back of Lindsey's neck stand up.

"*Little Women*," Marion said. She turned and darted to a bookcase on the far side of the room. She snatched the old volume off the shelf and hugged it to her chest.

Lindsey followed her slowly so as not to frighten her. "Which one of the sisters was your favorite? Jo?"

Marion shook her head. "Amy."

"Oh, I like her, too," Lindsey said. "She was the youngest sister, wasn't she?"

"You look like her," Marion said. She reached out and touched Lindsey's hair, fingering the long blond curls. Her face became serene.

Mrs. Sutcliff stepped forward, clearly planning to take

advantage of the calm moment to lead Marion out of the room. Marion saw her and tightened her fingers in Lindsey's hair. She yanked and Lindsey yelped.

Marion's lips became tense, disappearing into one thin line. Her eyes were wide and she whispered, "It's you, isn't it? After all this time, you're here."

"Who?" Lindsey asked. She put her hand over Marion's to keep her from yanking her hair again.

"You're her," Marion said. Her voice sounded frightened. "The runaway bride. You've come back."

"That is enough!" William said. He strode forward. He took his mother's hand and unclenched her fingers from Lindsey's hair. "Let go. This is Lindsey Norris, not Grace. Mrs. Sutcliff, take Mother to her room, please. She needs to rest."

Marion looked down at the book in her arms. Her shoulders slumped in defeat, and she let Mrs. Sutcliff lead her from the room. At the doorway, she looked back at Lindsey and said, "I'm sorry."

"It's all right," Lindsey said. She forced her lips to curve into a small smile. "No harm done."

But if she was honest with herself, she wasn't sure if Marion was apologizing to her or the person she thought Lindsey was . . . the runaway bride. But if the apology was intended for Grace Little, then *why* was Marion apologizing? After all these years, was she sorry that she hadn't let her son marry Grace? How differently would her and William's lives have played out if they had? How sad for all of them that they would never know.

This is going to be an endeavor," Violet declared. She was crouched on the floor beside a half-filled box. "If my estimates are correct, we're going to need a lot more boxes."

"A lot more," said Nancy, who was squatting beside her. She had a streak of dust on her cheek, and she'd shoved up her sweatshirt sleeves to her elbows.

"I don't know how we'll get this all moved in a month if we're only here a few days a week," Paula said. She was across the room, which was roughly the same size as Lindsey's cottage, inventorying the low shelves under the windows. "Are we planning to rent a moving truck?"

"That's an excellent suggestion," Lindsey said. "When we get back to the library, I'll figure out the logistics and draw up a detailed plan."

Lindsey was assessing the bookcase with the rare volumes. There was so much more than just the Mark Twain volume that William had shown her. There were first print editions, special editions, and limited print runs of many of Connecticut's most famous authors. Her archivist's head was spinning at the magnitude of the collection.

If the library was going to take on these rare items, they had to be preserved correctly. She knew William didn't care what happened to them, but it was important to her that the collection was treated appropriately. If the town couldn't manage to insure it and house it properly, then she would donate it to a larger public or academic library that could.

William had left the room when they set to work. Lindsey wasn't sure if it was because he was embarrassed by the scene with his mother earlier or because he just wasn't interested in the library.

"I can scrounge up more boxes," Sully said.

"Thanks," Lindsey replied. "But I don't think we'll need them today since we can't pack it all up in one go. Besides, I really need to figure out where we're going to store the books while we sort them and add them to the library."

"Plus, you feel guilty," Sully said. His bright blue eyes were studying her with a tenderness that Lindsey wanted to lean into like a hug.

"You know me so well," she said. "These books are worth a small fortune. I feel like I'm stealing them."

"You're not—" Sully began but was interrupted by a yelp from Paula.

Lindsey turned around to see Paula standing absolutely

still. Her eyes were wide and her face had drained of color. She looked like she was going to faint.

"Paula, are you all right?" Lindsey asked.

Paula was staring at the heavy brocade cloth that covered the window. "There's something behind the drapes," she whispered. "It tried to grab me."

Sully took a step forward to investigate, and the long curtain billowed as if pushed by a gust of wind.

"Ah!" Nancy cried. She and Violet ducked down behind their short shelf so that just their eyes were visible.

Sully stopped. Lindsey suspected it was because, like her, he remembered that William had said they kept the windows latched to protect the materials. This was not a breeze from outside. What or who was it, then?

"Get over here," Violet whispered to Paula.

Paula didn't hesitate. She slowly crept backward around the short shelf to crouch beside Violet and Nancy.

"Now what?" Nancy said.

"This is ridiculous," Sully said. "I'm sure there's a logical reason as to why the curtain moved. The house is almost two hundred years old. There's obviously a draft in the window frame or the wall, or perhaps there's a heating vent in the floor."

"Or it's the spirit of someone who died in this house," Paula said. She blinked at them, looking remarkably like a little owl. "How many generations have lived here? It could be more than one spirit."

"Right," Lindsey said. "In any event, we should look."

No one moved. They all stared at Sully, who blew out a breath and nodded.

"I'll just peek behind it," he said. Still, he didn't move.

Lindsey glanced at him. Was her husband afraid of ghosts? Could it be? The former Navy officer who regularly took on Mother Nature and all of her peculiarities while running his boat tours and water taxis, and a now billowy curtain caused him to pause. This was brand-new information!

"I'm closer. I can check," she said. She moved toward the window, but Sully fell in right beside her. He might be freaking out, but he wasn't letting her go in alone.

Lindsey glanced at her friends. She could practically feel their collective nerves tighten with suspense. This was crazy. Sully was right. It had to be a draft of some sort. Just like the library door locking had to have a reasonable explanation as well. She just didn't know what it was yet.

She reached out to move the curtain, but Sully stretched around her and beat her to it. His fingers wrapped around the thick brocade, and he jerked it aside with one swift motion.

There, sitting on the narrow windowsill, was a dark gray cat with light green eyes and a black tipped tail that swished back and forth. It blinked at them and then began to lick its shoulder.

"Ha!" Paula let out a cry and sagged to the floor, disappearing behind the shelf.

"It's a cat," Sully said. He let out a deep breath. "A cat."

Lindsey leaned into him and gave him a half hug. She let

him go and approached the cat, who didn't scamper away but continued preening as if perfectly at home with an audience.

Lindsey held out her hand just as she would with a dog. The cat didn't sniff her. Instead, it rubbed the side of its face against the backs of Lindsey's fingers as if it needed a good chin scratching. Lindsey was happy to oblige.

"It must be the Dorchesters' pet," Nancy said. "Although—"

"What?" Violet asked.

"Well, the door was stuck," Nancy said. "So, the cat must have been trapped inside here. You'd think it would head right for the open door."

The cat did not seem to be in a hurry to go anywhere. It arched its back and purred, demanding more pets from Lindsey. When that wasn't enough, it hopped down and rubbed its face against Sully's shins. He bent over and scratched its ears. Its green eyes closed in bliss.

"Maybe the cat was asleep while the door was stuck," Lindsey said. She glanced at the windowsill. It seemed a bit narrow for a nap spot, but cats were known for napping in odd places.

"Either way, mystery solved," Sully said. He straightened up, and the cat strode toward the door with its tail in the air.

They all watched it go. Lindsey glanced back at the window, which was now half uncovered and letting in the early afternoon sunlight. It streamed into the room, lighting up the dust motes that drifted through the air, disturbed by all of the activity in the room, no doubt.

And then the other curtain moved. Lindsey stared. She

had to be imagining it. But no. It billowed just as the other one had. Without turning away, she reached out and grabbed Sully's arm. She felt him turn and stiffen behind her when the curtain billowed again.

"Is it another cat?" Paula asked. Her voice sounded very faint.

"Only one way to know for certain," Sully said. He reached forward and yanked the curtain aside. The windowsill was empty.

They all agreed it must have been caused by a draft, although there was no evidence of one. It was late afternoon when Lindsey suggested they call it a day, and no one protested. In fact, the crafternooners and Sully hustled out of the room with decided alacrity.

Sully walked their friends out while Lindsey looked for William. She wanted to let him know that they were leaving but that she'd be back tomorrow with more helpers. She found him sitting at a desk in a small office at the front of the house.

"Finished?" he asked. He turned away from a laptop computer and rose to his feet.

"For today," she said. "Is tomorrow at noon a convenient time for us to come back and continue?"

"Absolutely," he said. "I'll try and have Mother occupied elsewhere if at all possible."

Lindsey didn't know what to say to that. She didn't want to sound rude and thank him, but there was no doubt it would make things easier if they didn't have to worry about Mrs. Dorchester being distressed by their presence.

"We found your mother's cat," Lindsey said. "It appeared to have been shut in the room."

William shook his head slowly from side to side. "She doesn't have a cat, hasn't had one for years."

"Oh, I suppose it must be a stray who got into the house," Lindsey said. "I'm afraid it wandered out of the library and we just assumed it belonged here." She glanced around the room but there was no sign of it. "It must be somewhere inside. It has beautiful charcoal gray fur and light green eyes and a black-tipped tail."

William went very still and his eyebrows rose. "Are you sure?"

"Yes, it was a gorgeous cat," she said. "And friendly."

"My mother's last cat Percy looked exactly like the cat you've described, but he went missing some time ago," he said.

"Oh, I'm sorry," Lindsey said. "That must have been very upsetting for her."

"It was," he said. He glanced across the room, and his eyes held a faraway look as if he were seeing something happening somewhere else. "Particularly because it was the same day that Grace disappeared."

Lindsey shivered. She didn't mean to, but the coincidence was extraordinary. Her mouth was dry, probably from the aridness of the library, and she swallowed.

"Perhaps the cat we found is from the same genetic line," she said. "It could be a fourth or fifth generation of the late Percy if he sired any litters in his time."

William turned to look at her and shook his head as if trying to bring himself back to the present. "I'm sure you're right. That must be it. Cats do get around. It's likely just a remarkable coincidence."

Sully appeared in the doorway. "Are you ready, Lindsey?"

"Yes," she said. She turned back to William. "See you tomorrow."

"I'll be here." He sounded resigned, but he forced a small smile and waved to Sully, who nodded in return.

Lindsey walked around the ornate furniture to the front door, looking for the cat on the way. There was no sign of it. It had to be a coincidence that it looked like Marion's old cat. It had to be. Still, she was relieved when she stepped out onto the front porch and Sully shut the door behind them.

"Feels better out here, doesn't it?" he asked.

He held out his hand and Lindsey took it. They walked down the steps together, and she said, "The Dorchesters don't have a cat."

"Then the cat belongs to . . ." Sully's voice trailed off as if he hoped she'd fill in the blank.

"No idea. William said they haven't had a cat in years," Lindsey said. They continued down the walkway toward the street.

"A neighbor's, then?" Sully suggested.

"Perhaps."

"What's wrong?" Sully came to a halt in the middle of the path. "I can tell by your voice something is weird."

"It's probably nothing," Lindsey said.

She glanced back at the house. Her gaze ran over its worn facade. It had the fatigued disposition of a grande dame whose prime had passed and was now content to sit in a squashy chair against the wall with her soft midsection, lip lines, crow's-feet, and arthritic hip, while the younger ones carried on around her. What joys and sorrows had this house witnessed? Lindsey wondered.

"And yet you're looking at the house as if it holds answers," Sully said. "What's going on, darling?"

Lindsey turned to face him. "It probably means nothing, but William told me that the last cat that Marion owned disappeared on the same day that Grace, the runaway bride, vanished."

"Okay, that's odd," he said. "But probably coincidence."

"Maybe," Lindsey said. "But I also described the cat we saw, and William said his mother's cat looked exactly like that."

"Exactly?" he asked. Sully looked ill at ease, which was precisely how Lindsey felt.

"Exactly," she confirmed.

Sully glanced back at the house, and Lindsey saw him shiver. "It's getting late. We'd better go," he said.

They continued down the walkway, and Lindsey felt the uncomfortable feeling that had been with her all day slowly start to recede. She felt as if she could breathe again. She wondered if it was the house. Could a house invoke feelings of foreboding? And if so, what did it mean?

They'd just reached Sully's old truck when Lindsey turned to him and asked, "Are you feeling better?"

"If you mean less creeped out," he clarified, "then yes. The farther we get from the house, the better I feel."

"Me, too," Lindsey said. "It's strange, isn't it? I don't *think* I'm being swept up in the season of Halloween, but with the locked door and the unexplained draft in the library, I feel as if the Dorchester mansion is—"

"Don't say it," he said.

Lindsey lifted her eyebrows. He opened the passenger side door for her, but Lindsey didn't climb in. Instead, she tipped her head back and studied his face. "Are you going to tell me about it?"

"About what?" he asked.

"About why you're afraid of ghosts."

"I'm not—" he protested, but she interrupted.

"I saw your face," she said. "When the curtain moved, you looked like you wanted to run out of there screaming."

He huffed a laugh. "Run, yes, scream, no. I have my dignity."

"Talk to me, Sully," she said.

"For the record, I am not afraid of ghosts because I do not believe in ghosts," he said. Then he squinted one eye. "Do you?"

Lindsey shrugged. "I'm open to the idea that there might be supernatural oddities that can't be explained away, whether they're ghosts or something else."

"How are we married and I didn't know this about you?" he asked.

"It never came up," she said. "But this is about you. If

you're not afraid of ghosts, what was happening in there that had you looking so freaked out?"

"Not a ghost," he insisted.

"Yes, you've been very clear about that," she said, trying not to smile.

"Fine." He sighed. "When I was nine, the local Boy Scouts put on a haunted house. It was dark, it smelled like gym socks, and they were very into the jump scares. Every time you turned a corner, something jumped out at you and tried to grab you."

"Sounds fun."

"It was," he said. "I loved it. My friends and I went in on a continuous loop. Get through it, go stand in line, do it again."

He paused. Lindsey leaned against the truck and waited for him to continue. A long moment passed, and she was wondering if he was ever going to finish his story when he said, "And then a little boy went missing."

Lindsey straightened up. "Oh, no."

"It's okay, they found him," Sully assured her. "He'd wandered out of the haunted house and curled up on a hay bale around the corner and had fallen asleep."

"Phew," Lindsey said. She sagged against the truck. "So, how does that relate to today?"

"I'm not sure," he said. "But the gut-churning feeling I had when the boy's mom was screaming for her little guy and no one could find him in the dark maze was unforget-table. It felt as if two giant fists were wringing out my insides like a sponge. It was awful." He glanced from the house back to Lindsey. His bright blue eyes were serious as they held hers, and he said, "I'd never felt anything like that before or since, until we were standing in that library today. There is something wrong in that house. I felt it."

Lindsey stepped forward and hugged him. It was clear that he was deeply disturbed by the vibes in the mansion. He held her close and rested his chin on the top of her head.

"Promise me one thing?" he asked.

"Sure," she said.

"You won't go in there alone. Not ever. Not once," he said. "The Dorchesters have to be there and preferably with someone from the library or the crafternooners or one of our friends."

She leaned back to look at him, studying the face that had become so dear to her over the past few years. Without hesitation, she said, "I promise."

Sully squeezed her tight one more time before she got into the passenger seat. He closed her door and circled the front of the truck to the driver's side. Lindsey glanced back at the house while she waited for him. Sitting in the window of the library was the cat. It stared at Lindsey, meeting her gaze, and then very slowly blinked.

Lindsey turned when Sully opened the door and climbed in. She grabbed his arm and said, "Look who's in the library window."

"Who?" Sully asked. He stared past her at the house, and Lindsey turned to look, too. The window where the cat had been sitting was empty.

CHAPTER
5

BRIAR CREEK
PUBLIC LIBRARY

Where do you think the cat went?" Beth asked.

"No idea," Lindsey said.

It was Monday afternoon, and Beth had come in to help Lindsey interview candidates for the children's librarian job share. The human resources department had approved temporarily splitting Beth's job into two part-time positions so that she could keep her job at the library, sharing her position and benefits with another part-time children's librarian. They'd had several promising applicants, and Lindsey was pleased that it looked like it was going to be a seamless transition. In between interviews, she'd been telling Beth all about Saturday's events at the Dorchester house.

On Sunday, Lindsey had met up with Carrie Rushton and several Friends of the Library members. Since half of the collection had already been inventoried, they'd concentrated on packing those sections. Sully was there with his truck, and he and Robbie Vine—a semiretired actor who lived in Briar Creek—had made several trips to the library storage room with the boxes. Even though they'd managed to move only a small portion of the collection, Lindsey told herself they were making progress.

Weirdly, there had been no sign of the cat on Sunday. Lindsey didn't know what to think about that.

"Do you think it's feral?" Beth asked. "If it's a bit wild, it might know a secret entrance into the house."

"It let me pet it, which makes me think it's tame," Lindsey said. "And it certainly seemed to feel at home in the mansion, as if it was born to live a pampered life."

"Like Daisy Buchanan in *The Great Gatsby*," Beth said.

"Just like that. Fitzgerald based the character of Daisy on his wife Zelda," Lindsey said, "and I definitely see a Zelda vibe in that cat. It's a beauty."

"Are you talking about the ghost cat again?" Robbie Vine appeared in the doorway carrying a tea tray.

"I'm just catching Beth up," Lindsey said. "And you have to admit it's odd that the cat was there one day and not the next, that it looks exactly like their old cat, and that it was shut in the library for who knows how long. I know for a fact that we let it out of the library on Saturday, and I closed the door behind us when Sully and I left, and yet, there it was sitting in the window when we got in the car."

Robbie set the tray down on the corner of Lindsey's desk. He handed a pretty floral mug to Beth.

"No caffeine for the nursing mom," he said. "I made you an herbal tea."

She sighed and said, "Thank you."

He then held out a plate of cookies. "But you can have all the biscuits you want."

"That seems only fair," she said. She took three.

"Where is our darling baby Bee?" Robbie asked. He poured tea from the pot for Lindsey and himself. They'd been sharing this afternoon ritual for a while now, and it had become a bright spot in her day.

"With her dad while I catch up on work stuff," Beth said. She took a nibble of a cookie, swallowed, and then said to Robbie, "You were at the Dorchester house yesterday—did you get any ghostly vibes?"

"No, but how could I with Lindsey's taskmaster of a husband cracking the whip?" He bit a cookie and settled back in his chair to eat.

"Really? A taskmaster?" Lindsey asked. "Is that why when I looked out the window, the two of you were playing soccer in the street with a bunch of neighborhood kids?"

"We were just being friendly," Robbie said. "Apparently, there's little to no traffic on that cul-de-sac because the Dorchester house is the only one on it. The kids play there all the time."

"Is it bad of me to say I'm surprised Mrs. Dorchester doesn't run them off?" Beth asked. "I know I haven't met her properly, but from what I heard about her reaction to having people in her house on Saturday, I'm amazed she's so accommodating to children playing in the street."

Lindsey took a sip of her tea. It was perfection. "I don't think she minded us being in the house so much as she was trying to protect her library. If I had one as spectacular as that, I would have had the same reaction. I feel sorry for her."

"Me, too," Beth said. "I can't imagine watching people take my books away from me. It would be like having them chip away at pieces of my soul."

"It was difficult," Lindsey said. "I talked to William about it on Sunday, and he agreed that Mrs. Dorchester can take any of the books she wants before we finish packing them all up. The assisted-living facility where she's going has said her apartment can fit a substantial bookcase in it, so that makes me feel slightly less guilty."

"No need for you to feel bad," Robbie said. "It's her son who's sticking her in a home."

"She requires more care than he can give," Lindsey said.

"Does she?" Robbie asked. "Or does he just not want to do it?"

Lindsey didn't answer because she didn't know. William had admitted that there was no love lost between him and his mother, but Lindsey had seen how overwrought his mother had become, and while she completely understood it in regard to the books, she didn't know if this was a constant state for the older lady.

"Her housekeeper, Mrs. Sutcliff, is retiring, so I think William feels that this is a good time to transition her to a place where she can be cared for as she ages," Lindsey said.

"I still say that he could find a new housekeeper or move

in and take care of her himself," Robbie said. His voice was heavy with disapproval.

Lindsey pursed her lips and blew the steam off her tea. Robbie sounded rather vehement even though he didn't know Marion or William personally.

"Are you being critical of William Dorchester because of your friendship with Tim Little? I understand your loyalty, but caring for a person with dementia is difficult, and if you're estranged, it's probably even harder. I don't think William knows his mother that well after all these years," Lindsey said. She knew that Robbie and Tim worked together on the sets of the community theater, and she also knew that Robbie was loyal to a fault toward anyone he considered a friend.

Robbie's blond eyebrows rose. He had pale green eyes, fair skin, and strawberry blond hair that was gradually becoming threaded with white. He was handsome in a ruddy-cheeked, square-jawed, lanky-build, God-save-the-queen sort of way. In other words, he looked very British.

"Pfft." He puffed out a breath. "I have no idea what you mean."

"Oh, come on," Lindsey said. "Tim's been building the sets for the community theater for years. I know he's a friend of yours, and I know the rumors about the runaway bride have started up again ever since William's arrival in town."

"The tongue wags have been busy, and it's bloody unfair to Tim," Robbie said.

"I agree," Lindsey said. "But Briar Creek is a small town."

"With a very long memory," Beth said.

"If someone just knew where Grace Little had gone, then the whole thing would have played out very differently," Robbie said.

"Assuming she went anywhere," Beth countered. "People don't just vanish into thin air. Not even in nineteen eighty-nine."

"They never found a body or any other trace of her," Lindsey said. "So in the case of the runaway bride, it seems that's exactly what happened. She disappeared."

"It'll be best for everyone involved if William Dorchester gets his mother settled and goes back to Florida where he belongs," Robbie declared.

"William says he wants his mother moved and the house on the market within a month, so you'll likely get your wish," Lindsey said. "And since you're so motivated to get him gone, what are you doing tonight?"

"Tonight?" he asked.

"Yes." Lindsey nodded. "Sully and Ian are in the middle of their haunted boat tour schedule, so he's booked every night. I've already tapped the crafternooners and the Friends of the Library for this weekend, but if I really want to get the library moved, I'm going to have to do some packing during the evenings."

"Emma is on duty," Robbie said. He'd been dating the Briar Creek chief of police for a while now. "And rehearsals for the community theater holiday show don't start until next week, so I suppose I can help out tonight."

"You sound reluctant," Beth said. "What gives?"

"The creep factor was pretty high in broad daylight yesterday," he said. "I can't even imagine what that place is going to be like at night."

"We'll only be there for a couple of hours at most," Lindsey said. She sipped her tea and reached for another cookie. "What could possibly happen in the space of a couple of hours?"

Lindsey and Robbie arrived at seven in the evening. The late October air was chilly, and Lindsey was wearing a warm corduroy coat over jeans and a turtleneck sweater. When she rang the bell, William met them at the door. She had called earlier to say she'd be coming by.

William informed her that Mrs. Dorchester was up in her room for the night and Mrs. Sutcliff, who slept in the bedroom adjacent to hers, had also retired for the evening. He invited them in and led the way into the main room. He was drinking a scotch neat while listening to jazz on vinyl, which was spinning on an old-school turntable. His cheeks were flushed, and there was a glint in his eye that made Lindsey suspect this wasn't his first drink of the evening. She was glad Sully had made her promise not to come here alone. She had no interest in dealing with the ramblings of a drunken man.

William seemed to suddenly notice Robbie standing behind Lindsey and visibly straightened. "Mr. Vine, good to see you."

"Evening," Robbie said. His voice had the same chilly

nip as the autumn air. He did not invite the man to call him Robbie. Lindsey refrained from rolling her eyes. Barely.

"I hope we didn't come at a bad time," said Lindsey.

"Not at all," he said. He gestured to the library. "The library is all yours. Let me know if I can be of help."

He strode back to his armchair by the fireplace and proceeded to tip his head back with his eyes shut, listening to his music and ignoring them. Robbie and Lindsey exchanged a glance and a shrug.

Lindsey opened the door to the library and was greeted by the singular smell of a roomful of books. The faint scent was that of almond and vanilla, which, as a former archivist, Lindsey knew came from the aging pages of the books. As the organic compounds in the pages broke down, they released chemicals that gave off those particular scents. It was comforting, and she felt her shoulders relax as she breathed it in.

She flipped on the light switch, and the soft glow from the old-fashioned overhead light fixture enveloped the space in cozy warmth. Robbie planted his hands on his hips and surveyed the room. Piles of books were everywhere, along with empty boxes waiting to be filled.

Lindsey picked her way around them until she was standing at the glassed-in bookcases. These were the most precious items, and she wanted to focus on them when just two of them were there so that she could ensure the integrity of the packing. In other words, be a complete control freak.

"Given how much hauling we did yesterday, it feels as if this project should be further along," Robbie said.

"It's like the books multiply when we're not looking," Lindsey agreed. Of course, the librarian in her loved the idea of a never-ending book collection, but she didn't say that out loud.

"Which section are we sorting tonight?" Robbie asked.

"The rare ones," Lindsey said. "I have acid-free archival boxes for them since I don't know how long it will take for the specialty cases to be installed in the library."

She led the way to a stack of small boxes beside the glassed-in cases. Each book would have its own acid-free box. They would put those boxes inside the larger plastic crates she'd brought from the library.

Robbie watched Lindsey pack a book and label the outside with the author and title. He opened a different case, and just when he reached for a volume, the overhead light flickered and then went out.

The music in the other room stopped, and William let out a muttered oath.

"You all right, Lindsey?" Robbie asked.

"I'm fine," she said, although she could feel her heart racing.

"I'll go see—" Robbie began, but then the lights flickered back on and the music started to play again. "Is it just me or was that spectacularly creepy?"

"Not just you," she confirmed.

"Let's get this done." Robbie started packing the shelves

near him, and Lindsey noticed he was moving more quickly than he had been before. She couldn't blame him.

They worked silently. It was quiet in the library but, surprisingly, not in an eerie way. It was actually peaceful, listening to William's jazz music from the other room with the only noise being the occasional ruffle of pages as she and Robbie worked.

They'd cleared off several shelves when they heard a noise come from the front of the house. There was a brisk knock and then a muffled shout.

Lindsey was bent over a crate and paused to listen. Robbie was marking the outside of a box, and he, too, went still. He met her gaze, and his right eyebrow lifted. They both turned toward the open door. Lindsey saw William striding to the front door. The knock sounded again, louder this time.

"Should we . . . ?"

"Yes."

They put their materials down and crossed the library with Lindsey in the lead. She stepped into the main room and moved aside to give Robbie space when William opened the front door.

"How dare you, Dorchester?" a voice boomed.

Lindsey craned her neck to see Tim Little standing on the front porch, and he looked furious.

William crossed his arms over his chest. "How dare I what?"

"You know what you did," Tim yelled. "You called the president of the Little League association and the head of the local scout troop and told them they had a murderer for a coach and scoutmaster and that I should be let go as I was unfit to be around children."

"Prove it," Dorchester said. He stuck his chin out as if inviting Tim to take a swing at him.

Tim was tall and broad, his silver hair was cut short, and his belly betrayed his love of a pint or two at the Blue Anchor every weekend. He was dressed in a flannel shirt over a T-shirt and jeans, which stood in sharp contrast to William's creased trousers and cardigan sweater.

"I don't have to prove anything," Tim said. "You've

been gone for thirty-three years, and no one ever accused me of murder in all that time. Now you're back for a couple of weeks, and suddenly anonymous calls are coming to the president of the league and my fellow scoutmaster, accusing me of murder. Of course it's you."

William took a sip of his scotch. "Maybe it's your guilty conscience."

"Why you . . ." Tim stomped into the house.

William wisely backed up. Tim glanced at Robbie and Lindsey, but other than a jerk of his chin in their direction, he didn't greet them.

"We should do something," Lindsey said.

"Like what?" Robbie asked. "Film it? I bet it'd go viral."

"No, I meant do something to stop it from escalating," she said.

"Oh, right." Robbie stepped forward and said, "Hey there, let's all just calm down and get things sorted in a civilized manner."

"Sorry, Robbie, but this has been a long time coming," Tim said. He started to roll up his sleeves.

William's eyebrows rose. "Are you planning to hit me?"

"Nope," Tim said. "I'm planning to beat you to a pulp."

"Oy!" Robbie cried. He moved closer, while still staying out of striking range. "Emotions are running high, I understand, but a fight isn't the answer."

"Don't worry," Tim said. "There's not going to be a fight."

"There's not?" Robbie straightened up, looking pleased that he'd managed to talk Tim out of it.

"No, there's just going to be two hits," Tim said. "Me hitting him and him hitting the ground."

"You are a Neanderthal," William declared. "What did Grace ever see in you?"

Lindsey saw a flash of pain pass over Tim's face before it turned into a sneer. "She saw a man who wasn't a mama's boy. You were too afraid to marry her, but I wasn't. She was *my* wife."

William's face turned blotchy red. He very carefully set his drink down on a nearby table and then raised his fists, looking like a kid on a playground trying to be brave when he really wanted to run.

Lindsey opened her phone and sent a text to the chief of police asking her to send a car to the house as things were getting dicey.

"Yeah, she was your wife until she didn't want to be married to you anymore, and you killed her," William taunted.

Tim let out a low growl. He raised his fists and started to stalk William, slowly walking around him as if looking for his weak spot. "I loved her. I would never have hurt her."

"And yet, she disappeared," William said. He began to dance on his feet, hopping from side to side, as if anticipating a punch. "Or was she murdered?"

"Good question," Tim said. "She was my wife. I'd never hurt her, but you never got over her, did you? Why did you run to Florida anyway? What did you have to hide?"

"Are you insinuating that *I* had something to do with Grace's disappearance?" William's voice was outraged.

Tim took the opportunity to feint a punch, and William let out a yelp and scurried back out of reach.

"That's right, run, you coward," Tim said.

"I am not a coward," William snarled.

"Really? I'm shocked you're not hiding behind your mother's skirts right now," Tim said, baiting him.

"Leave my mother out of this," William snapped.

"Fine," Tim said. "Then step outside like a man, and we'll settle this once and for all."

"Now, now, gentlemen, I think this has gone far enough," Robbie said. He found an opening and stepped neatly in between them with his arms up. They weren't listening.

"You want a fight?" William asked. "I'll give you a fight."

And just like that, he lowered his head and charged, plowing right past Robbie and into Tim's middle, taking Tim down and landing on top of him. Tim wasn't having it, and he flipped them over so he was on top. He grabbed William by his shirtfront with one hand and drew back his other fist.

"Oy!" Robbie cried. He leapt forward and grabbed Tim's arm, holding him back.

Lindsey moved forward to help, but before she could get there, William lurched up from the floor, and with his eyes squeezed shut, he threw a roundhouse punch. Tim saw it coming and ducked, but Robbie didn't, and it clocked him right in the face.

"Ow!" He dropped Tim's arm and fell back on the floor. "Bloody hell!"

"Robbie!" Lindsey cried. She glanced at Tim and William, who were both frozen in surprise. She glared at William and ordered, "Go get him some ice."

"Yes, of course, right away." William disentangled himself from Tim and hurried to the kitchen.

"Oh, man, I'm sorry," Tim said. He grabbed Robbie's arm, helping him onto the couch.

"A bit late for that, isn't it?" Robbie asked. He sounded salty, and Lindsey couldn't blame him. He had his hand clapped over his eye while he glared at Tim with the other one.

"I just got so mad when I heard what he'd done," Tim said. "I had to come over here and have it out with him."

"Which, while understandable, was the exact worst thing you could do," Robbie said. "If you're trying to convince people you're not a violent person, punching out your old nemesis is not the way to do it."

"Let me see your eye," Lindsey said. Robbie moved his hand and she winced. It was already swelling.

"That bad?" Robbie asked.

"Pretty bad," Tim said.

"All right, you all have five seconds to tell me who I'm arresting for assaulting my boyfriend." Emma Plewicki stood in the open front door, and she looked furious.

William entered the room with a bag of ice and said, "It was an accident, I swear." He handed the ice to Lindsey and then pointed at Tim. "It was his fault."

"My fault?" Tim roared. "You're the one who hit him!"

"I was aiming for you!" William fired back.

Emma raised her hands in a *stop* gesture. "Tim—outside."

"What? Why me?" he asked.

"Because it's Mr. Dorchester's house," she said. "And you two need to stay away from each other."

"Fine." Tim stomped outside. "I'm sorry, Robbie, it should have been me. Call me if you need anything."

"I will, mate," Robbie said.

"And you," Emma said to William. "Sit down." She didn't say please, which Lindsey felt was interesting. She then lifted the bag of ice off Robbie's eye and looked at it. Her lips pursed as she considered the damage.

"Nice timing, love," Robbie said.

"A little birdie told me to send a car over, and thankfully I happened to be on patrol nearby."

"Little birdie?" Robbie asked.

"Tweet, tweet," Lindsey said.

Robbie grinned and then grimaced. "Bollocks, that hurts."

"I don't think you're going to have full capacity of your face for a while," Emma said.

Robbie muttered another curse, to which William said, "I really am sorry."

Emma looked at Robbie. "Do you want to press charges?"

William went pasty pale and swallowed hard. Clearly he wasn't comfortable with the thought of being arrested. Robbie was silent for a moment.

"I'm really so sorry," William said. He sounded nervous. "Whatever you need from me to make amends, I'm happy to do it."

Robbie gave him an annoyed look. He then glanced at Emma. "I don't know. Do you think it will help me to have a police report if I decide to sue for damages?"

"Hey! It was an accident!" William protested. "And I said I was sorry."

"Might lose out on some acting work with this face though," Robbie said.

Emma grunted. "Good thing you don't get by on your looks."

"Hey!" Robbie protested. She winked at him to let him know she was teasing, and he smiled back. "All right, I don't suppose I need to file any charges."

"Thank you," William said. He looked so relieved Lindsey thought he might wilt into the upholstery. "I'm normally a very peaceful man, but that guy . . ." He stopped talking, seeming out of words.

"I'm still writing up the incident," Emma said. "And I'm filing it, so there had better not be any more nonsense between you and Tim Little, or I'll arrest you both for disturbing the peace, brawling and whatever else I can think of."

"But what about Tim storming into my house?" William asked. "Isn't that breaking and entering? Can't I have him arrested or take out a restraining order on him?"

"You really want to do that?" Robbie asked. "We were here and saw the whole thing. You opened the door and practically invited him in."

William opened his mouth, then shut it. He glanced back at Emma and said, "Just tell him to stay away from me."

Emma nodded. "And I'd advise you to do the same." She glanced at Robbie. "See you at home?"

"I'll make sure he gets there all right," Lindsey said.

"Thanks," Emma said. She leaned close to Robbie and whispered, "Try to stay out of trouble, Vine." Then she kissed him on the head and left.

Lindsey waited until Emma had given Tim a stern talking-to and they'd both departed before she and Robbie called it an evening. She didn't want to risk opening the door and having Tim and William get an eyeful of each other. Who knew what could happen.

"Again, I'm sorry about your eye," William said. "I really didn't mean to hit you."

"These things happen," Robbie said. He adjusted the bag of ice on his eye. "Not usually to me, but . . ."

"Good night, William," Lindsey said. "I'll be back for the boxes tomorrow."

He stood, looking uncertain, and Lindsey wondered how hard it was for him to be in a place he hadn't lived in over thirty years, facing feelings he obviously hadn't dealt with during his time away. She supposed that explained the scotch. In her opinion, he'd have been better served by just reading a good book. Something like Walter Mosley's Easy Rawlins mysteries. Maybe she'd bring one over with her the next time she came.

Lindsey and Robbie walked silently to the car. Robbie didn't say anything until they were seated inside and Lindsey had started the engine. She was driving his car since his vision was hampered by his swollen eye.

"Well, what do you make of that?" he asked.

"I have no idea," she said. She drove down the cul-de-sac toward a main road. "On the one hand, Tim was furious."

"Defending himself against a slur to his character, as one does," Robbie said.

"But on the other hand, William was ready to fight him," she said. "He didn't run, even though that seemed to be his first inclination."

"There is bad blood between them," Robbie acknowledged. "They each think the other one had something to do with the disappearance of Grace Little."

Lindsey drove to the end of the cul-de-sac and turned onto the main road back to town. She glanced at Robbie and asked, "But which one is right? Or are they both wrong?"

Sully arrived home after his haunted boat tour smelling of the sea. Lindsey hugged him when he leaned over the couch to kiss her head. Heathcliff, their dog, danced around Sully's feet until Sully bent over and gave him all the back scratches his doggy self could handle.

"How did the tour go?" Lindsey asked. She slid her bookmark in between the pages she was reading and closed the novel. Dealing with the Dorchester mansion had inspired her to pick Simone St. James's *The Sun Down Motel*.

"Ian was in rare form," Sully said. "When we passed Horseshoe Island, he convinced half the people on the boat that there was a headless horseman out there. He even managed to make whinnying noises over the PA. One lady screamed that she saw it galloping across the water at us. It helped that it was foggy."

Lindsey laughed. Ian Murphy was Sully's business partner in the boat company and owned the Blue Anchor with his wife, Mary, who was Sully's younger sister. Most often found behind the bar of the restaurant, Ian was the pipeline of gossip for their small town. Lindsey made a mental note to ask him what he'd seen and heard about the history between Tim and William. Not that it was her business, but after tonight's altercation, she wanted more information in case there was another brawl while packing up the Dorchester library.

"How about your night?" Sully asked. "Did you manage to get the rare books packed up?"

He lifted her legs and sat on the couch, replacing her long limbs across his lap. Not to be left out, Heathcliff jumped up onto the couch to sit on Sully's other side. This was Lindsey's favorite part of the day, when everyone was home and they were all safe and sound in their cozy little house.

"Not exactly," she said.

"Uh-oh," Sully said. "Why do I have a feeling there's a story here? Did a door without a lock become locked? Any curtains over closed windows start billowing? You didn't see the ghost cat again, did you?"

"No, nothing like that. But you're not completely wrong. There is a dramatic story to report," she said. She proceeded to tell him about Tim's arrival at the Dorchester mansion and the chaos that ensued.

"I suppose they were bound to meet up at some point," Sully said. "Not that I'm taking sides, but if it was William calling the scoutmaster and the Little League president, that was a rotten thing to do."

"I think so, too. I suppose a scuffle was inevitable, regardless of the slanderous phone calls. Briar Creek is too small to avoid anyone for long."

"Exactly how bad is Robbie's eye?"

"Bigger than a chicken egg but smaller than a goose egg."

"Ouch."

"William felt bad about it," she said. "I got the feeling that he isn't one to get violent very often—if ever. He looked as if he might be physically ill when he realized what he'd done, and he was desperate to make amends."

"You think Tim just brought out the worst in him?" he asked.

"Apparently," she agreed. "Tim was furious. I've never seen him look like that. It was very intimidating."

Sully's bright blue eyes narrowed as he studied her face. "Were you afraid of him?"

Lindsey blinked. "You mean did I think Tim was going to hurt me?"

"Yeah," he said.

"No, not at all," she said. There was something in her husband's voice that put her on high alert. "Is there a reason I would think that Tim would hurt me?"

Sully sighed and tipped his head so it rested on the back

of the couch. "The thing about living in a small town is that once the population has a particular perception of you, it's hard to craft a new image."

"So, if you're a handsome and dashing boat captain in your youth, you're seen that way forever?" she asked.

Sully turned to her and smiled. She felt the warmth of his regard bloom in her chest. "Exactly," he said. "Just like if you're a beautiful bicycling librarian when you arrive in town, you remain so in the collective consciousness permanently."

"This seems okay to me," she said.

"Ah, but the flip side is that if you're a troubled youth with a hot temper, you're always seen as such, no matter how much you contribute to the community," he said.

"Like Tim?" she guessed. "I take it there is more turmoil in his past than just a missing wife?"

"Let's just say he spent a lot of his youth cooling his heels in the town jail," Sully said.

Lindsey nodded. She liked Tim and his wife Barbara. They were regular library users. Tim was always in the sports or scouts section studying up for his coaching and scoutmaster gigs. Barbara was a literacy teacher and a literary reader. She read the highbrow stuff that Lindsey wanted to enjoy but just couldn't quite get there. She was a genre girl through and through, but she admired Barbara's willingness to slog through the stream-of-consciousness jungle that generally left Lindsey longing for something more accessible.

"Do you suppose that's why he went to the Dorchester

mansion tonight?" she asked. "If he's worked so hard to have his reputation rehabilitated, having William show up and remind everyone what he was once like could have set him off."

"That's what I'm worried about," Sully admitted. "I have no reason to think Tim would hurt anyone, but again, small towns have long memories, and he definitely had anger issues as a young man."

Lindsey thought about the Tim Little she knew. It was hard to reconcile that man, the father of two, grandfather of five, devoted husband and all-around nice guy, as a person with a temper that had caused him to be locked up. The man she knew was always the model of patience with the kids he coached and, well, everyone. She'd never seen him so much as roll his eyes at another person.

She glanced at her husband. His forehead was creased in concern. She put her hand on his arm to get his attention, and when he turned back to her, she said, "Straight talk. Do you think Tim killed his bride?"

Sully's face was grim when he answered, "I can't imagine it, I really can't, but ultimately, I just don't know."

CHAPTER

7

BRIAR CREEK
PUBLIC LIBRARY

ast one," Violet La Rue announced as she closed the lid
on the plastic crate. "What time did you say Sully and
Ian were coming to pick these up?"

Lindsey glanced at her watch. It was seven thirty.
"They're supposed to come by at eight," she said. "So we
have a half hour."

"Good." Nancy Peyton stretched out on the floor. "I
need to unkink my spine."

Lindsey smiled at her former landlord while she surveyed the room, making certain they hadn't missed anything. This was the last of the general collection. Lindsey
was still working on the rare books, but it felt good to have
the bulk of the volumes packed up.

She'd been at the mansion every night this week with
different volunteers, and all of the helping hands had

cleared the library out. It felt like a major achievement. As for the rare books, she was hoping to have them finished over the weekend. She glanced at the glassed-in shelves. Not much progress had been made since she and Robbie were here.

There were four large shelving units behind glass, and they'd only managed to empty half of two of them. There had been an emergency meeting of the library board to see if they could accommodate rare books in the Briar Creek Public Library or if the appropriate action would be to send them to Yale University's Beinecke Rare Book and Manuscript Library, which also happened to be Lindsey's former workplace.

She didn't think she was selfish, but she didn't like the idea of moving the books out of town. She glanced at the shelves and saw the mint-condition, first edition set of Andrew Lang's Rainbow Fairy series, published in the early nineteen hundreds. It was such a score that it was hard not to shout from the rooftops. And if the books went to a university library, then the public lost easy access to the collection, which didn't sit well with her.

A movement in the corner of her eye caught Lindsey's attention. She turned to see what appeared to be a cat's tail disappearing behind one of the freestanding bookcases. The cat! There'd been no sightings of it all week, but that had to be it.

Lindsey hurried across the room to the dimly lit corner. She glanced at the drapes in front of the window. Did they move? Was the cat hiding back there again? The fabric billowed, and she reached forward to pull it aside. There was nothing there. She felt the hair on the back of her neck prickle.

There'd been no randomly stuck doors or strange drafts lately, and she'd convinced herself that the other incidents had been the eccentricities of a very old house. But now, she wasn't so sure. The window was shut. There was no logical reason for the curtain to have moved. Maybe the cat was just that quick. She followed the wall, checking behind all of the drapes. There was no sign of it.

"Did you lose something?" Violet asked.

"I thought I saw the cat," Lindsey said.

Nancy rolled up to a seated position. "We need to find it. In a house this large, it could get shut up in a room and die of dehydration."

Violet held out a hand and pulled her friend to her feet. "We'll take this side of the room."

She and Nancy began to search for the cat, and Lindsey continued along the wall, which was just a row of empty built-in bookcases now. She reached the end and paused. She glanced at the last shelving unit and noticed that it stuck out farther than the others. It was just a half-inch difference, but it was definitely noticeable. She walked back to the shelving unit on the other end. It was flush with the others, not sticking out at all. Weird.

She walked back, forgetting about the cat for the moment, and ran her hands over the bookcase.

"Violet, Nancy, come here," she said. "I think I found something odd."

The two women gave up their search for the cat and joined her.

"Odd in this house?" Violet asked, her tone steeped in sarcasm. "How extraordinary."

Nancy laughed and Lindsey smiled. She supposed that it was a tremendous understatement.

"Do you see anything strange about this shelving unit?" Lindsey asked.

The two women studied the shelves.

"It doesn't fit," Nancy said immediately. "It looks narrower than the others."

"It appears to be an add-on," Violet agreed. "Look at the top. The others all reach the ceiling, but this one doesn't."

Lindsey knocked on the inside back panel of the bookcase. It sounded hollow. She knocked on the inside panel of the one beside it. It made a deeper thud as if it were up against something solid.

Nancy's eyes went wide. "Do you think this shelving unit was built over a closet or something?"

"Or something, for sure," Violet said. "But what and why?"

Lindsey stepped back and examined it. There wasn't a visible doorknob or latch. She ran her fingers along the gap at the top. There was nothing but a thick coating of dust and a cobweb. *Blech!* She wiped her fingers on her jeans.

Nancy crouched down and checked the lower shelves while Violet looked at the sides. Lindsey tried to think of what she would do if she wanted access to a room behind a bookcase. It would have books on it, and she wouldn't want them to fall and make a mess if she tried to open the door, so how would she make the door movable when it was full?

"Should we ask William or Marion about this bookcase?" Violet suggested. "Maybe they know why it doesn't fit."

"William and Mrs. Sutcliff took Marion to tour an assisted-living facility," Lindsey said. "Since our packing up the library distresses her so much, William thought it would be a good time for her to be absent."

"I'm pretty sure the assisted-living facility is going to distress her, too," Nancy said. She shook her head. "So many years wasted between them in anger."

"Do you think this time together is bringing them closer?" Violet asked.

Lindsey shook her head. "Not that I've seen. William is intent on doing his duty by his mother, but that's it."

"I guess this is up to us, then," Violet said. She continued running her fingers along the sides.

"Maybe this was the work of a handyman who didn't get it right," Nancy said. She sat back on her heels and frowned.

"That could be," Lindsey said. "Perhaps it was part of a remodel, and they couldn't match it to the original bookcases, although that seems unlikely."

She ran her hands over the shelves, comparing them to the wood of the shelves on the adjacent bookcase. They were very similar, but the shelf in the middle of the add-on felt loose. Lindsey jiggled it and realized it wasn't loose—it was a lever. She carefully lifted it, and with a pop and then a sucking sound as if a seal were being broken, the bookcase detached from the wall.

"You found it!" Violet cried.

"Well, look at that!" Nancy stood up. "Can we open it? Should we open it?"

"Of course we're going to open it," Violet said. "Maybe there are even more books in there. If William is giving the Dorchester collection to the library, that would include whatever is in this secret room. Maybe it's a vault with even more rare materials, like a Mesopotamian tablet or a Shakespeare folio."

"Let's see if it actually opens first," Lindsey said. "Maybe it's just a poorly built shelving unit that's about to fall down on us."

Both Nancy and Violet stepped back, putting their hands up as if to catch it if it fell on Lindsey. She was more concerned that they'd get hurt, but she appreciated the gesture.

"All right, here goes," she said. Holding on to the middle shelf, Lindsey pulled and the door swung open with a high-pitched screech of protest, as if it hadn't been used in years. A pungent malodor of dank dirt and rot wafted out of the empty space, and Lindsey let go of the shelf and pulled the front of her shirt up over her nose. She didn't know what she'd be inhaling, but safety precautions seemed advisable.

She glanced at Violet and Nancy and saw that they did the same. Lindsey glanced back into the space. It was pitch black with only the light from the library behind her illuminating the first few feet of the gaping hole.

"We need a light," she said.

Violet used her free hand to pull her phone out of the pocket of her wide-legged wool pants. She thumbed open the light app and shone it into the opening. The three of them huddled close together as they stared into the room.

The light didn't extend far into the gloom, but the yellow glow illuminated the edge of a braided rug and a table leg. Violet swept the light across the space, and Lindsey saw the tail of the cat.

"Point the light that way!" she cried.

"Which way? Where?" Violet asked.

"To the left," Lindsey said. "I swear I saw the cat."

"The cat?" Nancy asked. "But how did it get in there? We just opened the door!"

"Maybe it snuck in by our feet when we weren't looking," Lindsey said. "I don't know, but we can't let the cat get shut inside." She took a steadying breath. "I'm going in."

"We're going with you," Nancy said.

Violet nodded. She handed Lindsey her phone. "But you can lead."

"Thanks," Lindsey said. For a moment she wondered if she should wait for the Dorchesters to return, but then she thought of the cat. Who knew what was in the rank little room. She didn't want it on her conscience if the cat devoured some rat poison.

She stepped into the dark space, and Violet and Nancy followed her. They were pressed right up against her back as she aimed the light to the left where she thought she'd seen the cat. There was no sign of it.

"Hey, little fella," she crooned. "It's okay. We're not here to hurt you."

Nancy made kissy noises but there was no response. No sign of a twitching tail or a plaintive meow.

"Are we sure we should be in here?" Violet asked. "I'm getting a very creepy feeling."

"I'm not sure of anything," Lindsey admitted. "But I can't stand to think of the cat trapped in here."

"We could leave the door open," Nancy suggested. "Maybe it will come out on its own."

"But the smell," Lindsey said. "I don't think the Dorchesters want this musty, dusty smell to infiltrate their house."

"There aren't enough scented candles to burn to make this dankness go away," Violet agreed.

Lindsey swept the light across the room. She followed the leg of the table up to the tabletop. There sat a lamp and a book. Maybe this was a reading nook that the Dorchesters had forgotten about. Wouldn't that be a find?

Intrigued by the book, she stepped forward to see the title. Was it another rare book? Were there more in here? Was Violet right in assuming there might be a treasure trove of rare books? She felt a tingle of excitement at the possibilities.

Directing the light at the book, she saw the author's name, Poe, on the spine. Edgar Allan Poe, no doubt, but the thick coating of dust obscured the title. Given that it was late October, it seemed a very seasonal choice of book to find in a hidden room. She thought of the master of the macabre and knew he would appreciate what they'd found.

The book was thin, so Lindsey assumed it was a collection of his stories. She reached out to pick up the book but stopped. A flash of white reflected the phone's light. She moved the cell phone and gasped. There was a hand on the table beside the book. Except it wasn't a hand, not really. It was all bones, no flesh.

"Ah!" Violet cried. "Oh my God! What is that?"

"It's a hand!" Nancy shrieked. "A skeleton's hand!"

As one, they jumped back from the table and scurried to the door, tripping over each other in their haste to get out. Nancy reached it first, but just as she was about to exit, the door slammed shut, knocking her back into the hidden room. Violet caught her before she fell.

"Did you see that?" Nancy asked. Her voice was shaky. "Someone or *something* slammed the door."

"I have a really bad feeling about this," Violet said.

The two women huddled together. They looked terrified. Lindsey was right there with them, but she refused to succumb to the fear coursing through her. Instead, she directed her light onto the door. She ran her hands over the cold, smooth surface of the steel. Her heart was racing, and her skin felt tight. Her shoulder blades were pinched as if she expected whatever might be sitting at the table behind her to fly across the room and stab her in the back. She could feel a scream in her throat, but she refused to let it out.

The light from Violet's phone lit up the interior side of

the door. The light shook as Lindsey trembled, and she tried to calm down. She ran her fingers over the surface, looking for a latch of any sort, but there was nothing. She noticed there were deep gouges in the metal, as if someone had tried to pry their way out. She felt woozy and rested her forehead against the door for a moment.

"Open the door," Nancy begged. "Hurry."

"I can't," Lindsey said. "There's no doorknob or handle or anything. We're trapped."

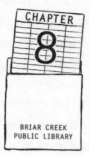

CHAPTER

8

BRIAR CREEK
PUBLIC LIBRARY

W e're going to die," Nancy said. Her voice was high and
tight and tinged with hysteria. "There's something in
here with us, and I bet it wants us to die, too! Its spirit
probably slammed the door shut!"

Violet let out a little noise that sounded like a whimper.

"Let's take a beat," Lindsey said. "Take a breath, slow
your heartbeat, we're okay, and we'll figure this out."

"But the door," Violet said. "How can we be okay if
something locked us in here?"

"I don't think that's what happened," Lindsey said. She
was pleased that her voice came out so steady when she was
positively quaking on the inside. "I'm sure the bookcase
just swung back to its usual position. Who knows how long
it's been shut. I'm guessing years." She tried to remain calm
and reasonable. It was a struggle, knowing that there was

a skeletal hand on the table just feet from where they stood. Lindsey's hand was shaking, bouncing the light all over the wall, creating a strobe effect that was making her nauseous. She noticed that they were all faced away from the table . . . or what might be sitting at the table.

In fact, they were pressed up against the closed door, trying to get as far away as possible from the skeletal hand. Lindsey could feel her heart pounding in her chest. She tried to take calming breaths, but the air was thick and musty even through her shirt, which she'd yanked back up over her nose and mouth, and it felt as if the grit and dirt were coating her throat. Her mouth was dry, making the sensation even worse.

"There has to be another way out of here," Nancy said. "Maybe there's a window." She nudged Violet. "Why don't you go look?"

"Me?" Violet asked. "Why not you?"

"You're taller," Nancy said.

"What does that have to do with anything?"

"You can see more from up there than I can from down here," Nancy said.

Lindsey closed her eyes, steeling herself for what she knew she had to do. Her heart rate was slowing. Weirdly, the bickering was calming her down. She turned and leaned her back against the door.

Violet and Nancy stopped arguing, and Lindsey heard them turn around and shift closer together. When she glanced over, they were hanging on to each other, eyes wide and mouths compressed into firm lines as if to keep in their screams.

She slowly lifted her phone flashlight up to get a better look at the hand on the table. Maybe it was just a silly prop. Perhaps it was left here decades ago by a Dorchester who was into pranks or realistic Halloween decorations. Lindsey let out a wheezy breath. Now that her initial fright had passed, she was certain there had to be a reasonable explanation.

"It's probably not what we thought it was," she said. "Maybe one of the Dorchesters is a doctor and this was something from their office."

"You're right," Nancy said. "Why didn't we think of that?"

"Could be a prop," Violet said.

"Or a decoration, given that Halloween is coming up fast," Nancy added. She visibly relaxed and let out a small laugh. "Oh, geez, I feel ridiculous."

"Me, too," Violet said.

Lindsey was glad they were calmer, but her stomach was still in knots. They needed to figure out how to get out of there. Maybe another part of the room would offer them a clue. With a steadier hand, she moved the circle of light from the tabletop with the book to the skeletal hand. She swallowed and moved the light up the hand to see that, yes, it was attached to an arm, then a body, a neck, until finally the skull was revealed. The full skeleton was slumped across the table as the bones succumbed to gravity without the ligaments holding them together. When Lindsey shone the light on the skull, where it rested on the table as if taking a nap, it stared back at them with its jaw sagging, its eye sockets vacant, and a knot of blond hair hanging off the back of its skull.

This was no prop, or medical school study aid, or Halloween decoration. This had once been a flesh-and-blood person, and Lindsey suspected that he or she had died exactly where they were sitting.

"Dear God," Violet muttered while Nancy spun around and started banging on the door.

"Help!" she cried. "Help! We're trapped and we can't get out!" She pounded it with her fists and then kicked the door with the toe of her sneaker for good measure.

There was no response from the other side of the bookcase. Nancy drooped against it. She was shaking, and Lindsey reached out and took her hand in her free one. Her voice was very firm when she said, "It's all right. We're together and we're okay. That skeleton can't hurt us."

She handed the phone to Violet, who was holding Nancy's other hand.

"Can you open your phone and try to call the police?" Lindsey asked. "I don't know if we can get a signal in here, but it's worth a try."

Violet let go of Nancy. Her hands were shaking, and her eyes kept darting to the skeleton as if she expected it to speak or move or something. Lindsey understood that completely.

"No, no signal," Violet said. She kept the light on the skeleton, who was wearing the tattered remnants of a dress with a wide white collar and shoulder pads. She glanced down at the skeleton's feet and saw they were encased in white leather sneakers. A dress with sneakers? It seemed so *Working Girl*, the movie where career girls would wear sneakers during their commute and then switch to heels for the office. She stared more closely at the dress. The bright colored fabric definitely had an eighties vibe to it.

Maybe it was because of the recent dustup between William Dorchester and Tim Little, but Lindsey couldn't help but wonder if this was her. Was this Grace Little? Had they inadvertently just solved the thirty-three-year-old cold case of where the runaway bride had gone?

"I think I know—" Lindsey began, but Nancy shushed her.

There was a muffled noise coming from the other side of the door.

"Someone's out there!" Nancy said. "Let's make some noise!"

All three of them started banging on the door and yelling at the top of their lungs. Lindsey thought about the claw marks. Had those been made by the woman behind her in a desperate bid to get out? The thought made her sick to her stomach.

"Lindsey!" Sully shouted just outside the door.

"Yes, I'm here!"

"What in the . . ." His voice became muffled as they heard him trying to move the bookcase. There was another male voice that Lindsey assumed belonged to Ian.

She leaned close and said, "The middle shelf."

"What?" Sully shouted.

"The middle shelf!" Lindsey cried. "Lift it!"

There was the low murmur of voices, some banging, and

then a pop. The bookcase swung forward, and the three women fell out of the dark, dank room into the bright light of the library.

Ian caught Nancy, and Sully reached for Violet, helping them out of the hidden room. When Violet was steady, Sully grabbed Lindsey and pulled her into a hug.

"Are you all right?" he asked. His hands ran over her shoulders and arms as if he were taking inventory, ensuring that she was in one piece.

"I'm okay," she said. "We're okay."

"Nothing a bottle of scotch and three hours of therapy won't cure at any rate," Nancy said.

"Is that really a secret room?" Ian asked. He blinked behind his glasses as if he couldn't believe what he was seeing.

"Not so much a secret room as a tomb," Violet said.

"What?" Sully asked. His gaze shot to Lindsey's. She nodded.

"There's a body in there," Nancy whispered as if she didn't want to wake the skeletal remains up.

"No way!" Ian gasped. He clapped his hands onto his balding head and stared at the dark space behind the bookcase. "Who is it?"

Lindsey didn't say what she suspected. She glanced at Violet and Nancy.

"No one we could recognize," Nancy said. Her voice was shaky, and she glanced around the library. "Where do they keep the booze in this place?"

"Come on," Violet said. "Let's go to the kitchen and get you a cool glass of water or something."

"'Or something' sounds about right," Nancy said.

"I'm going to call Emma," Lindsey said. "The police will have to investigate."

Ian crept closer to the opening. He flicked on the flashlight app on his phone and aimed it into the room. When the light reflected the skull's white bones with the vacant eye sockets and sagging jaw, he swore and jumped back, dropping his phone into the room. It illuminated the skeleton sitting at the table. The light shining on it from below made the skull look even creepier, if that was possible.

Lindsey glanced away. Sully, clearly sensing she was upset, moved her behind him as he peered into the room.

"Why don't I call Emma?" he asked. "You can check on Violet and Nancy."

Lindsey desperately wanted to get away from the claustrophobic little space, but she didn't want to make this situation his problem. "No, I can call her. I just need to catch my breath."

"It's all right," he said. "You're safe and we can help. Ian, why don't you go grab your phone?"

"Nope." Ian shook his head. "I don't need it. It's fine. I was planning to get a new one anyway."

His freckles stood out on his pale face, and Lindsey knew exactly how he felt. She stepped close and gave him a quick hug.

"I can't believe you were trapped in there with that," Ian said. He hugged her back. "I'd have stroked out in terror."

Sully stepped into the room and grabbed Ian's phone from the floor. He moved the light around the room, taking in the old carpet and the lone table, with an empty jug of water and some unidentifiable food items, two chairs and the skeleton. He lingered on her as if he was trying to see who she might have been. Lindsey stayed in the library, admiring his fortitude from afar.

"I think this must have been an old bomb shelter or panic room of some sort," he said. "There're no windows or doors, and the only way in or out is through this bookcase door."

"There's no latch or doorknob on the inside," Lindsey said. "In fact . . ." She paused to take a steadying breath. "On the inside of the door, it looks as though someone tried to claw their way out."

"That's it," Ian declared. "I'm out." He backed away from them and then turned and fled in the same direction Violet and Nancy had departed.

"Okay, now that everyone's gone, tell me exactly what happened as you remember it," Sully said. He stepped back into the library and switched off the light on Ian's phone.

Lindsey described the events of the evening. She was pleased that her voice sounded composed, even when a shiver rippled through her at the recollection of finding the body.

"Where are the Dorchesters?" Sully asked.

"William and Mrs. Sutcliff took Marion to visit an assisted-living home," she said. "They should be back soon."

"Good," Sully said. "I have no doubt Emma is going to want to talk to them."

"Emma, right." Lindsey shook her head. "I'll call her now."

"Should we close the bookcase door until she gets here?"

"We can't," Lindsey said. "The whole reason we went in there was because I saw the cat. It was prowling through the room, and then we found the door and . . ."

"The body," he finished for her.

"Yeah," she said. "But now I don't know where the cat is, and I don't want to risk shutting it inside there."

Lindsey crossed the room to where she'd left her handbag and took her phone out of the side pocket. She opened her contacts and pressed Emma's personal number. She walked back to Sully and put the call on speakerphone so he could hear the conversation, too.

"Lindsey, please do not tell me there's been another fight," Emma answered.

"No, no fight," Lindsey said.

Emma let out a relieved sigh. "Okay, then, shoot."

"There's a body," Lindsey said. "In the Dorchester mansion."

Emma let out a string of profanity that made Ian's previous expletive sound like that of an altar boy.

"Explain," Emma demanded.

"We found a secret room behind one of the bookcases in the library, and when we went inside, we found a skeleton."

"Did you touch anything?"

"No, just the door," Lindsey said.

"Is everyone safe? No one is injured?"

"We're all fine," Lindsey said. "Rattled but fine."

"Okay, don't let anyone else go in there," Emma ordered.

"Got it."

"I'm on my way," Emma said. She ended the call.

Lindsey lowered the phone. She glanced at Sully, who had taken one of the packed boxes and wedged it in the gap to keep the door open.

"She always sounds so happy to hear from me," Lindsey said. "I wonder when she's going to stop taking my calls."

He put an arm around her shoulders and pulled her close, comforting her with his solid presence. Lindsey leaned in. This was definitely the biggest perk to being married to her best friend. She didn't have to manage the scary stuff all alone anymore.

"It's going to be all right," he said. "I'm sure Emma will call in a crime scene team, and they'll be able to identify the remains."

Lindsey glanced at him. "I think I know who it is."

He looked surprised. "Who?"

"The runaway bride."

Sully let out a low whistle. "What makes you think it's her?"

"A quick glance at what's left of her clothes," she said. "It reminded me of the outfits I've seen in pictures of my parents before they had kids, very nineteen eighties."

"That fits," he agreed. "Grace Little, who'd have thought she'd be found here after all these years?"

"Grace?" a voice interrupted them. They turned to see

William standing in the doorway to the library. "Did you say Grace was found?"

"Um . . ." Lindsey didn't know what to say.

"Uh," Sully echoed. Obviously, he was at a loss as well.

"What's going on in here?" William demanded. He planted his hands on his hips and glanced from her to Sully and back.

Lindsey felt her heart drop into her feet. She did not want to be the one to tell William what they'd found in a secret room. Did he even know the room existed?

If he did, could he have been the one to murder Grace and put her in there? Is that why he disappeared to Florida for so many years? Was he escaping the scene of his crime?

But why would he have killed her when, by all accounts, he had broken up with her because his mother didn't approve of the relationship? Maybe he couldn't bear the thought of her being married to Tim, and he'd had one of those "if I can't have you, no one can" ex-boyfriend episodes.

But if he had murdered her and shoved her in the bomb shelter / panic room or whatever it was, then why would he have invited Lindsey to come and clear out the library? He couldn't have forgotten what he'd done. Or, because no one had ever found the room, had he just assumed that no one ever would? Lindsey felt as if her head were spinning with all of the possibilities. Of course, it could be that it wasn't Grace Little, and that there was an entirely different mystery to solve.

Sully shifted to stand in front of the open bookcase, as

if he could hide what was behind the open door. She reached for his hand. How were they going to stall William until Emma arrived?

"William, you're just in time." Nancy came back into the library. She was brandishing a snifter of scotch. "If ever a day needed a nightcap at the end of it, it's this one."

Violet was right behind her, clutching her own glass, and Ian followed them, looking much better than he had a few minutes ago.

"Is that my good scotch?" William demanded.

"It is," Ian said. He raised his glass to William. "You have excellent taste, sir."

William stood gaping at them. He turned to Lindsey and demanded, "What is the meaning of this?"

Emma strode into the room, looking grumpy. She glanced at all of them and then focused on Lindsey. "Show me."

"Show you what?" William demanded. "What is going on? This is my house, you know. I deserve an explanation."

Emma glanced at him and then at Lindsey. "You didn't tell him?"

"Didn't get the chance," she said.

"That's for the best," Emma said. She turned to Violet, Nancy and Ian. "Out . . . please."

"Back to the kitchen, ladies," Ian said. He held out both of his arms, and Violet looped her hand through one while Nancy took the other. The three of them headed for the door, turning sideways to fit through the narrow opening, and disappeared from sight.

"Mr. Dorchester, an unfortunate discovery has been

made in your home," Emma said. She strode toward Sully, who moved aside.

"Is that—?" William started when he saw the opening. "Is that a secret door?"

"Yes," Lindsey said.

Emma took the flashlight off her utility belt. She flicked it on and shone it into the room. She stepped inside, disappearing from view.

"How . . . when . . . I don't understand," William said. "Has that always been there?"

"You didn't know about it?" Lindsey asked. She studied his face. She didn't know him well enough to tell if he was lying, but he looked genuinely perplexed. Then again, if he were a cold-blooded killer, he would, wouldn't he?

"No, I had no idea." He glanced at the doorway behind him. His face was creased with concern. "My mother . . . Mrs. Sutcliff is putting her to bed. Tonight was difficult, and I don't—"

Emma reentered the room. Her face was grim, the lines around her eyes and mouth tight with tension. "Mr. Dorchester, I have a lot of questions for you. Is there a private place where we can talk?"

"I have a study," he said. He looked wary.

"That'll do," she said. Emma turned to Sully. "Can you keep everyone out of the room until the crime scene people are here?"

"Sure thing," he said.

"Crime scene?" William echoed. "What are you talking about? What crime?"

"I'll explain," Emma said. She gestured to the door.

William looked from her to the bookcase. Then he surprised them all by shoving past her and storming across the room.

"Mr. Dorchester, stop!" Emma snapped. She followed him, and Sully and Lindsey joined her.

William ignored them. He fumbled with his phone and turned on the flashlight. When he aimed the light into the room, he gave a cry of fright and then reared back away from the door.

Emma caught him by the elbow. "I'm sorry. I know it's a shock."

"A shock?" he cried. He looked at her as if she was not appreciating his distress. "There's a skeleton in my house!"

"Yes," Emma said.

"Is it real?" he asked. His voice was thin, as if he barely had enough air to push the words out.

"Yes."

He drooped and Sully caught him by the arm. He helped him over to one of the armchairs in front of the fireplace. William bent forward, putting his head between his knees while he dragged in long breaths of air through his nose.

Emma put her hand on his back. "I'm sorry, Mr. Dorchester, but it appears your home was potentially the scene of a murder, and I will be investigating it accordingly."

CHAPTER

9

BRIAR CREEK
PUBLIC LIBRARY

Sully and Lindsey waited in the library while Emma took William to his study. She'd said she wanted to talk to them after she spoke with William, and they agreed to wait. Officer Kirkland arrived and took their statements. When Lindsey got to the part about finding the skeleton, he put on his blue latex gloves and entered the secret room.

A big, rawboned redhead, Kirkland had the height and the breadth that made him seem as immovable as a mountain. When he came out of the secret room, however, he was pasty pale, shaking and, if Lindsey wasn't mistaken, about to throw up.

Sully took one look at him before grabbing Kirkland by the arm and dragging him out of the room to the nearby bathroom. He came back without him and Lindsey asked, "Is he all right?"

"He will be," Sully said. "He's still pretty new to the force, and while he's dealt with some grisly stuff, this was his first close encounter with this sort of thing."

"He's not alone there," Lindsey said. She didn't know if it was just because it was so close to Halloween or if finding a skeleton would have freaked her out this much any other time of the year, but with the chill in the air and jack-o'-lanterns springing up all over town, it seemed particularly ghoulish to have found skeletal remains.

Once he'd recovered, Kirkland took statements from Nancy, Violet and Ian. When they were done, Nancy's nephew Charlie picked them up and took them home as none of them were in a fit state to drive. Lindsey didn't blame them a bit. She had a feeling that the skeleton in the library was going to haunt her dreams for many nights to come.

She and Sully sat in the two armchairs at the end of the library away from the secret room. While they waited for Emma, Lindsey felt something brush against her ankle. The anxiety of the evening caused her to jump, and Sully looked at her in surprise.

"Are you all right?" he asked.

"Yeah, I just thought I felt something," she said. She forced a smile. Then she leaned forward and glanced down. Peeking out from beneath the chair was the cat. Its bright green eyes and beautiful gray fur were just as she remembered. "Oh, it's the cat."

Sully's eyebrows lifted. "The one that led you to the hidden room?"

She nodded. Making her voice soft, she addressed the cat, "Hello there. Where did you come from?"

Lindsey didn't want to scare it away, so she very slowly lowered her hand. The cat watched her. It didn't move. She stayed perfectly still, and then, just as it had before, it leaned into her fingers and let her rub the sides of its face.

"What should we do?" Lindsey asked. "William said they don't own a cat, but this one keeps appearing in the house. We should take it to Tom, our veterinarian, or a shelter or something, shouldn't we?"

"Definitely," Sully said. He watched as the cat rubbed against Lindsey and purred. "It looks thin."

Lindsey reached down and gently put her hand beneath the cat and lifted it up onto her lap. To her surprise, it let her. In fact, it arched its back, yawned and then started to knead her jeans as if it belonged there.

"Aw," Lindsey said. She stroked the cat's back. The fur was thick and soft and the most beautiful shade of charcoal gray with just the tip of its tail dark black, as if it had been dipped in a bucket of paint. She glanced up at Sully, and he gave her a rueful look as he reached over and held out his hand so the cat could nuzzle the backs of his fingers. It purred loudly in approval of all the attention.

"Why do I get the feeling we've just been claimed?" he asked. The cat grabbed his hand with its two front paws and blinked at him.

Sully's handsome face crumbled at the onslaught of cuteness and he said, "I'll call Tom and see if he can take him or her in tonight."

Lindsey nodded. "We'll have to see if it belongs to any-one. It could be a neighborhood cat that just likes to come here."

"Because of the incredibly welcoming atmosphere, no doubt," Sully said. His tone was dry and Lindsey chuckled.

"Exactly, who could resist this creeptastic ambience?" she asked.

A knock on the front door interrupted their conversation, and Sully went to answer it. The cat did not seem to care. It yawned and burrowed into Lindsey's lap, content to nap while the humans hurried around the house doing whatever it was humans felt compelled to do.

Lindsey could hear Sully talking with whoever was at the door, and he returned shortly with what appeared to be crime scene investigators from the state police. At least, that's what she assumed since they were wearing standard-issue white Tyvek coveralls, booties and latex gloves. There was an older man with a full beard—brown going gray—wearing black rectangular glasses, and a younger woman with a ball of dark hair pinned on top of her head, a tattoo of a dragonfly on her neck and a silver ring through her eyebrow. She was playing with a flashlight. She held it up under her chin, making her face ghoulish.

"This is so cool, Dr. Rogers," she said to the man. "We never get called for skeletons."

The older man put his hand on hers and lowered the flashlight so that it shone on the floor.

"Callie, remember when I told you that you needed to be more sensitive while on-site?" Dr. Rogers asked.

"Yeah." Callie nodded. She scratched the side of her nose and bit her lip.

"This would be one of those times, and that"—he gestured to the flashlight and then her face—"is not sensitive."

"Oh." She pursed her lips. "Sorry."

"Hmm." He made a noise in the back of his throat that sounded like he was out of patience.

"This is Lindsey Norris, our local librarian. She's also the one who found the remains," Sully said, introducing her. "This is Dr. Rogers and his assistant, Callie Bristow."

"Thanks for coming out," Lindsey said. "I know it's late."

"Crime doesn't sleep," Callie said. She grinned. Lindsey found herself smiling back, which felt weird given the circumstance. The woman had an infectious personality, which was good because Dr. Rogers was very dour and very intimidating.

"I may have some questions for you, Ms. Norris," Dr. Rogers said. "If that's all right?"

"Of course," Lindsey said. "Anything I can do to help."

"Chief Plewicki is talking with the homeowner, and Officer Kirkland is . . . on his way," Sully said. Lindsey knew he was being careful not to embarrass Kirkland by mentioning he'd gotten sick. "I can show you the hidden room, and then I'll go get the chief."

"Thank you," Dr. Rogers said. He followed Sully across the room, but Callie paused and glanced at the cat in Lindsey's lap.

"She's a pretty cat," she said.

"She?"

"It looks like it," Callie said. "No visible boy parts."

"Oh," Lindsey said. That seemed reasonable. "We found her wandering around the house."

"Well, that makes sense," Callie said. "Cats are more in tune with the spiritual world than us mere humans."

Lindsey studied the cat—she had her paw over her nose, completely relaxed even though she was twisted up into a tight circle that would have broken Lindsey's spine if she attempted such a position. Was that why the cat was here? Did it sense something otherworldly in the house? Lindsey thought about all of the weird things that had happened while they packed up the library. Locked doors, billowing curtains, lights going out, all things that they hadn't been able to explain, and yet the cat had shown no fear.

"Callie!" Dr. Rogers called from the hidden room.

"Oh, gotta go!" Callie patted the cat on the head and dashed across the room.

Sully returned carrying a cardboard box. He set it down beside Lindsey and said, "Let's put the cat in here so we don't lose it. I made plenty of air holes."

"Good idea," Lindsey said.

She glanced inside the box and noticed that Sully had put his hooded sweatshirt in the bottom so that it was more comfortable. She gently lifted the cat and set her inside. Surprisingly, the cat settled into the sweatshirt as if she'd been waiting for just such an accommodation.

"Good girl," Lindsey said.

"Girl?" Sully asked as he closed the lid, taping it shut.

"Callie said she's a girl," Lindsey explained.

"Well, okay, then," he said. "I'm going to let Emma know that the crime scene investigators are here. Do you mind looping Kirkland in when he returns?"

"Not at all," she said.

He smiled. Then he kissed her head and said, "I'll be right back."

Lindsey watched him leave the library to go to the study, where Emma was still talking to William. She wondered how that was going. William had looked horrified at the sight of the skeleton. If it was Grace, there were so many questions that needed answers. How she got in there was the first one that sprang to mind. She glanced at the secret room to see how Callie and Dr. Rogers were doing inside. There was a glow coming from the room because of the spotlight they'd set up.

"He did it," a soft voice said.

Lindsey started and turned away from the hidden room. She found Marion Dorchester standing beside her chair, almost looming over her. She was barefoot, wearing her nightgown and a thick pale blue bathrobe, which was hanging off her shoulders as if she had just slipped it on but hadn't bothered to tie it. Her black hair was flat on one side as if she'd just been asleep. Her eyes, pale blue and wide, stared at Lindsey as if trying to make her understand.

"I'm sorry, what?" Lindsey asked. How had Marion gotten into the room without her noticing?

"Timothy Little did it," Marion said.

"Did what?" Lindsey asked.

"He killed you," Marion replied. She reached out a hand as if she would stroke Lindsey's hair, but then she snatched it back. Her eyes narrowed and she said, "I'm glad he did. You weren't good enough for my William."

"I . . . um . . . I'm not her," Lindsey said. She realized Marion was having another episode and didn't recognize her, but she also wanted Marion to keep talking. Maybe she knew something about Grace being in the hidden room.

"Mother, what are you doing down here?" William strode into the library with Emma and Sully following him.

"I had to see," Marion said. "I had to see Grace. And look, she's come back and everything is fine. Now you can come back, too."

William's face went pale. He looked like he might be sick. "She's not Grace. Her name is Lindsey. She's a librarian here in town. She's married to this man, Mike Sullivan."

Marion glanced from Lindsey to Sully. Her expression was confused. "But I heard the people talking in the kitchen. They said they found her." She waved her hands at Lindsey. "And here she is."

"What were you doing in the kitchen?" William asked.

"I wanted a cookie," Marion said. She had an impish expression, like a child caught sneaking out of bed. "I like cookies. I heard the man say that Grace is here, that she's been here all along."

Lindsey glanced at Sully. He looked as uncomfortable as she felt. Marion Dorchester was failing mentally, and it was awful to see her struggle to differentiate the present and the past.

"I'm not Grace, Mrs. Dorchester," Lindsey said. "I'm Lindsey."

Marion seemed to consider this. Then she shook her head decisively. "No, I remember you. You're her, and you're *not* our kind of people." She sniffed and lifted her nose in the air.

Lindsey didn't know what to say to that. It was odd being snubbed for being someone else, and it didn't feel any less lousy.

"Mother, you're talking nonsense," William said. "I've told you, this is Lindsey. She doesn't look anything like Grace."

Marion turned toward her son. Her face was furious. "You want to marry *her*? A Hartwell? They're nothing but liars and thieves. Her own mother ran out on her father after stealing everything he owned. I forbid it. Do you hear me? I forbid it."

Emma stepped forward. She narrowed her eyes at Marion. "When was the last time you saw Grace, Mrs. Dorchester?"

Marion looked at her in confusion. "What do you mean? She's right there." She gestured to Lindsey.

"She isn't Grace!" William exploded. "That is Lindsey. You said she was Grace the other day, and we corrected you then, too. Grace is dead, Mother. Dead."

"I said that?" Marion's face crumpled. A tear slid down her wrinkled cheek. She glanced at them all, looking lost and confused. Lindsey felt her heart pinch. How awful it must be to feel trapped in your own mind.

"Mrs. Dorchester, there you are." Mrs. Sutcliff entered

the room. She put her hand over her heart as if to calm it. "I popped in to check on her before retiring for the night, and she was gone."

"She went to the kitchen," William said.

"So our guests told me when I stopped in there looking for her," Mrs. Sutcliff said. "I think she scared a year off me." She shook her head. "Let's get you back to bed, Mrs. Dorchester. I'll bring you a cookie and some warm milk."

"Oh, that would be nice," Marion said. She let Mrs. Sutcliff take her arm, and she smiled up at her. "You're so good to me. You're the only one who cares, Nanny."

Silently, they watched as the two women made their way to the stairs. When they were out of earshot, William said, "Nanny. She's begun calling Mrs. Sutcliff that as if she's a child and has her beloved nanny back." He squeezed the bridge of his nose between his fingers as if trying to gather his wits. He then turned to Lindsey and said, "I'm sorry. Her dementia is getting worse by the day. I need to get her into an assisted-living facility and soon."

"It's all right," Lindsey said. "No harm done."

William glanced at the staircase where his mother had departed. He looked wary and horrified as if he was besieged by thoughts he found deeply disturbing. Then he turned back to Lindsey and said, "I'm not so sure about that."

CHAPTER

10

BRIAR CREEK
PUBLIC LIBRARY

When Sully knocked, Tom Rubinski, the vet, answered the door to his clinic, with his golden retriever Sam by his side. With a wide warm smile, he waved for them to enter.

"Thank you so much, Tom," Lindsey said. "Sorry to come by so late, but we found this cat and she looks thin and we have no idea what to do with her. Beth is my only hard-core cat friend, but I didn't want to burden her since she's a new mom."

"It's fine," Tom said. "Anything for Heathcliff's parents. How is my boy?"

Sully grinned like a proud father. "Smartest dog in town, present company excluded."

Lindsey bent over to scratch Sam's ears just the way he liked it.

"So, you have a new pet?" Tom asked. "Another rescue from the library?"

"Sort of," Lindsey said. "Zelda keeps appearing—"

"Zelda?" Sully interrupted.

"Just trying it out," Lindsey said. "When I described the cat to Beth, she said the way the cat trolled around the Dorchester mansion, obviously enjoying the finer things, reminded her of Daisy Buchanan."

"She doesn't look like a Daisy," Sully said. "So, I'm guessing you went with Zelda because . . ."

"F. Scott modeled Daisy after his wife Zelda," Tom finished.

Lindsey glanced between them. "I'm impressed. Neither of you thought it was from the name of that video game."

"That was my second guess," Tom teased.

Lindsey smiled. "Anyway, the cat keeps appearing inside the Dorchester mansion, but the residents said they don't own a cat."

"Does anyone really 'own' a cat?" Tom asked. "It's generally more a matter of the cat owning you."

Lindsey smiled. "Well, there is that."

"Let's have a look," Tom said. He sent a pointed look at Sam, who went and curled up on his dog bed in the corner. "Good boy."

Sully placed the cardboard box on the exam table and popped open the top. Tom looked inside and said, "Aren't you a beauty? She's a Russian Blue, very rare, not the sort of cat that you usually find as a stray."

"Have you heard anyone say they're missing one?"

Lindsey asked. She was surprised by how much she didn't want anyone to own the cat. Why? She had Heathcliff. She did not need another pet.

"Not to me," he said. "But you can always put up flyers. I'll bet there are any number of cat lovers who would love to take her."

Tom lifted her out of the box. Zelda offered minimal protest apart from a soft "mew." He checked her over while Sully and Lindsey stood to the side like anxious parents.

"She is on the thin side," he said. "But she has been spayed, I can see the faint line of the scar, so she must have belonged to someone at some point. I can check for a microchip, which may solve the whole mystery of who her family is."

Lindsey felt her heart drop. She reached out and scratched the feline's head. Zelda purred in response and blinked her green eyes at her.

"I can keep her overnight for observation and run some blood work on her," Tom said. "We'll also make certain she doesn't have any life-threatening illnesses. If she has feline leukemia virus or something worse, it could be that her owners just booted her out."

"What?" Sully cried. "Who does that sort of thing?"

"The same type who shoved a puppy in a book drop a few years ago," Lindsey said.

He grumbled under his breath, and Lindsey knew he was cussing out the heartless people who didn't value their animals.

"When would we get the test results back?" Lindsey asked.

"Two days at most," Tom said. "I can rush them through while you search for her owners, assuming there is no microchip."

"That'd be great," Sully said. "And, of course, you can bill us for her care."

"That's generous of you," Tom said. "Given that you might just be giving her back to her people."

"If we find them," Sully said. "It seems to me if they really wanted her back, we'd have seen MISSING signs for her posted around town or on the online neighborhood bulletin board."

"We'll think of it as an investment in our future pet," Lindsey said. Sully glanced at her in surprise, and she shrugged. "I can't help it. I just think she belongs with us."

Sully nodded. He took her hand in his and gave her fingers a squeeze. "I do, too."

After several more pets of the cat, they left Tom with thanks. Lindsey felt bad that they had to leave her, but she knew Tom would take excellent care of her.

On the ride home, she said, "So, this night was unexpected."

"In so many ways," Sully agreed. He glanced from the road to her. "How are you doing? That had to be terrifying, getting trapped in that room with those remains."

"If I hadn't had Violet and Nancy with me, I might have died of fright or claustrophobia," she said. "And that is not hyperbole. There was something about that skeleton sitting at the table with its hand resting beside a book that was like something out of a horror film."

"Halloween is coming," he said. "You don't think it was an elaborate prank, do you?"

"No, but finding a skeleton this close to the holiday is a little too on point," Lindsey said. "Do you think Violet, Nancy and Ian are going to be okay?"

"Charlie texted that he managed to get them into his van all right," he said. "Although, I imagine they might not be feeling too great tomorrow."

"Hopefully they won't be seeing that skeleton in their dreams," she said. "I can't seem to get the image out of my mind. Thank goodness the cat came along to give me something else to think about. How long do you think it will take them to confirm that the remains belong to Grace Little?"

"You sound as if you've already made up your mind," he said.

"I just feel like it has to be her," she said. "The clothes clinched it for me. Wide collars and shoulder pads. I wonder if Tim gave a description of what she was wearing when she went missing?"

"I'm sure he must have," he said.

"And Emma would have that in the old case report," she said. "I'll bet we know something soon. I hope so at any rate. She told me that I'd have to halt moving the library books until their investigation is complete. I'm worried the books might get damaged."

"Hopefully there is an old case report," Sully said. "We've been through a few chiefs of police since then."

"Right." Lindsey stared out the window, studying their

night-draped village as they drove to their small gray cottage by the water. Briar Creek was the sort of place where everyone knew their neighbor's business, families dated back to the settling of the area, and being a "Creeker," meaning you were born and raised there, stood for something.

"What are you thinking?" Sully asked.

"That someone had to have overheard the fight between Tim and Grace at the restaurant that night," she said. "Otherwise how would everyone know about it? But what was said? What did they fight about? Did he seem violent?"

"I've known him for a long time, and it's hard for me to picture Tim as a violent man," Sully said. He turned his truck onto their street. "He's been the scoutmaster and Little League coach for forever."

"That doesn't mean he didn't hurt his wife," Lindsey said. "He was a young man back then. It could have been a horrible mistake that he's been trying to make amends for ever since."

"But how did Grace, assuming that was Grace in the hidden room, end up at the Dorchester mansion?" Sully asked. "How would Tim have access to the house, and how would he have known about the secret room?"

Lindsey shrugged. "Maybe he heard about it from her. She did date William and must have been in the house at some point, and maybe he planted her there to make it look like it was William who murdered her."

"That's more than a guy who made a horrible mistake, then." Sully shook his head. "That's a guy who killed someone and actively tried to hide the evidence and blame it on someone else."

"That does make it feel like a much darker crime," she said. "If that's even possible."

"You know who I feel terrible for?" Sully asked. "Tim's wife, Barbara. This is going to be a nightmare for her. All the old gossip will be back in full force."

"She's such a nice lady," Lindsey agreed. "Always involved in the community, she teaches an adult literacy class at the library once a week, and she's always willing to help in any way she can. Tim is like that, too. Despite our conversation, I really do have a hard time believing him capable of murder."

Sully parked in their driveway. Lindsey glanced at the house. A little face peered out the window at them. His black nose was pressed up against the glass, leaving a puff of hot breath against the window.

"Assuming no one claims the cat," Lindsey said, "do you think Heathcliff can handle sharing his parents with a feline?"

"Yes, absolutely," Sully said. "He's a good boy, and look at it this way, now when we're gone at work, he'll have a buddy."

They climbed out of the truck and followed the path to the front door. The already fallen leaves crunched under Lindsey's shoes, and the late October air nipped her ears and her nose. She danced from foot to foot, trying to stay warm while waiting for Sully to unlock the door.

As usual, Sully warned her and said, "Incoming!"

Lindsey bent her knees slightly in anticipation of the impact. Sure enough, Heathcliff shot out the door, as exuberant in his greeting as if they'd been parted for months instead of just hours. He jumped up on his back feet, hugging her around the knees while he wagged his tail off.

"Who's a good boy?" Lindsey asked. "Who's Mama's good boy?"

Heathcliff barked and then spun around and greeted Sully in the same affectionate way. After sufficient pets, he shot out to the yard to patrol the perimeter. Sully draped his arm around Lindsey's shoulders and pulled her into his side.

"He's going to make a great big brother," he said. "You'll see."

Lindsey laughed. She hoped so because there was no going back now.

The next day Lindsey spent her lunch hour looking up old articles on "the runaway bride." The story had garnered local attention with a flurry of stories in all of the Connecticut newspapers, which had dwindled over the years to the odd mention of it as an unsolved case in the local village weekly. By and large, Grace Little, having no living family members except for her new husband, was forgotten.

Lindsey studied the accompanying professional portrait of Grace Little, who was in her early twenties at the time. She wore a light blue sweater with a pearl necklace, her rouge had been applied in bold streaks across her cheeks, her lips were shiny and pink, and her blue eye shadow was thick. Her hair was a big permed mass of honey blond curls that reached past her shoulders, with her bangs sprayed into one big curl across her forehead.

Raised by her father, a train conductor who worked the commuter train to New York and back every day, Grace had been orphaned at seventeen when he suffered complications from a stroke and passed away. There was no other family, and she was left to fend for herself, which she did. A graduate of the Katharine Gibbs School, she worked as an administrative assistant for a local financial planning company, Felder Investments.

Lindsey wondered if the business was still in operation and, if so, whether anyone remembered Grace. She made a note to check into it. The articles mentioned that Tim Little had been considered a person of interest, but with no evidence of foul play or a body, he was never arrested.

Lindsey thought about Tim and how he had stormed into the Dorchester mansion the other night. He'd been furious that the old rumors were starting up again because of William's presence in town. Lindsey could only speculate how he was going to handle the news that Grace's body had been found in the mansion.

Had Tim been agitated that William was back because he feared William would discover Grace's remains, or had it really been because William was stoking the fires of the old gossip?

Lindsey leaned back in her chair at the reference desk. It

was a quiet morning at the library. The regulars who popped in every day were going about their business while the staff checked in the books returned overnight and braced themselves for their peak busy hours, which lasted from midmorning until right before dinner. Afternoons were hectic, for sure, but the time flew by.

She thought about the two men in Grace Little's life. Either one of them could be her murderer. William had vanished right after she did. This could absolutely be a sign of guilt, and he had access to the secret room, since he lived in the Dorchester mansion at the time of her disappearance. Tim, too, was a prime suspect. He was her spouse, and he'd been seen arguing with her on the evening of her disappearance.

Then again, it could have been neither of them. Maybe it was Mrs. Dorchester. She would have been much younger in nineteen eighty-nine. She clearly didn't approve of her son's attachment to Grace. Could she have murdered Grace and hidden her in the secret room? But if Grace was already married to Tim, why would Marion care? Unless she feared that William was trying to win Grace back? There was no way to know what was true and what was false as Marion's dementia made her unreliable at best. Of course, the dementia hadn't caused her to confess yet either.

Lindsey made a note of the name of the witness in the article who saw Grace and Tim arguing. Sarah Bessette. When she looked her up, Lindsey discovered Sarah lived on the outskirts of town in a retirement community of town-homes, where she acted as the social director. Perfect. Lindsey decided it was time to do some outreach and visit the retirement residence with brochures and pamphlets about the benefits of using the library.

The other name she noted was David Felder. Grace had reported directly to him, and Lindsey did some digging and discovered that he'd sold off his company in the nineties but still resided in Briar Creek in a big house along the shore. Winter hadn't arrived yet, so Lindsey hoped he hadn't fled to Florida for the season, because she wanted to ask him what he remembered, if anything, about Grace Little.

It was easy to come up with an excuse to visit the retirement home, but she had a harder time devising a reason to reach out to Mr. Felder. Of course, their annual fund-raiser, Dinner in the Stacks, would be happening soon, and she supposed she could stop by and see if he was willing to contribute. And if she brought Robbie Vine, Briar Creek's resident celebrity, with her, she might be able to finagle a meeting.

She supposed the cold case was really none of her business, but she couldn't help but try to move the investigation along. Besides, as long as the Dorchesters' library was closed off as a crime scene, she couldn't access the collection. Her primary concern was that the books that had yet to be moved from the mansion were the rare ones. While she didn't think that the crime scene investigation would hurt the materials, she didn't want to take any chances. It was best to get the books out as quickly as possible.

Beyond that, being one of the people who'd found the remains that were potentially—probably—those of Grace

Little had made the situation more personal. Lindsey wanted to know what had happened to the runaway bride. Had Grace been murdered, or was it just a horrible accident? Lindsey's gut was telling her it was murder, but there was no proof . . . yet.

During her afternoon hours on the reference desk, Lindsey pondered everything she had learned about Grace. She couldn't get the picture of the young woman out of her mind. Newly married, she'd had her whole life ahead of her. How had she ended up in a sealed-off room in the Dorchester mansion with just a thin volume of Poe by her side? To say it was as macabre as anything Poe had ever written was an understatement.

Lindsey walked back into the short story collection in the nonfiction area. She scanned the shelves until she reached 818.309. There were a few collected works by Poe, the father of the modern mystery, on the shelf, and Lindsey took them back to her desk. She didn't really think there were any answers for her in these stories, but she was curious about what Grace had been reading when she met her end.

She skimmed the familiar stories, "The Pit and the Pendulum," "The Tell-Tale Heart," "The Cask of Amontillado" and the poem "The Raven." She read the brief biography of Edgar Allan Poe on the book jacket and wondered at the short, tragic life of the American writer. Was it the amount of personal loss he suffered—his mother, foster mother and young wife, all from tuberculosis—that made his stories so sinister and dark? Or was that just the lens through which he viewed the world?

Lindsey glanced out the big picture window at the bay and noted that the blue skies of the morning were disappearing beneath a steely gray layer of clouds. It was very much a Poe day outside, with a certain feeling of menace in the chilly air. The wind had picked up, and the large maple tree on the library lawn was dropping the last of its leaves in a steady rain of red and brown.

Walking along the sidewalk with her body tipping forward into the wind was Barbara Little, Tim's wife. Like Tim, she was in her fifties. Her figure was pleasantly plump, her ash blond hair slowly fading to gray. She wore yoga pants and a pale gray quilted coat, the sort made to withstand the mercurial New England weather. As Lindsey watched, Barbara turned up the walkway, heading straight for the library.

Lindsey tried to read her body language. Did she seem upset? Worried? She couldn't tell.

Briar Creek was a small community, and she suspected that the Littles must know about the body that was found in the Dorchester mansion last night. Then again, today was the day that Barbara met with her literacy group at the library every week. Clearly, she either hadn't heard the news, or she didn't think it significant enough to alter her schedule. Or perhaps, she felt that she had to maintain appearances for her husband's sake. Lindsey wondered which it was and how she could approach Barbara without being too obvious. Hmm.

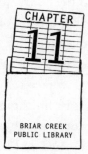

Lindsey watched Barbara stride into the library. Her head was held high as she unzipped her coat and pulled off the ruby red scarf from around her neck. She waved to Paula, who was working the circulation desk, and headed right to the study room, where her three literacy students were waiting.

She didn't stop to talk to Lindsey as she usually did, which made Lindsey suspect that she had heard about the remains being discovered in the Dorchester mansion. Lindsey scanned the library to see if anyone else had noted Barbara's arrival. She saw Peggy Jones and Sonya Taylor watching Barbara from their spot by the new magazine rack. Peggy was a knitter and waited, impatiently, for each new issue of *Vogue Knitting* to arrive. Sonya was her neighbor and was plugged into the gossip pipeline of the village through her work at the elementary school's front office.

Sure enough, as Lindsey watched, Sonya leaned down and whispered something in Peggy's ear, which caused Peggy's eyes to widen and then dart to the study room, where Barbara was. Lindsey felt a pang of sympathy for Barbara as Lindsey had been the subject of town gossip before and knew it was not fun to have your every move scrutinized.

Thankfully, the two women left before Barbara finished her class. Lindsey was just finishing up reviewing her book order to Baker & Taylor, the bookseller to libraries, when the study room door opened and Barbara stepped out.

She said good-bye to her students, two older men and one woman, and one of them made a joke at which they all laughed—even Barbara. As soon as the students left, Barbara turned and glanced at the reference desk. When she saw Lindsey, a look of relief passed over her face, and she approached the desk.

"Hi, Lindsey," she said.

"Hi, Barbara. Good class today?"

Barbara nodded. "They're getting it. Even Saul, who was certain he could never learn to read, is beginning to read at a second-grade level." A look of pride crossed her face. "He's worked so hard. I'm very proud of him."

"You've made a tremendous difference in his life," Lindsey said.

"I like to think so." Barbara glanced around the desk as if to be certain that no one was in the area.

"Can I help you with something?" Lindsey asked.

Barbara sank down in the seat next to Lindsey's desk. "I hope so."

"Is it materials for your class?" Lindsey asked. "Do you need something special?"

"No, it's a personal matter," Barbara said. She bit her lip, and a worry line appeared between her eyebrows.

"That's all right." Lindsey kept her expression blank. "How can I help?"

"I know that you found the remains at the Dorchester mansion," Barbara said.

Lindsey expelled a breath. "Yes, but I don't think I'm allowed to talk about it."

"That's fine," Barbara said. "I don't want to."

"Okay." Lindsey tipped her head to the side, wondering where this conversation was going.

"I know you've been involved in solving a number of murders in the community, and I was hoping that maybe you could help with this one," Barbara said.

"I . . ." Lindsey hesitated. She didn't know what to say. No one had ever asked her to get involved before. It had always been a matter of the crime affecting her life or the life of someone she cared about. "I don't know that there's much I can do beyond what the chief of police and the crime scene investigators are doing."

"But you're a librarian," Barbara said. "You know things."

Lindsey smiled. It was true. Librarians did spend their lives accumulating random bits of knowledge. "I'm not sure how that can help in this situation."

"People are going to start talking again," Barbara said. "Just like they did last time." Her eyes got watery and her lip trembled. "My husband is a good man."

"I know," Lindsey said. "Tim is a great guy."

"But that won't matter," Barbara said. Her voice was high and tight. "Just because Grace went missing right after they were married, people blamed Tim because he was the spouse. I can't have that. I can't have our kids and grand-kids go through that. Sure, they heard rumors while grow-ing up, but Tim worked so hard in the community to prove that he wasn't a wife-killing maniac, I just can't bear it if all of that is swept away because Grace's body was found and it's a salacious bit of gossip for the nightly news."

Lindsey nodded. She could only imagine the panic Bar-bara was feeling that the life she and Tim had built was go-ing to be demolished by the discovery of his first wife's body.

"They haven't identified the body yet," Lindsey said. "It might not even be Grace."

Barbara stared at her. "You don't believe that."

Lindsey shrugged. "I don't know anything for certain."

"But you could," Barbara insisted. "You're working on moving the Dorchester library collection. You have access to the house. You could look around and look for clues. You could prove that she did it."

"She?" Lindsey asked.

"Mrs. Dorchester," Barbara said. "Don't you see? It has to be her. She hated Grace. She forbade William from marrying her. She must have lured Grace to the mansion and murdered her. That poor girl. She must have been scared to death."

Lindsey noted the compassion in Barbara's voice for her husband's first wife. She wasn't surprised. That was the sort of woman Barbara was. But still, her theory didn't add up.

"But why would Marion do that if Grace was already married to Tim?" Lindsey asked. "I mean, William was safe from her clutches, right?"

Barbara stared down at her hands, where they twisted the red scarf in her lap. "I don't want to speak ill of the dead, but there were rumors about Grace."

Lindsey's eyebrows went up. "Rumors?"

"Yes, that she was cheating on Tim and planning to leave him," Barbara whispered. "Please don't tell anyone I told you. Tim gets very upset when he hears this because he was certain that she loved him, and it hurts him to think that she didn't."

"But you think she was going to leave him?" Lindsey asked.

Looking miserable, Barbara nodded. "I don't think Grace ever got over William. He was her first love. He was the catch of the town. She thought she was going to marry him and live in the big house with everything her heart desired. It wouldn't surprise me at all if she carried a torch for William, and if he gave her any encouragement, Mrs. Dorchester would have panicked. I know she's frail now, but back in the day, she was a force."

"I don't know what I can do," Lindsey hedged. She felt uncomfortable with Barbara's request, which seemed to single out Marion Dorchester. "The chief has instructed me not to move any more materials until after the investigation is complete."

"I'm sorry. I know I'm putting you in a terrible position," Barbara said. "I'm just . . . I love my husband so much. This could destroy him. So, I'm asking for him."

The misery on Barbara's face made Lindsey's heart pinch. How could she possibly refuse? Barbara and Tim had built the perfect life in Briar Creek. Their roots were deep, they'd raised their family here, and they were civically minded, helping whenever someone in the community needed it. Everything Barbara had worked for in her life—her home, her family, her place in the community—was now in jeopardy.

"Of course, if I see or hear anything that I think might help with the investigation, I will tell the chief of police, absolutely."

"Thank you." Barbara heaved a deep sigh. "I really appreciate your support. I'm worried about Tim. He's taking the news of the discovery of a body in the Dorchester mansion very hard. He's already had one altercation with William. If they should cross paths again, well, I don't want to think about it."

Lindsey didn't mention that she had been there for the first altercation, not wanting to rehash the events of that evening. Instead, she reached across the desk and patted Barbara's arm. "It's going to be all right, really."

Barbara gave her a brave smile and nodded. She rose from her seat and headed to the door. Lindsey noted that she avoided meeting the gaze of anyone else in the library, which was unusual for the usually gregarious woman who was always quick with a smile or a hug.

Lindsey mulled over what Barbara had told her. Was it possible that Grace had been seeing William? It would explain why Grace was in the Dorchester mansion, but how did she get into the hidden room? What had happened on

the day she disappeared? Lindsey thought of Marion confusing Lindsey for Grace. Did Marion actually believe Lindsey was the return of the girl she had murdered? A shiver
raced down Lindsey's spine. It was impossible to know.

I appreciate you coming with me to see Sarah Bessette,"
Lindsey said. "I promise it won't take long."

Sully had picked Lindsey up after work that day, and
they were headed to the retirement home to meet with
Sarah, the lone witness to the argument between Tim and
Grace on the evening that she disappeared. Lindsey had
called Sarah after her talk with Barbara and said she was
doing outreach to determine how the retirement community
could best be served by the library, which wasn't a total lie,
and Sarah had been eager to have her drop by for a visit.

"Do you think she'll remember the argument between
Tim and Grace?" Sully asked.

"I don't know. She was the only witness listed in the
paper, and while they quoted her as saying she saw the couple arguing, she didn't say what the argument was about,"
Lindsey said. "I feel like the subject might be critical."

"In what way?"

"If it was simple cap-on, seat-down issues like all mar-
riages have, then I don't feel like Tim is as likely a suspect,"
she said. "But if they were arguing about money, or if
someone was cheating—"

"Hadn't they only been married for a few weeks?" he
asked.

"Six," she said.

"That seems awfully early in the game to be cheating," he said.

Lindsey turned to look at him with one eyebrow raised inquisitively. "Is there an acceptable time frame for cheating?"

Sully laughed. "That came out wrong."

"I should hope so."

He turned onto the road that wound through Oak Crest—the community of retirees. The small houses were clustered into groups of four and shared a common number but a different letter of the alphabet.

"We're looking for 14B," Lindsey said.

They followed the signs until they reached that number, and Sully parked his truck in the lot designated for guests.

"Does Sarah know we're coming?" he asked.

"Yes, I called her, and she said she'd be happy to talk with us," Lindsey said.

He fell into step beside her as they approached Sarah's door. It was decorated for Halloween with a vine wreath sporting mini pumpkins and fabric autumn leaves.

"This could be unpleasant," Sully warned her. "She might know more unsavory details about Tim's past than I do."

Lindsey shrugged as she knocked on the thick wooden door. "Perhaps."

She could hear the sound of someone approaching, and she burrowed into her coat as a bitter wind blew past them, sending leaves twirling on the air.

"Hello!" A petite, softly rounded woman with short gray hair opened the door. "Lindsey?"

"Yes, and this is my husband, Sully," Lindsey said.

"The boat captain?" Sarah asked.

"Yes, ma'am," he said.

"Come in, come in," Sarah said, inviting them. She gestured to a coatrack by the door. "Hang up your coats. I just put the coffeepot on."

Lindsey and Sully stepped inside and were immediately engulfed in the warmth of the house, which smelled faintly of vanilla and cinnamon. Lindsey took off her coat, hanging it on the rack, and Sully did the same.

They stepped into the main room, which had a fire crackling in the corner, and took a seat on the brown leather sofa, while Sarah disappeared into the kitchen. The walls were painted the color of rich cream on top with deep blue on the bottom. It was such a pleasant room; Lindsey felt the tension in her shoulders ease.

Sarah came bustling back in carrying a tray with three mugs of coffee, cream and sugar and some oatmeal raisin cookies, which looked delicious.

"I am so glad you reached out to me," Sarah said. "I am by far the youngest resident in Oak Crest, and I have to tell you, we need more outreach to the citizens here."

She was wearing a sweatshirt with a quilted cat on the front, and her eyeglasses turned up at the corners in a very feline way. Lindsey noted there was a scratching post in the corner and several cat toys on the floor. It occurred to her that these were clues that would help her steer the conversation in the direction she wanted it to go.

"What do you think would be most beneficial to the

residents?" Lindsey asked. "With a new mayor coming into office, I am thinking that a shuttle bus from Oak Crest to the library would be handy, or we could have a librarian do weekly visits to the community, bringing the materials they've requested or just the books that are most popular?"

"Oh, I like both of those ideas," Sarah said. She handed them each a mug of coffee and gestured to the milk and sugar on the tray. "We have a wide variety of needs here. Am I being greedy if I say both?"

She laughed, and it was a lighthearted musical sound. Lindsey like Sarah. She glanced at Sully and noticed that he was smiling while he sipped his coffee, so she suspected he liked her, too.

"We have so many programs at the library that the residents here might enjoy," Lindsey said. "If we could arrange a shuttle bus, they could attend our quarterly cooking programs, our winter concert series, and in the spring, we have several gardening lectures."

"Those sound amazing," Sarah said. She gestured at her window. "We have a community garden, and last year, we had so much zucchini even the rabbits got sick of it. I'm sure our garden lovers would like to be instructed on what else to grow. It's so important for your mental health to have things to look forward to, don't you think?"

"Definitely," Lindsey agreed. "The library has a terrific collection on gardening, and we work with a local cooperative extension that offers guidance on how to humanely deter pests."

"Brilliant," Sarah said. "Now if I can just come up with

some more excursions for the residents who need to get out a bit more." She sipped her coffee, staring pointedly at Sully over the rim of her mug.

He laughed, taking her meaning immediately. "Maybe we can arrange for a boat tour in the summer," he suggested.

Sarah put down her mug and clasped her hands together. "That would be wonderful. So many of our residents don't have family nearby and have few opportunities to get out of the house and do fun things."

Sully nodded. "We can talk again in the spring and set a date."

Lindsey reached into her bag and handed Sarah a fat stack of library materials with information about how to get a library card, upcoming programs, and the different services the library provided.

"These might be of interest to your residents," Lindsey said.

"Oh, perfect," Sarah said. She flipped through the stack of pamphlets. "We're having a residents' meeting next week, and I'll be sure to bring them."

Just then, a chubby gray tabby with a white belly jumped up onto the back of Sarah's chair and meowed.

"Sebastian, company manners, please," Sarah said. He laid across the top of her chair, letting his belly droop onto each side. He was the picture of contentment.

"He is beautiful," Lindsey said.

"King of the house," Sarah said. "And he knows it."

"We just found a cat," Sully said. "She's with Dr. Rubinski now, but if we don't find her owner, she'll become ours. We've named her Zelda."

"Oh, that's a perfect cat name. They are wonderful pets, exasperating but wonderful. Where did you find Zelda?" Sarah asked.

"The Dorchester mansion," Lindsey said. She sent Sully an appreciative glance. Clearly they were doing the spousal mind meld, and he knew she was going to use Zelda as her segue into asking about Grace and Tim. "The Dorchesters have donated their personal book collection to the town library, and while I was there packing up the materials, she just appeared."

"In the house?" Sarah asked.

"In the library," Lindsey confirmed. "I asked the Dorchesters about her, but they said they don't have a cat."

"How odd for her to be in the house," Sarah said. "I hope she's all right."

"She's in good health according to the vet," Lindsey said. "If a little on the thin side."

"Oh, dear." Sarah looked concerned. "She's lucky that you found her." She glanced at the fireplace, lost in thought for a moment. "It's strange, isn't it, when you haven't heard a name in years, and then suddenly, it's all anyone is talking about?"

"Do you mean the Dorchesters?" Lindsey asked.

"And Grace Little." Sarah nodded. Her voice was soft when she said, "I was the last one to see her . . . that night."

"Really?" Lindsey asked. She made her best surprised look.

Sarah nodded. "I always felt bad that I didn't do something or say something that night, but I just thought it was a lovers' spat. It didn't occur to me that she'd disappear, and now, well, I have a confession to make."

Lindsey straightened up, her curiosity fully engaged. Was Sarah going to confess to knowing something she hadn't told the police?

"What's that?"

"When you called earlier today, I knew that you were there when they discovered the skeleton of the woman," Sarah said. She put down her coffee and clutched her hands in her lap. She twisted her fingers. "When you suggested we meet to talk about outreach, I thought it would be the perfect opportunity to ask you . . ." Sarah's voice trailed off and she stared into the fire.

"Ask me what?" Lindsey said. She put down her mug, too.

"Do you think it's Grace Hartwell, I'm sorry, Grace Little that they found?" Sarah asked. Her cheerfulness vanished beneath the high-pitched strain in her voice.

Lindsey shook her head with regret. Emma would be furious if she said anything about the investigation, so she wouldn't. "I don't know for certain, but it seems likely."

"Oh," Sarah said. "I just keep replaying that night in my head. If only I'd known what was going to happen, I would have done something, anything, different."

Her eyes became watery, and she looked like she was about to cry. Lindsey felt her heart plummet. She'd wanted information, but not at the expense of causing Sarah distress.

"I have a confession, too," Lindsey said. "I came here hoping you could tell me about that night. I'm sorry. It's a horrible thing to ask of you. They've closed down the Dorchester mansion because of the investigation, and I can't get inside to pack up the remaining books, which are all rare and valuable. I'm worried that they might get damaged before I can get back there."

Lindsey met Sarah's wide-eyed gaze. She knew because of her promise to Barbara that she couldn't tell Sarah the other reason she was asking about that night—to find suspects other than Tim—which made her feel even worse for causing Sarah to cry. "I certainly never meant to upset you. I'm very sorry. I've been completely selfish."

Sully shifted beside her as if getting ready to defend her, but Sarah spoke first.

"No, you haven't," Sarah said. "You're just a book lover who is concerned about a valuable collection. I understand."

"Can you tell us what you remember about that night?" Sully asked. "Maybe we can figure out what happened, if it turns out that it is Grace that was found."

Sarah nodded. "I've already spoken to the chief of police—she was going through the old file and found my name—so I don't suppose it matters if I tell you, too."

She took a bracing sip of coffee. She stared into the mug for a moment, collecting her thoughts. "I was working as a waitress at the Dockside Café back before it was called the Blue Anchor. It was autumn, I remember, because it was cold when I left the restaurant. I'd worked a double and was just punching out as the dinner crew came on.

"I'd parked my car in the lot, and as I walked to it, I heard raised voices. I paused to make sure everything was okay, and I noticed it was Tim and Grace Little. I knew they'd recently gotten married and assumed it was a lovers' quarrel. Those happen a lot in the beginning when you re-alize you've promised to spend your life with someone who is incapable of picking their socks up off the floor."

Lindsey glanced at Sully, and his eyes cut to her. She remembered their growing pains when they'd first started to live together. The man whistled—whistled!—in the morning, and she read too late at night and kept the light on. They'd worked it out, but for a while there, she wasn't so sure they could cohabitate peacefully. Now he winked at her and she winked back.

"My Doug and I certainly had our share of dustups back in the day," Sarah said. "God rest his soul. Anyway, I didn't want to eavesdrop, and it didn't look like it was serious. Oh, Tim looked upset, and I heard him ask, 'Who is sending you flowers at work? Is it your ex-boyfriend, William Dorchester? Someone else?' and Grace responded with a very sincere 'I don't know.' He then asked her who kept calling their house and hanging up when he answered. She didn't have an answer for that one either.

"Honestly, I felt bad for Tim. He was clearly jealous, and Grace didn't seem to have any answers for him. It was awkward. She was a very pretty girl and had clearly caught the eye of someone who didn't care that she was married. When Tim said he didn't believe her, she lost her temper and yelled at him. She said she loved him, but if he doubted her, then she didn't want to be with him anymore. He looked shocked, and she turned and stomped off into the night. He stared after her for a minute and then yelled, 'Fine. Good riddance.'"

Sarah sighed. Her shoulders drooped and she looked sad. "If only I'd known, I would have chased her down and offered her a ride home, but I really thought she was just going to cool off."

"Did you notice how Tim looked when she left?" Lindsey asked.

"Yeah, he looked really . . . sad," Sarah said. "I wanted to assure him that it would be all right, but I didn't want to intrude more than I had, and I really believed they'd work it out."

"I would have done the same thing," Sully said.

Sarah's gaze darted to his face, and she searched his eyes as if to be sure he was telling the truth. "Would you?"

"Yes, definitely," he said. "It doesn't sound as if it was anything a stranger should get involved in."

"I agree," Lindsey said. "As you say, it sounds like it was the sort of tiff newlyweds have."

"I try to tell myself that," Sarah said. "But there's just one thing I can't let go of."

"What's that?" Lindsey asked.

"What if Tim killed her that night, and I could have stopped it, but I didn't?" Sarah asked.

CHAPTER

12

BRIAR CREEK
PUBLIC LIBRARY

Lindsey and Sully left Sarah Bessette with all of the reas-surances they could muster. Lindsey suspected it was cold comfort.

Lindsey thought about what Sarah had told them, mulling over all the information at home that evening and again the next morning while Sully drove her to work. It was Lindsey's day to work the Saturday shift, which she didn't mind because it gave her a weekday off.

Sarah's story didn't portray Tim as the killer—he never threatened his wife, at least not that Sarah had heard during the argument. But it was clear that whatever was happening between the couple was serious. Grace was receiving flowers, and a man was calling the house and hanging up. Was Grace having an affair? Was she lying to Tim about it? And if Tim thought his wife was cheating and he was a hothead at the time, could he have followed her that night and murdered her?

It was impossible to know, but Lindsey still had a very hard time believing that the Tim Little she knew was capable of murder. If he were a violent man, wouldn't something have happened during the past thirty years of his marriage to Barbara? But by all accounts, he was the nice guy he'd always seemed to be.

She thought about the night he'd arrived at the Dorchester mansion. How far would things have gone if William hadn't clobbered Robbie by accident? Was that the real Tim Little, the man with the fiery temper lurking just beneath the surface? Had he kept it under wraps all these years? Lindsey simply didn't know.

Sully put the truck in park at the staff entrance. "Pick you up at six?"

"Yes, please," Lindsey said. She leaned across the console and kissed him, lingering just for a moment so she could inhale the scent that was unique to her husband. After so many years on the sea, he seemed to have absorbed the fresh clean scent of the ocean air, and it had begun to smell like home to her.

"I know it's a waste of breath to tell you to be careful when you ask questions about Grace Little, but remember that we have no idea who murdered her, and if they've gotten away with it for over thirty years, they most likely do not want to get found out now."

"I'm working all day," Lindsey said. "The most I can do is research old articles and stuff."

Sully gave her an assessing stare. "Your research never seems to go as simply as you think it will."

"Information is power," Lindsey said with a grin.

"Spoken like a true librarian," Sully said.

Lindsey climbed out of the truck cab with a wave, and Sully waited until she was inside before he drove off. When she entered the library through the staff entrance, she could smell the coffee that was already brewing in the staff room. It was a welcome scent, along with a hint of lemon left over from the cleaner's furniture polish, the faint note of antiseptic, and of course the aroma she most associated with the library, that of books.

The lights were still off and the library was quiet. Lindsey stored her handbag in her desk in her office and followed the scent to the break room. Standing by the machine, bouncing on her toes as if she could speed it up through sheer force of will, was Ann Marie.

Dressed in a Black Watch plaid dress with black suede ankle boots, she was holding her mug in front of her as if she could not wait for the caffeine to appear.

"Morning, Ann Marie," Lindsey said. She grabbed her *Book Lover* mug and joined her in the wait.

"Hi," Ann Marie said. "Word of warning, I made it strong today. The boys had to go to school dressed as characters from ancient Egypt, and they told me about this grade-saving project at ten o'clock the night before last. I should have left them to flunk out and suffer the consequences, but I'm not that good a mom."

Lindsey laughed. "Is that what a good mom does?"

"Apparently. Instead, I took the risk of having them grow up to be entitled knuckleheads, because I stayed up until two in the morning crafting a pharaoh and an Anubis, which looks like a big gold rat, in case you're wondering."

"I don't think they'll be too entitled because you helped them with their Egypt project," Lindsey said. She glanced at Ann Marie and added, "Since I suspect there is a payback happening?"

"Oh, yeah." Ann Marie nodded. "They'll be raking leaves until the very last one falls from the tree. Have you seen how many maple and oak trees surround my house? And on the off chance they do manage to get them all, I'll be sending them to the neighbors' yards."

Lindsey laughed. Ann Marie was creative with her punishments. The last time one of the boys got in trouble at school, he had to pick up dog poop in the rain. He never sassed that teacher again.

"So what's your sleep-deprived story?" Ann Marie asked.

"Do I look that rough?" Lindsey asked.

"Will I get fired if I'm honest?"

"Ouch."

Ann Marie waved a hand at her. "I'm just teasing, but the usual spring in your step is missing."

"I didn't sleep well either, but not for such a noble purpose as crafting an Egyptian king or the god of mummification," Lindsey said. "I was up late thinking about who could've killed Grace Little."

"So, it's true?" Ann Marie asked. Her brown eyes were bright, and she reminded Lindsey of an inquisitive little bird. "The remains found in the Dorchester house are Grace Little's?"

"Not conclusively, but from what I saw . . ." Lindsey paused to try to blink that image out of her mind. "The clothes, what was left of them, certainly indicated that the person was from the eighties."

The coffee beeped and Ann Marie turned to grab the carafe. She poured the steaming liquid into Lindsey's mug first and then poured her own.

As Lindsey took the communal creamer out of the refrigerator, Ann Marie said, "I knew her. Grace Little." Lindsey turned and stared at her in surprise. "Oh, not well," Ann Marie clarified.

"But you would have been just a child when she disappeared," Lindsey said.

"I was six," Ann Marie said. "She would babysit me and my sister every now and then. It was quite traumatic to have her vanish like that."

"I'll bet." Lindsey's curiosity took hold of her good manners, and she asked, "What was Grace like? Do you remember?"

"She was kind. I remember she would read to us before she put us to bed, and she never got impatient if we wanted more water or another hug," Ann Marie said. "I wish I remembered more about her, but it was so long ago. My impression was that she was pretty, but that could be because I was at the height of my princess phase back then and saw every woman through a Cinderella lens."

"Did you ever see her with her husband?" Lindsey asked.

"Tim Little," Ann Marie nodded. "I never spent time with them. I mean, he never babysat with her or anything, but I remember seeing them slow dancing in the gazebo in the park one time. My sister and I were at the beach with our parents, and we snuck up to the gazebo to watch when we recognized Grace."

Ann Marie stared out the window as if bringing the memory back into focus.

"There wasn't any music. But I remember he was humming Mellencamp's 'Jack & Diane' in her ear while they swayed back and forth, and then he spun her and she threw her head back and laughed. My sister and I were convinced they were the most romantic couple ever. Probably because she was our babysitter and we felt invested in her relationship."

"Did she ever talk about him?" Lindsey asked.

Ann Marie stared into her mug. "No, but right before she disappeared, she said something I've never forgotten. She said, 'Sometimes you think you're with the right person, but then you meet the actual right person and everything clicks.' I always assumed she meant that the real right person was Tim Little, they were so in love, but after she disappeared, I wondered if maybe she met someone else and ran off with him." She glanced at Lindsey with a sad expression. "I guess not, huh?"

"It doesn't look like it, no," Lindsey said.

"What happens now?" Ann Marie asked.

"The medical examiner will try to identify the remains and determine the cause of death," Lindsey said. "After that, I have no idea."

"Who would have wanted Grace Little dead?" Ann Marie asked. "She was so young and had her whole life ahead of her."

"I suppose it would be someone who didn't want her to have the life she wanted," Lindsey said.

Lindsey spent the rest of the day working on library business. She was in her office writing her weekly report for the mayor's office when there was a knock on the doorframe. She glanced up and saw Robbie standing there. His eye was a lovely shade of purple and gave him a bit of thuggish appeal.

"Nice eye," she said.

"You should see the other guy," he said. "Actually, he looks fine. Damn him."

Lindsey smiled. "If it's any consolation, I think William truly was horrified that he struck the famous Robbie Vine."

Robbie shrugged as he came into the office and took the seat across from her. "I'm surprised you're not at the Dorchester mansion defending your books."

"Believe me, I'd like to be," Lindsey said. "Emma has closed off the entire library as a crime scene. I can't go back until she opens it up."

"Any word on the identity of the body?" he asked.

"Not that I've heard," she said. "You?"

"Emma never discusses her cases," he said. "It's like she doesn't trust me."

"Imagine that," Lindsey said. "It's almost as if you've played amateur sleuth too often."

"Pot meet kettle."

"Indeed."

"Spill it. What have you discovered?" Robbie asked.

"What makes you think I've discovered anything?" she asked. She glanced at her computer and saved her document before shutting the program. She could proofread it later.

"Because it's who you are," he said. "There's no way you're not going to try and figure out the identity of the body, especially when an unsolved case impedes your progress on moving the Dorchester library here."

"You make me sound awfully cold-blooded," Lindsey said.

Robbie stared at her. He knew her so well.

"All right, fine, I did read up on the runaway bride," Lindsey confessed.

"And?"

"Grace Little seems to have been very well liked," she said. "There doesn't seem to be anyone who'd want to harm her, except . . ."

Robbie waited while Lindsey sorted through her thoughts.

"You saw William and Tim," she said. "There is bad blood there."

Robbie touched his eye and winced. "Clearly."

"It appears that someone was interested in Grace," Lindsey said. "Sarah, the woman who witnessed the argument between Tim and Grace on the night she died, said that Tim was upset that someone was calling their house and hanging up every time he answered the phone."

"A lover?"

Lindsey shrugged. "She was also getting flowers at her workplace from an unknown admirer."

"The plot thickens," Robbie said. "Any ideas?"

Lindsey shook her head. "I was thinking of talking to her old boss, David Felder. He used to own Felder Investments. He's retired but still living in town."

"Is that what you meant when you asked me to join you in a fund-raising excursion?"

"Asking for a contribution to our annual Dinner in the Stacks fund-raiser seems like a logical approach," Lindsey said.

"When do we leave?" he asked.

"My lunch hour is in five minutes," she said.

"Perfect," Robbie said. "I'll get my car and meet you at the back."

He rose from his seat and left the office. Lindsey took her handbag out of her desk drawer and grabbed her coat. She paused by the circulation desk to let Ms. Cole know she was stepping out.

When she exited the building, Robbie was parked by the curb in his Mercedes. The engine was running and she hopped into the passenger seat.

"Address?" Robbie asked.

"Two-eleven Marshall Street," she said.

"Oh, where the wealthy play," Robbie said. He drove out of the parking lot and through the village, minding his speed.

It was another gray day outside, and the wind blowing in off the water was brisk, warning that temperatures would be dropping. Lindsey adjusted the vents on her side of the car so that the heat washed over her in a steady stream. The road was narrow and twisty. The large houses hugged the curve of the coastline, standing bravely in the face of the hurricanes that frequently slammed the waterfront in the late summer and early autumn.

Felder's house was a large white columned colonial. Thick rosebushes, recently deadheaded, lined the driveway. Lindsey imagined they were quite a colorful sight in spring. Robbie stopped the car in front of the house, and they both climbed out.

A detached garage was off to the side, but with no windows, it was impossible to tell if anyone was home. Lindsey supposed she could always leave a message for Mr. Felder, but she really hoped she'd have a chance to speak with him. There were so few people remaining in town who had known Grace. Putting together the pieces of her life had left Lindsey with more questions than answers.

White pumpkins of varying sizes were perched on the wide steps that led to the front door. When Lindsey rang the doorbell, the sound of a dog barking gave her hope that someone was home. The front door was painted matte black, matching the shutters on every window. The look was tidy but the door itself seemed ominous.

She and Robbie waited, not speaking, until the sound of someone unlocking the door broke the silence. They exchanged a wary glance and then put on their game faces.

The door was pulled open, and a man in his late fifties, if Lindsey was to guess, stood in front of them, wearing a dark gray cardigan over a white dress shirt and pressed navy pants. Instead of shoes, he had on fur-lined slippers. Clutched in his teeth was a pipe, and he carried a thick book cradled to his chest. He looked like an extra sent by central casting to play the part of the retired financial advisor.

"May I help you?" he asked. He took the pipe out of his mouth when he spoke.

"I hope so," Lindsey said. "I'm looking for David Felder."

"You've found him," the man said. His gray hair had a precise part on the side, and his glasses were narrow readers that he wore perched on the end of this nose. He glanced over the top of them to study Lindsey. He gestured to the small sign in the window beside the door. "But I do not entertain solicitors of any kind."

"We're not selling anything," she said. "We're here about a fund-raiser."

Felder frowned. "That's even worse. At least if you're selling something, there's an exchange of goods and services. Fund-raising is you asking me for money with nothing to offer in return."

Lindsey had a feeling that this was not going to go as well as she'd hoped. Sensing his celebrity superpower was in need, Robbie stepped up beside her.

"Hello, Mr. Felder, I'm Robbie Vine." He held out his hand and gave the man his most charming smile. It seemed to do nothing to melt Felder's cold, cold heart.

"I used to watch you on that British show," Felder said. He didn't shake Robbie's hand, which Robbie managed by pretending to brush a bit of invisible lint off his coat.

"Did you?" Robbie asked. His voice was tight.

"Yes, you were an inspector of some sort," Felder said.

"Detective inspector," Robbie corrected him.

"Whatever." Felder waved his hand dismissively. "You weren't very convincing, were you?"

"I won several awards for that role," Robbie said. He sounded rightly annoyed.

"That doesn't signify," Felder said dismissively. "Those award shows are all popularity contests. Actors spend months lobbying to win awards. It's not really based on merit, is it? What happened to your eye? A disappointed fan let you know what they thought of you?"

"I just filmed an action sequence," Robbie lied. "I do my own stunts."

"Right." Felder's voice was full of doubt.

"I think we're getting off the subject," Lindsey said.

"We had a subject?" Felder asked. "Oh, yes, you're trying to rob me."

"No, we're not," she protested.

"Really? What do you call it when someone wants your money for nothing?" he asked.

"In this case, we call it fund-raising," Robbie said.

"Still feels like a shakedown."

"I assure you—" Lindsey began, but Felder interrupted.

"You're letting all the heat out," he said. "Please be quick. I can give you three minutes to make your case, but that's it, and don't think your imagined, self-important Hollywood glamour is going to sway me. It won't."

CHAPTER

13

BRIAR CREEK
PUBLIC LIBRARY

Robbie's mouth popped open in outrage, and Lindsey quickly moved in front of him. It would do them no good to have Robbie get into a spat with David Felder.

"About the fund-raiser," Lindsey said. "It's for the public library's annual Dinner in the Stacks event. You could donate an item for our auction, buy a ticket to attend, buy a whole table for you and your family and friends, or just make a monetary contribution."

Felder's eyes narrowed. "Why would I do that? Doesn't the library, which I never use, by the way, take enough of my money in taxes? What could you possibly need more money for?"

"The town's budget is generous, but the summer reading program for kids—"

"I don't have kids," Felder interrupted.

"Or the small business startup club—" she began, but he interrupted again.

"No one helped me start my business," he said. "I did it all by myself."

"Very admirable," Lindsey said. "But wouldn't it be amazing to be the person who makes a difference in another businessperson's life?"

She smiled at him, hoping to win him over. His face was devoid of expression, as if he found her incredibly tedious.

"Why would I waste my time? Either a person has what it takes or they don't," he said. "I don't do handouts. Is that clear?"

"So, you're a no on Dinner in the Stacks, then?" Robbie asked. He smiled at the man as if they hadn't just been thoroughly rejected.

"Yes," Felder said. He sounded thoroughly exasperated.

"Oh, then you're a yes," Robbie said. He grinned at Felder, who blinked. "Shall I put you down for a whole table, then?"

"No!" Felder cried.

"No?" Robbie asked. "Half of a table?"

Lindsey knew Robbie was having fun with him, undoubtedly as petty revenge for Felder's critique of him and his profession, but she felt she had to intervene.

"No!" Felder said again. "Not a whole table or a half table or a single seat. I will not contribute to this grift in any way, shape or form."

"Grift?" Lindsey went rigid. "Since when is contributing to the betterment of your community a grift?"

"When you're already taxing me into the poorhouse," Felder snapped.

Robbie stepped back and made a show of studying the very large house in front of them.

"Fancy that, Lindsey," he said. "We're in the poor section of town. Blimey, I had no idea."

His accent was so thick, she'd need a knife to spread it. She shook her head, but Robbie completely disregarded her.

"Beg pardon, sir," he said. "We didn't realize this was the slum. Clearly, we need to go where the toffs live and ask them to help provide the extra niceties for the local library."

"I know what you're doing," Felder said.

"Doubt it," Robbie bit out.

"You're trying to make me feel guilty that I live in a nice house in a nice neighborhood," he said. "Well, it won't work. I've earned everything I have with blood, sweat and tears."

"Did you?" Lindsey asked. "Did you really?"

Felder stared at her. "What's that supposed to mean?"

"I'm a librarian," she said. It came out on a sigh because, honestly, she was a bit tired of being underestimated. Librarians were all-powerful in the sense that their go-to method of dealing with any situation was to arm themselves with knowledge. Why didn't people understand that?

"So?" Felder asked.

"Do you really think I didn't look up your family history before I came here?" Lindsey asked. "Your father was a very successful businessman, making a fortune in utilities, and he invested heavily in your business, which you opened right out of college. He was also a beloved philanthropist, which is why the elementary school is named for him."

Felder's eyes narrowed. "I fail to see your point."

"The point," Robbie said, "is that you're only successful because your father gave you a head start, and the subtext, in case you're missing it, is that your father would have contributed to the library's Dinner in the Stacks."

"My father was a fool," Felder said. "He thought his generosity would bring him immortality."

"Well, his name is on the school," Lindsey said. "And his memory lives on. I don't suppose yours will though."

Felder's face went a splotchy shade of red. "My answer remains no."

Realizing he wasn't going to give in, Lindsey felt as if she had nothing left to lose, so she stated her real purpose, because what the heck. "What do you think happened to Grace Little?"

Felder gasped. "Why would you ask me?"

"Because you were her boss," Robbie said. "You saw her every day. Did she say anything or do anything that made you think someone would want to harm her?"

Felder glanced from side to side as if afraid that his neighbors would hear. "Is this why you're really here?"

Lindsey shrugged. "Dinner in the Stacks is a big deal, but, yes, I did want to ask you about Grace Little, too."

"Why do you care?" he asked.

"Because I'm the one who found what could possibly prove to be her remains," Lindsey said. "I'm a librarian and I want answers."

Felder met her gaze and held it. Whatever he was looking for, he must have found it, because he nodded once. He stepped back, opened the door wider and gestured for them to come inside.

The interior of Felder's house was much like the man himself, lacking in warmth. It had all the right aesthetics—fine art and expensive furniture in a neutral palette that showcased his expensive taste. But instead of feeling inviting, it made Lindsey feel like she was in a bank examiner's office asking for a loan. All she could think was that she wanted to escape.

Felder led them into his home office at the front of the house. The large windows looked over the tall trees in the front lawn, which were almost barren of leaves.

He sat behind his desk and gestured for Lindsey and Robbie to take the two seats opposite. He put his pipe in a holder and rested his forearms on his desk, clasping his hands on the glossy mahogany finish.

"Is it her?" he asked.

"The body that was found?" Lindsey clarified. He nodded. "I don't know. The medical examiner hasn't made an identification that I know of, but it's hard to imagine who else it could be."

"What was your relationship with her?" Robbie asked.

Felder whipped his head in Robbie's direction. "What are you insinuating?"

"Nothing," Robbie said. "I'm just wondering if you had the sort of employer-employee relationship where you shared bits about your personal lives."

"We were . . . friendly," Felder said. He stumbled over the word as if it wasn't quite right, but he couldn't think of a better one.

"She was married," Robbie said.

"I know," Felder said. His expression became one of profound sadness. "Tim Little was not worthy of her."

Lindsey glanced at him in surprise. "Do you think she should have been with William Dorchester?"

"No!" Felder said. "He's a sad little mama's boy. She deserved someone . . ."

"Like you?" Robbie supplied.

Felder glanced away from them and out the window. "That's a ridiculous thing to say. I was her boss. It would have been completely inappropriate to have any sort of relationship with her."

Lindsey noted that he didn't deny that he felt she deserved someone like him. She wondered how long he'd been in love with her and whether he still was.

"What do you know about her receiving flowers at work?" Lindsey asked.

Felder turned back from the window. He straightened a stack of papers on the side of his desk with complete absorption. "I'm sure I don't know anything."

"Really?" Robbie pressed. "A woman repeatedly receives flowers at work and then disappears, and you don't know anything about it?"

"Well . . . I . . . it's . . . how could I possibly know who they were from?" he asked. "They were from a secret admirer. How do you even know about the flowers?"

"A witness mentioned them," Lindsey said.

"What witness?" Felder asked. He looked alarmed. "Was it someone who worked in my office? What did they say about me?"

"They didn't say anything about you," Robbie said. "Should they have?"

"No! Listen, I'm feeling attacked here, and I don't like it," Felder said. "The truth is I liked Grace. She was lovely and kind and a pleasure to have in the office, but that's it."

"When you say 'to have'—" Robbie said, his voice laden with innuendo, but before he could go on, Lindsey interrupted. She needed to keep Felder talking. She wanted a fuller picture of Grace as a person, and he was one of the few people who could give that to her.

"Did she seem scared at work?" Lindsey asked. "Was she concerned about anyone in her life threatening to cause her harm?"

Felder stared at the top of his desk as if trying to remember. "No, I don't know, maybe? She wasn't herself during those last few weeks at work. She was quiet and she seemed anxious all the time. I thought she was regretting her marriage."

"Was there anyone in the office she would have confided in?" Lindsey asked.

"There were a couple of secretaries that she spent time with outside the office," he said. "I don't know how close they were, but I know they went to Toad's Place in New Haven a few times to see bands that were touring."

"Do you know how I could get in touch with any of those women?" Lindsey asked.

"No, I have no idea," he said. His tone was dismissive. "I don't even remember their names."

"But you remember Grace's?" Robbie asked.

"Well, she did disappear," Felder said. "It was very disconcerting at the time. Of course I remember. Her husband stormed into our office and demanded to talk to everyone who knew her. He was in a fury, convinced that someone knew where she was but they weren't telling. Naturally, he didn't fool us. We all knew it was an act."

"An act?" Lindsey asked.

"Yes, he was obviously the one who murdered her," Felder said.

"Frantically looking for his wife doesn't sound like the behavior of a man who committed murder," Robbie said. A deep V formed between his brows, and Lindsey knew he was still very resistant to the idea that Tim had killed Grace.

"Doesn't it though?" Felder asked. "He was clearly having a fit in public to try and make himself look innocent. It didn't work. Everyone knew it was him. Everyone talked about it. And now it seems, after all these years, the truth is finally coming out."

"But it doesn't make any sense. How would Tim have murdered Grace and left her in the Dorchester mansion?" Lindsey asked. "I mean how would he even get in there?"

"You'd have to ask him, wouldn't you?" Felder said. "The fact remains that most domestic murders are committed by the spouse, and there was clearly something wrong between Grace and Tim at the time of her disappearance."

"Did she say that specifically?" Robbie asked.

"No, I told you she didn't, but I could tell," Felder insisted. "She didn't really love him. She never should have married him. I imagine it's only a matter of time before they figure out how he did it and arrest him."

Robbie looked like he was about to argue, but Lindsey didn't want to antagonize Felder further in case she needed to talk to him again.

"I appreciate your input, Mr. Felder," Lindsey said. She rose from her seat and Robbie reluctantly did the same. "If you change your mind about contributing to our Dinner in the Stacks fund-raiser—"

"I won't," Felder interrupted.

"Well, then," Lindsey said. "Thanks for your time. We'll show ourselves out."

"Do." Felder didn't rise from his seat. He simply swiveled his chair to face the window, dismissing them.

As soon as they stepped out of the room, Robbie said, "What a wank—"

"Save it for outside," Lindsey said.

They left the house, closing the massive front door behind them. As soon as they were standing on the steps, Robbie exploded. "What a complete arse!"

"Agreed," Lindsey said. "Also, I think he's lying."

Robbie straightened up. "About?"

"I think he knows more about those flowers than he was saying," she said.

"Meaning?"

"I think he was the one sending them."

They walked down the steps to the car.

"How do you figure that?" Robbie asked.

"Because he said they were from a secret admirer," she said. "How could he know that unless the secret admirer was him?"

"Maybe Grace told him," Robbie said.

"Would she though?" Lindsey asked.

Robbie opened the passenger door for Lindsey, and she slid onto the seat. He shut the door and walked around the front. Lindsey glanced at the time on her cell phone and realized she would just make it back to work before her lunch hour was over. Excellent.

"I don't see Grace confiding in him," Lindsey said. "I suspect Felder's affection wasn't returned, and he was too thick to notice. He did say she wasn't herself, that she was quiet and anxious. I think she was afraid of whoever was sending the flowers. It was obviously causing a problem in her marriage, which Felder would have been fine with since he didn't think Tim deserved her anyway."

"If he was sending them, he wasn't doing it to be nice, he was interested in her and didn't care that she was married or that the flowers were disturbing for her," Robbie said.

"I think he was in love with her, and his own desire for her was more important than any discomfort he was causing her," Lindsey said. "Who knows how far he went. He might have been harassing her at work, and she didn't know how to handle it. She might have been afraid of losing her job or of telling her husband."

Robbie let out a low whistle. "If this theory is true, that makes Felder a suspect."

"Yes, it does," Lindsey said. "I'm planning on sharing what we've learned with Emma, but I think it's important to find one of the secretaries that Grace was friends with and ask them about Felder."

"Agreed," Robbie said. "But how are we supposed to find them without their names?"

"That's where you come in," Lindsey smiled at him. "You need to talk to Tim and see if he remembers any of Grace's friends from the office."

Robbie gaped at her. "And how the bloody hell am I supposed to work that into the conversation? It's not like I can just say, 'Oy, it looks like rain, and by the way, who were your dead wife's friends at work just before she was killed?'"

"I have every confidence that you will find a way to ease the question into a conversation," Lindsey said.

Robbie rolled his eyes. He started the engine and drove away from Felder's house and back to town. Lindsey pondered the different ways she could try to find out who had worked for Felder back in the day, but nothing came to mind. Tim was their best shot, and she really hoped Robbie could figure out a way to approach him without giving away their suspicions about Felder.

The last thing Tim needed was to go after Felder the way he had William. It would do him no good, and she suspected that Felder was the vindictive type who would sue Tim down to the change in his couch cushions if he made one false move. They were going to have to proceed with caution.

CHAPTER
14

BRIAR CREEK
PUBLIC LIBRARY

Lindsey returned to the library just in time to take her turn on the reference desk so that Ann Marie could take her lunch break.

"I'm here," she said as she speedwalked to the desk.

"You're fine," Ann Marie said. "With two minutes to spare."

"Phew," Lindsey said.

Ann Marie stood up and Lindsey slipped onto the desk chair. "Anything you need me to take over?"

"No, it's been quiet, mostly," Ann Marie said. "I do have Pete Cassela looking up how to rebuild a Chevy engine for that truck he's trying to restore. I set him up on the online car repair database, and he's been engrossed for the better part of an hour."

She pointed with her thumb to a computer terminal near

the reference desk. Lindsey glanced over and saw Pete. He was somewhere in his sixties, with gray hair and stooped shoulders, newly retired from the post office and looking for things to occupy his time. So far he'd tried gardening, beekeeping and pickleball. None of which had kept his interest. Maybe car restoration would do the trick.

"I'll keep an eye on him," Lindsey promised.

Ann Marie scooped up her things and headed to the workroom.

Lindsey settled in, opening up the file she had saved on the shared drive to look over the purchase requests from patrons. She was halfway through when she saw Tim and Barbara Little arrive with their twin grandsons. The boys were dressed identically in tan pants, plaid shirts, puffy blue coats and red hats. One had his coat unzipped while the other had his hat over his eyes. They started running for the children's area as soon as the automatic doors shut behind them.

Barbara hurried after them while Tim followed. He walked more slowly, as if the weight of the world were pressing him down. He glanced around the library, and when he spotted Lindsey, he changed course and approached the reference desk.

"Is it true?" he asked.

Lindsey didn't pretend not to understand. "That we found a skeleton in the Dorchester mansion?"

He nodded. His face was grave, and a look of deep hurt haunted his eyes.

"Yes, we did," she said. "But as far as I know, the remains haven't been identified."

"It's her," he said. "I can feel it." He rubbed his sternum with his knuckles as if trying to alleviate an ache. "I knew it. I knew it was him."

"Him?" Lindsey asked.

"William Dorchester," he said. "He killed her, I know he did."

"What makes you think that?" she asked.

"He hated that she married me," he said. "He wasn't man enough to stand up to his mother to marry her himself, but he didn't want anyone else to have her either."

"That's quite an accusation," Lindsey said.

Tim was a big man, and he loomed over the desk. Lindsey wasn't afraid but she felt a twinge of caution. She'd seen Tim when he charged William. His temper was fierce. Could he have lost it with Grace? Is that why she ran? Did she run? If so, how did she end up at the Dorchesters'?

"I know what you're thinking," Tim said. "It's what everyone has always thought."

"What's that?" she asked.

"That I killed her," he said. "After she disappeared, the gossip, the rumors, the suspicion followed me everywhere." With a heavy sigh, he sank into the chair across from her desk. Just like that, the fight went out of him and he looked utterly defeated. "I would never. I loved her. I would never have hurt her."

Lindsey didn't know what to say. This broken man in front of her didn't look as if he could harm a flea.

"The only person who believed me was Barbara," he said. He glanced across the library to where his wife had disappeared into the story time room. "She was with me that night. I was full of vitriol and outrage, convinced that Grace had wronged me. Barbara didn't try to talk me out of it or argue. She just listened."

Lindsey sat perfectly still. She didn't know where this conversation was going, but she didn't want to discourage him by being too interested or not interested enough, so she kept her expression neutral and hoped he kept talking.

"Grace let me have it," Tim said. "I was being a jealous idiot, and she called me out. I deserved it. But I didn't know how to tell her that I just felt like she was too good for me, you know? I could never believe that out of all the men she could have had, she chose me."

Lindsey nodded. She understood. She sometimes felt like that about Sully. He was such a good man, she frequently wondered what she'd done to deserve him.

"I was a young hothead back then," Tim said. "Anyway, Grace stormed off, and my stupid pride wouldn't let me go after her and beg for her forgiveness like I should have. Instead, I skulked around the pier, hugging my righteous indignation, telling myself I was better off without her."

Lindsey nodded again. She could see the argument playing out exactly as he described.

"Why do we choose anger?" Tim asked. "What is the gain in feeling 'right' and 'superior,' especially when we're arguing with someone we love? Wouldn't we be better served to be kind instead of right? Understanding instead of outraged?"

"You were young," Lindsey said.

Tim laughed but it was without mirth. "It's not just the

young who wrap themselves up in their pride. Let me tell you, it's cold comfort being right when you lose the one you love."

"I'm sorry," Lindsey said. She meant it. Whatever had happened between Tim and Grace, it was clear he had loved his first wife very much.

"Yeah, well, thank you for that," Tim said. "Not just for listening to me but for not looking at me as if I'm a cold-blooded killer. Since the body was found, it's started again. People stare and they whisper." He looked wrecked. "I don't want to put Barbara through that, not again, and my kids and grandkids. I just . . ."

His voice broke and his eyes took on a watery sheen. In that moment, Lindsey understood why Robbie believed in him so much. She couldn't see Tim hurting anyone. He was a big man, sure, but with a heart like marshmallow fluff. Unless, of course, he was a sociopath and this was a performance piece laying the groundwork to get people to believe he was innocent.

She wondered if she should take the opportunity to ask about Grace's coworkers, but she stopped herself, thinking it was better if it came from Robbie, who had more of a friendship with Tim.

"Tim, is everything all right?" Barbara asked as she approached the desk.

Tim cleared his throat and forced a small smile. "Of course, I just thought I'd check and see if . . ."

His voice trailed off, and Lindsey realized he was not a very good liar, so that was another check in the not-likely-a-murderer column. She broke the silence and said,

"If the new Nick Petrie thriller is in. It's not, but I'm adding your name to the list."

Tim sent her a relieved look. "Thanks, Lindsey, I appreciate it. I'd best go check on our grands. Those boys can find mischief in the most unlikely places."

He squeezed Barbara's shoulder as he walked by her. She watched him go, looking like she, too, wanted to cry.

"How are you doing, Barbara?" Lindsey asked.

"Not good," Barbara said. She sat on the edge of the seat Tim had just vacated. "It's starting again, just like I told you it would, and I don't know how to protect him."

"You don't have to," Lindsey said. "The medical examiner will identify the person, maybe it's not even Grace, and the cause of death will be determined. For all we know, it's someone else and they died of natural causes."

Barbara turned to look at her. "You are very kind to try and talk me out of my fears, but I've been through this before. People talk and they assign blame without proof. Everything we have worked for, our family, our place in the community, all of it, is once again in peril because of her."

"Grace?"

"Yes," Barbara said. "It's like she's reaching from beyond the grave to ruin Tim's life."

Lindsey tipped her head to the side. This didn't sound like the Barbara who had spoken to her before, calling Grace a "poor girl" and sympathizing with the tragic end that she met. Lindsey wondered if something had happened.

"Has someone approached Tim about Grace's death?" she asked.

Barbara flushed a deep shade of red. "Chief Plewicki wants Tim to come by the station today. She didn't say he was a person of interest, but I know, I just know, it's not good."

Barbara twisted her hands in her lap. She was obviously nervous, and Lindsey felt for her. To have the life one had built put at risk could make anyone worry.

"I'm no expert, but I think I can safely say that just because she wants to talk to Tim doesn't mean she suspects him of anything," Lindsey said. "I mean she calls me into the station all the time."

Barbara smiled at that. "I suppose you're right. Hopefully, I'm just being silly."

"I would call it concerned, not silly," Lindsey said. "And that's okay." She gestured to her computer and said, "I'm filling out my orders for books requested by patrons. If you have anything you want for your literacy class, let me know and I'll add it to my list."

"Thank you," Barbara said. She glanced across the library to where Tim was playing in the puppet theater in the children's area. Her face took on a softness when she gazed at her husband.

"You love him very much," Lindsey said.

Barbara nodded and then sighed. "I've loved him since I was six years old and he was eight. We grew up on the same street, and I used to follow him everywhere. He treated me like a pesky little sister until . . . well, no need to go there. Suffice to say, he finally noticed me."

"You've built a wonderful life together," Lindsey said.

"It's been everything I ever dreamed of," Barbara said. Her voice was wistful.

"Trust Emma," Lindsey said. "She's a wonderful chief of police. She'll figure out what happened to Grace, assuming that it is Grace, and everything will be okay."

"You're right," Barbara said. She stood and smiled at Lindsey. "I'll send you an email about the materials for my class."

"Terrific," Lindsey said.

Barbara turned and crossed the library, joining her husband and her two grandkids in the children's area. Tim was on all fours pretending to be a dragon, much to the boys' delight. As Lindsey watched them, she wondered how this family would manage whatever Emma discovered, and she hoped for all their sakes that Grace's death, if it was Grace, was just a horrible accident.

Sully picked up Lindsey after work, and they made their way to Dr. Rubinski's. Lindsey had been fretting about the cat ever since they dropped her off. It wasn't that she didn't want the poor thing to find her family, really; it was just that she felt as if the cat belonged with them. When Sully parked the car, she hopped out, eager to see how Zelda was doing.

Tom was waiting for them at the door with the cat in his arms. She looked quite content, which Lindsey took as a sign that she liked humans and wouldn't mind living with them. She refused to worry about the cat's introduction to Heathcliff. It would be fine.

"Hi, Tom. How is she?" Lindsey asked.

"In excellent health overall," Tom said. As if sensing that Lindsey was aching to hold the cat, he held her out to Lindsey. She took her carefully into her arms and was pleasantly surprised when the cat purred and rubbed her face against Lindsey's chin. "She's still a bit underweight, but I'm sure you can get her where she needs to be. I've given her all of her immunizations and examined her tip to tail. My guess is that she's about five months old."

"Has anyone reported missing a cat like her?" Sully asked. Lindsey could hear just a hint of anxiety in his voice, and she knew he was as attached as she was.

"No," Tom said. "I reached out to all of the local cat communities, and there's been no report of anyone missing a cat. I think, if you want her, she's yours."

Lindsey did a tiny hop for joy and grinned at Sully. "We have a cat."

He returned her smile and reached over to scratch the cat under her chin right where she liked it. "Good thing, because I have a cat carrier in the back of my truck. I'll go get it."

"You just happen to have a cat carrier," Lindsey said.

"I was feeling optimistic." He shrugged.

He ducked back outside and Lindsey turned to Tom. "Okay, you know Heathcliff. What's the best way to introduce the two of them?"

"Slowly," he said. "If you have a spare room, keep her in there on her own for a while. That way they can get used to the smell of each other through the door. Then you can slowly let them check each other out, maybe through a baby gate, and see how it goes. They'll grow accustomed to each other and will be snuggling up on the dog bed in no time."

"I hope you're right," she said. "At the very least, Heathcliff will have a friend while we're at work, so that should be good, right?"

"Absolutely," he said. "It just takes time. It usually takes a week or two, and then they settle in."

Lindsey glanced down at the feline in her arms. "We've got nothing but time."

Tom gave them all the supplies they needed to get started. Food, litter and the baby gate he had used when training his golden retriever pups. With the truck loaded, Lindsey and Sully headed for home.

The evening was spent getting the cat situated in the guest bedroom and calming Heathcliff, who was desperate to meet his new housemate. It was an adventure.

"Do you think she'll be okay in there by herself?" Lindsey asked. They were getting into bed after an evening spent with one of them playing with the cat in the guest room while the other entertained the dog, frequently switching places so the cat could get used to both of them, until the cat finally climbed onto the armchair in the corner and curled up in a tight ball to sleep.

"She has food and water, a litter box, a nice warm bed, windows to look out on the world, and a dog whose nose is pressed up against the bottom of the door," Sully said. "She'll be just fine."

"You're right," Lindsey said. "Heathcliff, bedtime."

With a grumble of protest, Heathcliff left his spot by the guest room door, entered their bedroom, and climbed onto his bed, which they kept on the floor beneath the window. He threw himself down onto the thick cushion with all the insolence of a teenager being forced to have a curfew. Lindsey smiled.

Sully switched out the light, and Lindsey lay there listening. If the cat cried, she wanted to be there to comfort her. But the cat never did cry, seeming to have accepted that this new place was home.

Lindsey was debating running home for lunch to check on the cat when Robbie popped up in the doorway to her office. It had been a few days since she'd seen him and his eye was no longer swollen. The deep purple had faded to a spectacular lavender.

"There are women who would kill for that shade of eye shadow," Lindsey said.

"But I wear it so well." Robbie tossed his head as if he had a mass of long glossy curls.

Lindsey grinned. "What's the good word?"

"Cat," he said. "I hear you've adopted one."

"Yes, we have, the one I kept seeing in the Dorchester mansion," Lindsey said.

"Ghost cat," Robbie said. Then he shivered. "Are you sure about this?"

"About adopting the cat?" Lindsey asked. "One hundred percent. She's so little and sweet."

"Until she morphs into a monster in the middle of the night and eats your face off," he said.

"Have you been watching too many Halloween horror movies?" Lindsey asked. "She's not going to morph into anything except a perfectly content house cat, and her name is Zelda."

"If you say so. Zelda, eh?" he said. "How's Heathcliff taking it?"

"You make it sound like I betrayed him," Lindsey said.

Robbie shrugged, indicating that's exactly what he thought.

"I had no idea that you were so anti-cat," Lindsey said.

"I'm not," he protested. "I'm anti–ghost cat."

"I've held her, she rubbed her head on my chin, she's not a ghost."

"We'll see, or maybe we won't," he said. His voice became eerie as he moaned, "Boo-oo-oooo."

Lindsey laughed and then forced herself to be serious. "Stop it, that's my cat you're maligning now. She's very docile and does not deserve to be reduced to being an antagonistic apparition."

"Fine," he said. He glanced at the expensive watch on his wrist. "Are you about to take your lunch?"

"Yes, I was thinking about going home to check on the pets," she said.

"You could do that, or you could come with me to speak with Michelle Womack," he said. "Former employee of Felder Investments."

Lindsey gave him the side-eye. "Would this Michelle be someone who worked with Grace?"

"Not only worked with her but considered her a close personal friend," he said.

"And Tim told you about her?"

"Sort of," Robbie said.

"I'm listening."

Robbie sighed. "I met up with Tim at the Blue Anchor for a beer last night, you know, in a support-my-friend sort of move. I hoped to get him talking about Grace and her job with Felder. Well, I stepped away for just a second to greet some fans down the bar, and before I got back, this woman approached Tim and tossed her wine into his face."

"No!"

"Yes, and then she told him that she knew he murdered his wife and tried to frame William by hiding the body in the mansion. She capped the scene off by telling Tim she hopes he's sent to the electric chair," Robbie said. "Poor Tim was sitting there sputtering, and then her husband appeared and dragged her out of there.

"I hurried back to join him, but the entire restaurant was staring at us. I took him outside to get him away from the whispers. After that, it was pretty easy to get him to tell me who she was and why she was angry. She worked with Grace, considered herself a close friend—although, according to Tim, Grace didn't reciprocate the affection—and this woman, Michelle Womack, is convinced because of the rumors and gossip that Tim murdered her friend."

"Wow," Lindsey said. "I'd say good work, but you did nothing to get all of that information. It fell into your lap like candy at a parade."

"Don't underestimate the power of being at the right place at the right time," he said.

"Meh." Lindsey shot down his bid for praise.

"Ingrate," he muttered.

"So where do we find Michelle today?" Lindsey asked. "Does she have a job in the area?"

"Yes, she works for Dr. Stanley as an office administrator," he said.

"The town dentist?" Lindsey asked.

"Yup," Robbie nodded. "We should head over there."

"Why?" Lindsey asked. The dentist was not her favorite out-of-work activity; in fact, she'd rather go anywhere but the dentist.

"Are you due for your cleaning?" he asked.

"No," Lindsey answered, but she didn't meet his gaze.

"Right," he said. "You're afraid you're going to get yelled at for not keeping up with your appointments."

"No, I'm not," she insisted. She absolutely was. Plus, they would undoubtedly try to schedule her next cleaning, and it took a bit for her to work up to these things.

"Then this visit should be no problem," he said. "In fact, you're giving us the perfect cover since Michelle works the front desk."

"I don't want to," Lindsey said. "Go without me."

"You're afraid of the dentist," he said.

"No, I'm not," she said. "I'm just not very good at it."

"What's there to be good at?" he said. "You just lie there with your mouth open, swish and spit, and it's all over."

"For you," she said. "But some of us are not comfortable with the scrape and the buff and—heaven forbid—the drill. Even the noise that it makes could cause some people to feel faint."

"Lindsey Norris Sullivan afraid of the dentist, I am shocked," Robbie said. "Shocked, I tell you."

"All right, fine, I'm afraid," Lindsey admitted. "Happy now?"

"I don't know that I'd say I'm happy so much as amused," Robbie said. "Listen, I'll do all of the talking. You hang back. I promise I won't let anyone come at you with a drill or a Novocain needle. Okay?"

"Ugh, you had to mention the needle." Lindsey pressed her lips together. She could feel her teeth and gums retract at the mere thought of dental work.

"This is bigger than you and your ridiculous phobia. We need to talk to Michelle Womack and see what she knows," he said. "With the body being found at the Dorchester mansion, she might have a whole new perspective."

"Or she's going to double down on the theory that Tim murdered his wife and somehow managed to hide her in the mansion to cast blame on William," Lindsey said.

"That seems so far-fetched," Robbie said. "How is anyone taking that theory seriously?"

"People in a panic will believe dumb things," Lindsey countered.

"But Tim has an alibi for the evening," Robbie said. "He was with Barbara. That right there proves he couldn't have done it. Now stop stalling. Let's go, or your lunch hour will be over before we know it."

Lindsey heaved a sigh. "All right." She grabbed her handbag and followed him out the door.

The dentist's office was on Post Road in an old redbrick building. Robbie parked in the lot and strolled toward the front door with the ease of someone not there to have any work done or make an appointment. Lindsey followed him with the enthusiasm of a hostage.

The automatic door swung open when Robbie stepped onto the mat, and they entered the office. Soft classical music was playing in the background. There were three people in the waiting room, looking at their phones, ignoring the television in the corner and the magazines on the table.

Robbie strode across the room to the reception desk. The woman behind the counter had a thick head of dark hair that was held up in a clip at the back of her head. She was wearing a pink sweater and glanced up at them over the top of her glasses when they approached.

"Hi, can I help you?"

"My friend needs to make an appointment," Robbie said.

The woman blinked at him. "You're Robbie Vine."

He smiled. "The one and only, thank goodness."

"I've seen all your movies." She put both of her hands over her heart. "I am such a big fan. I can't . . . I don't . . ."

Robbie's smile deepened. This was what he lived for. It occurred to Lindsey that she'd known him for so long, she actually forgot he was a famous actor.

"Would you like an autograph?" Robbie asked. He picked up a pen as the woman handed him a sheet of paper. He sent the woman a smoldering glance and then asked, "What's your name, love?"

"Michelle," she sighed. "And can I get a picture, too?"

"Of course," he said.

"How about I take it of the two of you?" Lindsey offered.

Michelle's eyes went wide. "That would be amazing."

She grabbed her phone and hurried around the desk. When she stood beside Robbie, he put his arm behind her but didn't touch her. Robbie was always very respectful of boundaries. It was one of the things Lindsey liked about him.

Michelle's grin lit up her whole face, and Lindsey snapped several pictures before handing it back to her. Michelle glanced at the phone and nodded. "These are great. Thank you."

"Sure," Lindsey said.

Michelle went back around her desk and said, "Now when did you want to make an appointment?"

Lindsey hesitated. She knew she needed to make one. She did. But . . . ugh.

"Do you know when you'll be finished moving the books from the Dorchester mansion? It would have to be after that, right?" Robbie asked. He gave Lindsey a pointed look, and she realized he was giving her their opening.

"I don't," she said. "The chief of police has to let me back into the library there."

The smile vanished off Michelle's face. "You're the librarian who discovered the body?"

"Yes," Lindsey said. She looked pained, which wasn't an act, as the second she remembered finding the skeleton in the sealed room, she felt a bit ill.

"That must have been horrible," Michelle said.

"It was. *Horrible* is a good word for it," Lindsey said.

"It was Grace Little, wasn't it?" Michelle asked.

"I don't know," Lindsey said. "As far as I know, the medical examiner hasn't made his findings public."

"I just know it's her," Michelle said. She put her head in her hands, and she took a deep breath as if trying to center herself. When she dropped her hands, there was a hard glint in her eye. "She was my friend. We worked together as secretaries right up until she disappeared."

"You did?" Robbie asked. Lindsey knew he was trying to sound surprised, but to her ears, he was overacting. Michelle didn't seem to notice.

"She was the nicest person," Michelle said. "Always re-membered everyone's birthdays and went out of her way to bring a cake or a pie, whichever the birthday person pre-ferred. She was so well liked by everyone because she was so positive, even though her life had pretty tough beginnings."

"So, no enemies at work, then?" Robbie asked.

"No, absolutely not. Everyone adored her."

"Was there anyone who showed a little too much inter-est in Grace?"

"Only every man we worked with," Michelle said. "Grace was so gentle, she had that way about her that made you want to protect her. She had a hard time with boundaries. There were several men who misinterpreted her friendliness for something more. She couldn't bear to make anyone feel bad, even when they were being inappropriate."

"Including her boss?" Lindsey asked.

"Oh, yes, he was interested in Grace," Michelle said. "But Grace never did anything to encourage him. I told her she didn't have to put up with that and to complain to the executive board, but she said she didn't want to cause any trouble. It came looking for her anyway, and then it killed her. And I know who did it."

Robbie straightened up. "You do?"

Again, Lindsey felt like he was overselling it, and she resisted the urge to check him with her elbow.

"I think so," Michelle said. She leaned over her desk and whispered, "For the longest time I thought it was her hus-band Tim. I even said as much to him last night when I saw him at the Blue Anchor."

She looked down at the top of her desk, and it was clear she felt remorse.

"But you don't anymore?" Robbie asked.

Michelle shook her head. "My husband and I had a big fight about it. He's friends with Tim, and he argued that Tim is a decent man. My husband doesn't think he's a murderer, and I have to admit I'm doubting it myself."

A door opened behind the reception desk, and a woman in scrubs handed Michelle a chart. "Here's the update on Mr. Gillespie."

"Thanks, I'll add it to his file," Michelle said. The woman nodded and left again. They all waited until the door shut behind her.

"If not her husband, then who?" Robbie asked. Lindsey knew he was waiting for Michelle to say William Dorchester, but she didn't.

"David Felder," Michelle said. She ducked her head as soon as she said it, as if she expected some sort of lightning strike to hit. "We used to work for his company. He was our boss. That's where Grace and I became friends."

"You think her boss murdered her?" Lindsey asked. She hoped she sounded like this was brand-new information.

"Yes," Michelle said. "I spent all night thinking about it, and I always got a creepy vibe off Felder. It wouldn't surprise me at all if he was a murderer. Miserable man."

Lindsey's certainty that David had been interested in Grace in more than a professional manner returned tenfold.

"What makes you think he had something to do with it?" Robbie asked.

"When Grace disappeared, he went a bit round the bend," Michelle said. "At first, we all thought she'd be back. I was certain she and Tim had just had a spat and that she'd return when they patched things up, but Felder didn't think she'd be back. The very first day after she disappeared, he vanished into his office and drank himself unconscious."

Robbie looked at me. "Trying to forget what he'd done?"

"Maybe," I said. "Or he was just grief-stricken."

"But if he was grieving, that implies he knew she was dead while the rest of us still thought she'd just left Tim for a while," Michelle said. "Why would he be that overwrought unless he knew?"

"Have you told anyone your theory about Felder?" Lindsey asked.

"No, I don't have any proof," Michelle said. "Honestly, I didn't even start to suspect him until last night, when my husband and I fought about it. He asked me to look back on my time with her at the office and think if there was anyone who was suspicious. That's when I remembered how Felder would linger around Grace's desk, making small talk, and . . ."

"And?" Robbie said.

"Touching her," Michelle said.

Robbie's eyebrows rose.

"Oh, not in any flagrant pinch-her-bottom sort of way, but he'd put his hand on her shoulder or her lower back," Michelle said. She glanced out the window as if she could see her memories like they were as tangible as the row of pine trees that lined the parking lot. "At the time, sexual harassment wasn't a thing. A woman, especially a secretary, was supposed to put up and shut up. There was very much a good old boys vibe about that place. I hated it. We all did."

"Who was in charge besides Felder?" Robbie asked.

"There was an executive board, which was basically a group of his own investors. They liked to drink whiskey and smoke cigars at the weekly meeting. I don't know that they contributed much to the overall well-being of the company. Practically speaking, it was just Felder who ran the place," Michelle said. "He was a generous boss, but when I reconsider it, there was a bit of possessiveness in the way he treated all of us, most especially Grace. He called her into his office all day long, asked her to stay late to take notes on meetings. He became very cold if she said no, and she fretted about losing her job."

"Were she and Tim in financial trouble?" Lindsey asked.

"No, Tim was making enough to support them, but Grace dreamed of having a family of her own. Losing her father so young, she yearned for babies, lots of them, and she wanted to put away plenty of money so that when the time came she could stay home with them. She always said she knew Tim was going to be an amazing father."

Lindsey felt her heart constrict. By all accounts, Tim was an amazing father and grandfather, but not to Grace's children and grandchildren.

"What about the flowers Grace received at work?" Lindsey asked. "I remember the woman who overheard Tim and Grace arguing that night mentioned that she'd been receiving flowers. Do you remember those?"

Michelle nodded. "Of course I do. That's why I suspected Tim to begin with. Grace kept receiving flowers from a secret admirer, and he was furious. He wanted to know who it was, but Grace had no idea. In fact, it was making her very skittish and uncomfortable, but she didn't know what to do."

"Could they have been from Felder?" Robbie asked.

Michelle shrugged. "Maybe. I remember he'd stop by her desk and ask her about them, whether she liked them or if she was more of a lingerie sort of girl." Michelle rolled her eyes. "So skeevy."

"Ew." Lindsey curled her lip in disgust.

"Like I said, it was back when sexual harassment was tolerated under the nonsensical notion of 'boys will be boys and they just can't help themselves.' Ugh."

"Gross," Robbie said. Both women looked at him and he asked, "What? I can't be an ally?"

Lindsey reached over and squeezed his arm. "The thought is appreciated."

"But I should close my mouth and open my ears," he said.

"That's the ticket," Michelle said.

Lindsey glanced at the clock on the wall. Her lunch hour was almost over, and she had to get back to work. She said as much to Robbie and Michelle.

"But what about your appointment for your cleaning?" Michelle asked. "I haven't even scheduled you."

"You know, I forgot to bring my planner," Lindsey said.

"It's not on your phone?" Michelle asked, looking skeptical.

"New phone," Lindsey said. "I'm still getting used to it." She took a business card out of the card rack on the counter. "But I'll give you a call as soon as I have my calendar in front of me."

"You do that," Michelle said. She turned to Robbie. "Thanks again for the picture."

"My pleasure," he said. "If you think of anything else that you remember about Grace, let me know. I happen to be good friends with the chief of police."

"Friends?" Michelle gave him a hard stare. "Right."

Robbie blinked, the picture of innocence. Lindsey turned away to hide her smile. Robbie and Emma had been dating for a while now; it was only natural that people were starting to talk.

"Very smooth," Robbie said once they were outside.

"I was," she said. "You? Not so much."

"What do you mean?" he asked. "I was totally cool."

"Right up until she questioned your friendship with the chief," Lindsey said. "I think people are wondering where your relationship is going."

"Going? It's a relationship, it doesn't go anywhere!" He sounded upset. "Why can't Emma and I just be exactly as we are for ten or fifteen or more years?"

"Have you asked Emma what she thinks?" Lindsey asked.

"No," he said. "Because I assume she'll tell me if she thinks things need to change in some way."

"That's not how it works," Lindsey said. "You need to ask her."

"Bollocks!"

CHAPTER

16

BRIAR CREEK
PUBLIC LIBRARY

Lindsey had fifteen more minutes until she was done for the day when her cell phone rang. She picked it up and saw Emma's name. She hoped this meant that the Dorchester library was open again.

"Hi, Emma, what's up?"

"You and Robbie had a busy lunch hour," she said.

So this was not about the library reopening.

"What makes you say that?"

"Michelle Womack just dropped by the station," she said.

"Oh, really?" Lindsey tried to keep her voice neutral. "What a coincidence. I was just in their office to make an appointment."

"And yet you didn't," Emma said.

"Forgot my calendar," she said.

"I'm sure," Emma said. "Listen, I know Robbie's taking the accusations against Tim personally, and I know you want back in the library, but I'm going to tell you the same thing I told him—stay away from this case."

"I hear what you're saying," Lindsey said. "But how helpful was your conversation with Michelle?"

"We can discuss that over dinner tonight," Emma said. "Your house. Robbie and I will be over at seven."

"I—"

"Bye."

The call ended and Lindsey stared at her phone. And that was why Emma was the chief of police; she had just completely outmaneuvered Lindsey. She opened her text messages and sent a quick note to Sully, telling him there'd be two more for dinner.

He texted back immediately that he was on it. Lindsey was grateful yet again that she'd married a man who liked to cook, because if it were up to her, they would be serving pizza with a side of tacos.

Despite the scolding she'd gotten from Emma, Lindsey was happy to have Robbie and Emma over for dinner. Over the past few years, they'd become close friends, and the four of them got together frequently. They didn't usually discuss Emma's investigations, but tonight Emma shared her own frustrations with the cold case and the lack of information from the original investigation back in the day.

"I'm not saying the chief back then didn't do his job," Emma said. "I mean there was no reason to think that Grace Little would be found in the Dorchesters' house, but the investigation itself is so full of holes, and they barely interviewed anyone."

"Well, they didn't have a body," Sully said. "It's hard to make a case for murder when there's no body."

"But it's more than that," Emma said. "The missing person's file is so thin. It's as if no one tried to find her. The only one who kept trying was Tim Little. He badgered the chief of police constantly for details, up to the point that the chief mentioned it in the file."

"Which proves my belief that there's no way he murdered his wife," Robbie said.

"Maybe," Emma said. "Or else he was really committed to making himself look innocent."

"Such a cynic," Robbie said.

"That's the job," she said. "Everyone is guilty until proven innocent."

"What about David Felder?" Lindsey asked. "Did Michelle convince you to look more closely?"

"He's definitely moved up on the suspect list," Emma said. "I—"

Whatever else she was going to say was interrupted by her cell phone ringing. She glanced at the display. Her face gave away nothing, but Lindsey could tell by the way her body tightened just a bit that the call was important.

"Excuse me, I have to take this," she said. She pushed back from the table and strode across the room to the doors that led out to their deck. She slid the door open and stepped outside into the cold night air.

They all watched her go, and Robbie turned back to the table and said, "That was her 'very important call' face."

"Do you think it's in regard to the Grace Little case?" Sully asked.

"As far as I know, it's the only case she's working on right now," Robbie said. "Things have been remarkably quiet in town since the spring, and with Ms. Cole running unopposed in the upcoming election, there's really not been anything out of the ordinary. Well, until you and the ladies fell into the secret room, that is."

The sliding glass doors opened, letting in a gust of chilly evening air. Emma was frowning as she resumed her seat at the table.

"Everything all right?" Sully asked.

"That was the medical examiner," Emma said. "He's positively identified the remains as belonging to Grace Little."

Lindsey felt her heart plummet in her chest. Even though she'd known it was most likely Grace, there had been a tiny part of her hoping that it wasn't the runaway bride. She hadn't wanted the story of the woman who had been so universally liked, with the exception of Marion Dorchester, to end in such a tragic way. She'd wanted to believe that maybe she'd just decided marriage wasn't for her and had taken off for Paris or Fiji or Antarctica.

"He called me to let me get ahead of the press," she said. "Because according to the tests he's run, there is no visible cause of death. No evidence of poison, no injury suggesting blunt trauma, and no bloodstains in the room to indicate a fatal wound. His best guess is that, because the room appears to be airtight, she suffocated to death."

"Dear God," Robbie said. "What an absolutely horrific way to die."

"According to the ME, it is pretty awful," Emma said. "Technically, the person dies from carbon monoxide toxicity or hypercapnia, which is what happens when there's too much carbon dioxide in the bloodstream, leading to labored breathing, fever, fatigue and loss of consciousness. And, not-so-fun fact, bodies decompose faster in a sealed space, like a coffin, or in this case the secret room. The only way to know for certain how she died is to find out how she ended up in that room and how long she was sealed inside it. After all these years, I just can't believe Lindsey, Nancy and Violet were the first people to have found her."

"You think someone knew there was a body in there but chose to ignore it?" Sully asked.

"If she was murdered, if her killer put her in there to die, then, yes," Emma said.

"The bigger question for me is why that room exists in the first place," Robbie said. "I mean, who puts such a dangerous room *in their house*?"

"According to William, his father had it built for the rare books and manuscripts he collected. It was supposed to be a low-moisture and airless space to keep his rare materials from disintegrating," Emma said. "But when his father died, Marion decided to extend the bookcase over it since it was no longer in use."

"Why was there no handle on the inside of the door?" Lindsey asked.

"There was one," Emma said. Her face turned grim. "But it was removed. No one seems to know when or by whom."

"Meaning that if it was done before she was put in there, then it was definitely premeditated murder," Sully said. "They knowingly removed the door handle to keep Grace trapped until she died."

"It seems so," Emma said. "She likely slid into a coma in a matter of days and then slowly died."

Lindsey glanced at Sully. His face was tight, as if he, too, was imagining how gruesome Grace's death had been.

"The media has been dogging the ME's office for details," she said. "He's going to hold them off as long as he can, but the news is going to break, and it'll cause a feeding frenzy of reporters in the village as they vie for the story."

"I don't know that I blame them," Robbie said. "Halloween is days away, and the salaciousness of finding a skeleton in a sealed room in a decrepit mansion would make even the most stalwart reporter salivate."

"This is a nightmare," Emma said. She put her hand on her forehead. She closed her eyes and visibly shook her head. Then she dropped her hand and said, "Well, now that they're done with the crime scene, you're welcome to go back to the Dorchester mansion and finish moving the books out."

Lindsey felt relief sweep through her. She'd been so worried that the stampede of crime scene personnel would disturb the integrity of the collection. "I'll be there tomorrow."

"Slow your roll, librarian," Emma said. "There are some conditions."

Lindsey gave her a side-eye. "Like what?"

"You are not to be there alone. If you go to pack up, I want either Robbie or Sully or one of your staff with you," Emma said.

"I wasn't planning on going there alone anyway, but is there a specific reason that I should be concerned?"

"Just precautionary," Emma said. "Whoever killed Grace has gotten away with it for over thirty years. They are not going to simply turn themselves in and will likely try to stop anyone they fear could reveal them."

"I'll be with her," Sully said.

Lindsey looked at him and saw the stubborn set to his chin. *Okay, then.*

Lindsey was ready to get back to the Dorchester mansion the next evening. She and Sully stopped at home for dinner and time with the pets before commencing the packing. Heathcliff was delighted to see them, and the cat, well, she seemed pleased, too, but Lindsey wasn't sure whether it was because of the food they gave her, possibly that was her love language, or if she was genuinely happy to see them.

During a phone call that morning, Emma reiterated her desire for Lindsey to have company at all times while at the Dorchester mansion. Lindsey promised she would. At this point if the lights went out, or a door got stuck, or a curtain billowed, she'd probably have a complete freak-out. They had agreed that it was best to keep the library free from too much foot traffic, so Sully and Lindsey were going to pack the remaining books by themselves. Lindsey hoped it would only take a few evenings at most.

When they arrived, Mrs. Sutcliff met them at the door. She looked tired, and Lindsey wondered if the strain of taking care of Marion was beginning to wear her down.

"How are you, Mrs. Sutcliff?" she asked.

"Ready to retire," she answered. "These last few days have been exhausting. Mrs. Dorchester has started sleepwalking in the middle of the night, so there's no peace. Mr. Dorchester is out with friends for the evening, and I feel as if I'm constantly on alert. I don't want to complain as the Dorchesters have been very good to me, but I am exhausted."

"We're here," Lindsey said. "If you'd like to get some rest, we can keep an eye on Mrs. Dorchester."

Sully nodded. "It shouldn't be a problem."

"A cat nap would be lovely." Mrs. Sutcliff's eyes lit with hope. "Just twenty minutes and I'd be a new person."

"Go," Lindsey said. "Sully and I will keep watch. Where is Mrs. Dorchester now?"

"She's watching television in her room," Mrs. Sutcliff said. "It's her favorite program, *Wheel of Fortune*, so she likely won't leave her room for the next half hour."

"Is the main staircase the only exit from upstairs?" Sully asked.

"Yes." Mrs. Sutcliff nodded.

"We'll take turns watching it, then," he said.

"Thank you." She looked like she might weep, and Lindsey imagined her exhaustion must be beyond comprehension.

Mrs. Sutcliff left and Lindsey said, "Why don't I start packing and you can keep an eye on the stairs?"

"Sounds like a plan," he said. "Let me know when you want me to tag in."

"Will do," she said.

Lindsey picked up an archival box and headed for the glassed-in cases that ran along the wall. She opened the hinged door and began packing the materials, using the acid-free specialty packaging she'd ordered, since she didn't know how long these items would be in storage at the library. She wanted them to be secure for however long it took the town's maintenance department to install the glass-front shelves in the library.

She had two boxes packed and was just starting on the third when the lights went out. A clawing feeling of dread ripped through her. Not again. She couldn't do this again. She hoped the electricity would blink back on in a moment, but no. Instead, a scream of sheer terror ripped through the darkness, making Lindsey start.

"Sully? Are you all right?" she called.

"I'm fine. You?" he asked. A bright light shone from the doorway. It was Sully with his phone. He turned it on her, and Lindsey shielded her eyes against the glare.

"I'm okay," she said. She put her hands on the bookcase in front of her to keep her bearings. "That scream sounded like it came from upstairs."

"I'll check it out," he said. "The power outage probably caused Mrs. Dorchester a fright. I don't want her wandering around in the dark."

"Okay, I'll stay down here just in case she gets by you," Lindsey said.

"Do you need a light?" he asked.

"No, I have my phone," she said.

"All right, back in a minute," he said.

He vanished from the door and Lindsey yelled after him, "Be careful."

"Always."

Lindsey felt along the bookcase to the spot on the floor where she'd left her handbag. She patted the floor, thinking that was where it had to be. All she felt was the carpet. She closed her eyes, hoping that when she opened them, they would have adjusted to the darkness. They did not.

The room was so dark, she couldn't see the bookcase in front of her face until she smacked into it. *Ouch!* For a second, she wondered if this was the sort of darkness Grace had faced in the airless room. Had she been terrified? Undoubtedly. Lindsey hoped that Grace had been able to escape into unconsciousness before the terror got too bad.

Lindsey felt her heart thump hard in her chest. There was no reason for her to be afraid. Sully was here. Mrs. Sutcliff and Mrs. Dorchester were here. It wasn't as if she were alone. She just needed to find her phone and access the flashlight app.

She continued crawling along the floor. She patted the ground, seeking her bag. Nothing. Maybe the dark had her turned around, and it was on the floor by the other shelf. She crossed over and ran her hand along the thick carpet. Nothing.

She paused and listened, trying to hear Sully. If Mrs. Sutcliff was asleep, then she probably hadn't noticed the power outage. The scream had most likely been Mrs. Dorchester, scared when her show and the lights went out. Had Mrs. Sutcliff heard the scream? Was she on her way to help, too? Lindsey hoped so. She had no idea what Mrs. Dorchester would make of a strange man entering her room in the dark.

She felt her anxiety spike but then forced herself to inhale a deep breath. Everything was okay. Until she was informed otherwise, everything was fine. She exhaled nice and slow, hoping to settle her racing heart. It worked a little.

Lindsey kept crawling along the floor. Her purse had to be here somewhere. She tapped the floor and felt something. It wasn't her purse. It was a shoe. And judging by the feel of it, it had a foot in it.

"Ah!" she yelped, and leapt back.

The person to whom the shoe belonged also yelled. It was a man's voice, low and deep, and not Sully's. Lindsey scrambled away, slamming into a bookshelf. Luckily, it was empty, but it still hurt her shoulder, and she lost her balance and flopped onto the floor.

"Grace?" the man asked. His voice was tremulous. "Is that you?"

The lights snapped back on, and Lindsey stared up from her sprawled position on the floor into the sad, hopeful eyes of Tim Little.

"Tim? What are you doing here?" she asked. She put her hand over her racing heart, trying to steady herself while noting her purse was on the floor beside a bookcase behind Tim.

"Lindsey?" He blinked as recognition kicked in. "Oh, I'm sorry. I thought . . . well, never mind. I'm clearly losing my mind. I just stopped by to . . . and then the lights went out and I heard someone scream, so I came inside to see if everything was okay. Are you all right?"

He reached out a hand, and Lindsey took it, letting him pull her to her feet.

"I'm fine," she said. "It wasn't me who screamed. Sorry, I was so startled when I ran into your shoe. I thought you were Sully. He's upstairs checking on Mrs. Dorchester. We think she's the one who screamed."

"Should I go help?" Tim asked.

Lindsey pondered him for a second. She didn't know what to say except for the truth, but she didn't want to squash his feelings.

"I don't know that the sight of you would be that soothing for her," she said.

Tim nodded, pursing his lips in a rueful look. "You're not wrong."

"Why did you come by tonight, Tim?" she asked. "You were about to say but then you didn't."

"I just . . . it really doesn't matter . . ." His voice trailed off, and his gaze shifted to the hidden door behind the bookshelf, which was propped open.

"I think it does matter," she said. "I think it matters to you quite a lot."

"I wanted to see—" He stopped talking and put his hand to his throat. Lindsey suspected that it had gotten so tight with emotion, he was having a hard time speaking. His eyes glittered with a sheen of unshed tears, and he sniffed. "I wanted to see where my wife died."

CHAPTER

17

BRIAR CREEK
PUBLIC LIBRARY

Lindsey felt her own throat constrict. The anguish in
Tim's voice made it clear that his grief was as fresh today as it had been when Grace disappeared. It was probably
even worse now that he knew she was gone for good.

"You talked to Chief Plewicki?" she asked. She wanted
to verify that the chief had told him that Grace's remains
had been identified so that she didn't say anything out of
turn.

"She came by the house," he said. "She told me that
Grace likely suffocated in that room."

He pointed toward the dark maw of the hidden room at
the end of the library. They both studied the entrance.
Lindsey wasn't sure what to do, but she couldn't imagine
denying him his opportunity to see where Grace had spent
her final hours.

"Did Emma say it was all right for you to be here?" Lindsey asked. She hoped he said yes.

He didn't. He glanced at her, looking so much like one of his twin grandsons, caught on a technicality, that she almost smiled.

"She told me the area was no longer restricted," Lindsey said. "The medical examiner and crime scene unit are done, so I don't think it's a problem that you're here so long as you don't disturb anything."

"I just want to look," he said. "I want to see where she was all this time."

His voice was gruff, and Lindsey couldn't imagine how wrenching it must be to know that his wife had been here, close by, all this time.

"I suppose that would be okay," Lindsey said. She glanced out the door, wondering where Sully was. She could really use some backup here, but he was dealing with Marion, and that took priority. "Come on."

She led the way to the secret room. She kept up a steady stream of talk, trying to put Tim at ease. But really, how could she? The man had lost his first wife just weeks after they were married, he'd been a suspect in her disappearance, and then he'd gone on to build a nice life for himself in this town. All of that was about to come crashing down once the news got out that his wife had been murdered in this very house.

She paused beside the room. If she never went in there ever again, that was fine with her. Still, Tim deserved to see where his young wife had passed away.

"I don't want to upset you or be gruesome, but could

you describe what she looked like when you found her?"
he asked.

"Oh, Tim," Lindsey said. She clasped her hands together. She desperately didn't want to be the one to describe
the scene to him.

"Please, Lindsey, I need to know," he said. A tear streaked
down one of his cheeks, and Lindsey nodded. How could
she deny him this? A teeny tiny part of her reminded herself
that he could very well be the killer, but she pushed that
aside. It seemed implausible, whereas his grief appeared
quite genuine.

"She was sitting at the table, leaning against the wall,"
Lindsey said. Tim used his phone to illuminate the room.
Lindsey didn't look inside. She didn't want to remember. "She
had a book beside her hand as if she'd been reading. Apparently, the room once had lights, but they must have burnt out
a long time ago."

Tim's face crumpled as if this was too much information, coming at him hard and fast. "Thank you for telling
me that. I hate to think of her alone, trapped in the dark.
She didn't like the dark. Having a book would have been a
comfort."

Lindsey felt her chest ache. She didn't mention that the
book had been a collection of works by Edgar Allan Poe,
which was not exactly *Chicken Soup for the Soul*. She
thought of the picture of the runaway bride in the newspa-
per. Grace Little had been a lovely woman with a warm
light in her eyes. How awful for her to have met this end.

"According to the chief, she passed within a matter of

days of being shut up in there," Tim said. "Who could have done such a thing? She was so kind and thoughtful, funny but shy. It took me forever to get her to go out with me."

"But she did," she said. "And she married you."

"Yes, she did."

Lindsey watched the memories flit across his features. There was warmth and affection and something more. It hit her then that Tim Little was still very much in love with his first wife and probably always had been. Is that what happened when there was no closure, no proper ending to a relationship? Did a person just pine forever? The thought was heartbreaking.

"I have to know what happened to her," he said. "I have to know how she ended up here."

"I under—" she began, but he cut her off.

"No you don't, Lindsey. I appreciate the sympathy, but you can't comprehend how I felt. Grace was everything to me."

He glanced from her to the empty room. He drew in a long, shuddering breath, trying to calm his emotions. Lindsey didn't say anything. He was right. She couldn't comprehend such a loss. Her thoughts strayed to her husband, who was upstairs trying to soothe a confused old woman. What would her life be without him? She couldn't bear to think about it.

"I loved Grace so much. The way she laughed, her attempts to cook, how she always hummed little bits of songs over and over and didn't even realize she was doing it. She was everything I'd ever hoped for in a best friend, a partner, a wife. When she disappeared, I thought I'd driven her away. I thought she didn't love me. I was devastated." His voice cracked and more tears fell. "She was the love of my life, Lindsey. Not one day has passed that I don't think of her and miss her."

Lindsey felt her own eyes get damp. Tim and Grace's life together had been derailed by someone. The person sending Grace flowers? A stalker? Someone who wanted Grace for himself? Or someone like Marion, who just wanted Grace gone? Or maybe it was someone who just wanted to hurt Tim in the most powerful way that they could.

"What are you doing here, Little?" William Dorchester stormed into the room. His fists were clenched, and he looked like he was ready to have another go at Tim.

Tim drew himself up to his full height. "I came to see where my wife died."

"The wife you murdered," William spat. He moved so that a short bookshelf was between him and Tim.

"Stop saying that," Tim bellowed. "I would never have hurt her. Never."

"Right," William said. "Weird how she disappeared after a fight with you."

"It wasn't a fight," Tim said. "It was a disagreement over flowers that were being sent to her at work. Was it you, Dorchester?"

"What are you talking about?" William looked baffled.

"Were you the one sending her flowers?" Tim asked. "What were you trying to accomplish?"

"You're crazy!" William scoffed. "Why would I send her flowers? She was married to you."

"Because you wanted her back," Tim said.

"You honestly think I wanted her back after she married you?" William said. "Hardly. I was over her the minute she became Mrs. Little."

"Were you?" Tim asked. His tone indicated that he didn't believe him. "Were you really? Why don't I believe you?"

"Because it suits your purposes to try and make me look bad when we both know that you killed your wife."

"Really? Then why was she found in your house?" Tim said. "Why, Dorchester? How could I have possibly gotten her in here and into a room that I didn't even know existed?"

"So you say, but you might have known about it. And it's obvious that you planted her body here to make it look as if I had something to do with her death."

"Didn't you?" Tim asked. He began to pace around the room as if he was looking for an opening to attack. William sidled through the short bookcases to the door, trying to keep the space between them.

"I had nothing to do with what happened to Grace!" William protested.

"And yet she was found here in your house," Tim said. His eyes narrowed. "There's something rotten about this whole thing, and I'm going to find out what."

"Keep projecting, Little," William said. "The only reason Grace is dead is because of you, and everyone knows it."

"That's it! I'm going to—"

"Problem here?" Sully asked as he stepped into the room.

"You bet there is," William cried. "This man is trespassing. Again! Someone needs to call the police."

Sully moved in between the two men, making Lindsey nervous. She didn't want her husband in harm's way. Emotions were running high, and if one of them pulled a weapon, well, she didn't want to consider what could happen.

"Is Mrs. Dorchester all right?" she asked Sully.

"Yes," Sully said. "She was frightened by the blackout, but Mrs. Sutcliff is with her now."

"Good," Lindsey said. She met Sully's gaze. She didn't know how to de-escalate the situation that they were in, and judging by the way he was watching both men, he didn't either.

"I think it's best if you go now, Tim," Lindsey said. "You saw what you wanted to see."

Tim's jaw was hard, but he glanced at Lindsey and nodded. He looked like he was going to leave, but William had to chime in and ruin the little bit of peace Lindsey had managed to create.

"So, you came to revisit where you abandoned her?" William taunted Tim. "What? Did you forget where you stuffed her body?"

Sully opened his mouth to protest, but Tim beat him to it.

"Shut your mouth, Dorchester," Tim said. "Repeating a

lie over and over will never make it true. I loved Grace with all that I am. She was the love of my life—"

"Ha!" William interrupted, but Tim was undeterred.

"She was!" Tim argued. "Not only was Grace the love of my life, but I was the love of hers. She loved me more than she ever loved you, and that just eats at you, doesn't it?"

"Get out!" William bellowed.

Tim tipped his chin up. He'd made a direct hit and he knew it.

"Ahem." They all spun around to face the doorway and found Barbara Little standing there. She looked as if she'd just sustained a crushing blow, and Lindsey realized that she must have heard Tim. Hearing him profess his undying love for his first wife had to be devastating.

"Barbara—" Tim said. He sounded regretful, and Lindsey knew he must have come to the same realization.

"We have to go, Tim," she said. "The boys are expecting us at their soccer game."

"Right," he said. He cleared his throat and nodded at Lindsey. She watched them leave. Barbara and Tim walked side by side but didn't touch, as if there was now a chasm of raw hurt dividing them.

"And don't come back," William yelled after them. He turned to Lindsey and Sully. "Do you see? Do you see how he is? I'm certain he killed her. He's so full of anger and rage. He doesn't even try to hide it."

Sully exchanged an exasperated look with Lindsey and

said, "Well, when you accuse someone of murder, I imagine anger is a normal response."

William looked at him in reproach. "He's a killer, Sully. It's a darn good thing I showed up when I did, or your wife would have been alone with him, and there's no telling what he might have done. She could have been his next victim."

Lindsey felt the need to defend Tim, but she suspected she'd be wasting her breath. Still, she had to say something.

"I don't believe that Tim would have hurt me," she said. When William looked like he was about to argue, she raised her hand in a *stop* gesture. "The fact is, we'll never know. But that's not what's important right now. Your mother had a terrible fright, and you should probably go and check on her."

With a put-upon look, William glanced at the stairs. Lindsey knew that caregiving was exhausting, but it seemed to her that Mrs. Sutcliff was pulling more than her own weight, and William could step up a bit.

"I suppose you're right," he said. "Are you two done for the evening?"

Lindsey glanced at the boxes of books. She hadn't gotten as far as she would have liked, but her nerves were shot, and she just wanted to go home and hug her dog and her cat—even if the cat did not reciprocate the feeling just yet.

"Yes," Lindsey answered. She didn't think she imagined the loosening of Sully's shoulders. He was clearly happy to get out of there, too.

"If you don't mind showing yourselves out, I'll go check on Mother," William said.

"Not at all," Sully said. "We'll be sure to lock up after ourselves."

"Thank you. Good night," William said. He left the library, and they heard him walk slowly up the stairs as if bracing himself with each step.

As soon as he was out of earshot, Sully turned to Lindsey and pulled her in for a hug. "Are you all right?"

"I'm fine," she said. She melted into his arms, absorbing his warmth and his strength. "I was a little freaked out when Tim popped up in the darkness, but I believed him when he said he loved Grace. I don't know what happened between them, but his grief is devastating."

"Do you think Barbara knew?" Sully asked.

Lindsey pulled back and met his gaze. "That her husband is still in love with his first wife?" she asked. Sully nodded. "I don't think so, no. She looked crushed."

"And a bit angry," Sully added.

Lindsey frowned. She hadn't noticed anger in Barbara, but maybe she was seeing her through the filter of what her own feelings would be if she heard Sully profess his love for a wife who'd disappeared over thirty years ago.

"I can't really blame her if she is upset," Lindsey said. "She's been with Tim for over thirty years. She must feel as if that doesn't count for anything if he's still pining for his wife of just a few weeks."

"I'd pine for you forever," Sully said.

Lindsey felt her heart flip-flop just like it always did when her husband said something hopelessly romantic. She stood on her tiptoes and kissed him.

"I'd pine for you, too," she said when they broke apart.

"Poor Tim," Sully said. "I don't think he'll have any peace until he knows exactly what happened to Grace."

"Probably not," Lindsey agreed. "I hope Emma gets a break in the case before Tim has a breakdown."

"Speaking of the chief," Sully said. "We need to tell her what happened tonight."

"Agreed," Lindsey said. She picked up her purse from the floor. "I'll text her on the drive home."

"Home," Sully said. His tone was full of longing, and Lindsey felt exactly the same. They went to grab the boxes she'd left stacked up, and when she lifted them in her arms, a chill breeze blew through the room.

Lindsey glanced at the windows to see if any were open. They weren't. She looked at Sully and asked, "Did you feel that?"

He turned to her and nodded. "The temperature dropped." He frowned, glancing past her. "Did you close the bookcase?"

Lindsey peered over her shoulder at the door to the secret room. It was shut. A shiver rippled down her back. It had been open just moments ago, she was sure of it. She turned back to Sully and shook her head.

"Tim and I were standing there just a few minutes ago," she said. "Neither one of us shut the door. I'm positive."

Sully nodded slowly, as if taking in this information. "Let's get out of here."

"All right," she said.

Sully gestured for her to lead, and Lindsey didn't balk. The feeling of being watched followed her all the way to the car, and she didn't relax until the Dorchester mansion was far behind them.

CHAPTER

18

BRIAR CREEK
PUBLIC LIBRARY

When they pulled into their driveway, they found Emma waiting for them. Her patrol car was parked in front of the house, and Emma was in the driver's seat. She popped out when Sully parked.

Lindsey glanced at her phone. She'd texted Emma about the events of the evening, but she hadn't received a response. Clearly, Emma wanted to hear the story from them directly.

"Glass of wine?" Lindsey asked in lieu of a greeting.

"Can't," Emma said. "I'm on duty."

The sound of barking erupted from the house as Heathcliff heard them approach.

"Coffee?" Sully asked.

"Now you're speaking my language," Emma said.

Sully unlocked the door, and Lindsey and Emma assumed their stances. Emma had been over often enough that she knew to brace herself for the furry missile that was Heathcliff. Sure enough, as soon as the door opened, he rocketed out, demanding pets from all three humans before dashing out into the yard for his patrol.

"I take it you got my text," Lindsey said as they stepped into the house. Sully stayed outside to keep an eye on Heathcliff.

"Yes, and I was wondering if you had anything more to share about what you observed in the house?"

Lindsey knew that Emma was talking about her conversation with Tim, but there was a part of her that really wanted to mention the blackout, the sudden drop in temperature, and the bookcase door suddenly closing. She decided to wait and see if Sully brought it up.

In the meantime, she told Emma all about her conversation with Tim, the argument between Tim and William, Barbara's arrival, and the feeling that something was about to break. When Emma pressed her to explain what she meant, Lindsey couldn't quite find the words except to say that she felt like if they didn't solve the case of Grace's murder, the two men were going to have it out once and for all.

Emma sat at the counter while Lindsey went to check on the cat, who was asleep in the guest room. She had no interest in getting up and continued to snooze on her pillow, so Lindsey left her there. When she returned to the kitchen, Sully was there, making coffee, and recounting his time at the house.

"I have no idea why the lights went out," he said. "I went down to the basement and checked the circuit breaker, but there was nothing wrong. When I was upstairs, I looked out over the neighborhood, and everyone else had electricity."

"Are you about to tell me that you believe in ghosts?" Emma asked.

"No," he said. He glanced at Lindsey. She wasn't sure if he was looking for backup or what, but she figured they had nothing to lose.

"But the temperature suddenly dropped in the library," she said. "And I do mean dropped. It was fine when we arrived, but by the time we left, my teeth were chattering."

"And then there was the door," Sully said.

"What door?" Emma asked.

"The bookcase door was open all evening," Lindsey said. "While I worked, when Tim was there, through all of it, the door stayed open, but when Sully and I went to leave, we got hit with a frigid draft, and then he noticed that the bookcase was closed."

Emma frowned. "Do you think there was someone in there doing those things? Maybe trying to spook you?"

Lindsey shrugged. "Maybe. But who, and how wouldn't we have seen them?"

"Because of the blackout," Emma said. "Someone probably turned the heat off to the library, cut the lights, and then closed the bookcase while the lights were out."

"That could be, except the bookcase was still open

when the lights came back on, because I took Tim over to the hidden room to show him where we found Grace," Lindsey said. "He seems truly devastated, by the way."

"I'm sure he is," Emma said. "Still, if the two of you think the incidents tonight were the work of ghosts, I am telling you right now, that isn't possible. I have been a cop for a long time. There is no such thing as ghosts. People, on the other hand, can do some truly horrific things to one another."

Sully slid a coffee mug in front of her. She took a long, bracing sip, and Lindsey noted the dark circles under her eyes. This case was definitely running her into the ground. How could it not? There was no evidence, just a lot of rumor and speculation. It was possible they would never find out who sealed Grace up in the secret room. Lindsey shivered.

"There is a new problem with the case," Emma said.

"Oh?" Lindsey and Sully glanced at each other.

"After I got your text, I received a phone call from Barbara Little," she said. "She wanted me to know that on the night that Grace Little went missing, she lied. She'd told the former police chief that she was with Tim Little the entire evening after the spat with his wife. But she wasn't. She lingered to talk to him to make certain he was okay, but then she had to go home to take care of her father. She said she left Tim outside the Blue Anchor shortly after Grace left."

Lindsey felt her jaw drop. In the articles she'd read about Grace's disappearance, one of the main reasons Tim had never been charged with his wife's murder was because he had a witness who'd been with him the entire evening the night that Grace disappeared. If Barbara recanted, then Tim had no alibi.

"Did she say where she thought he'd gone after she left him?" Sully asked.

"Yes, she said he went after his wife," Emma answered.

Emma left shortly after dropping that bomb on them. Lindsey and Sully collapsed onto the couch with Heathcliff wedged between them. They opened the door to the guest room, and Zelda came out. Heathcliff wanted to go greet her, but Sully kept him close. Zelda kept her distance, ignoring the whimper and wag that Heathcliff sent her way while she moved around the perimeter of the room.

"I have no idea what to do about the Tim and Barbara situation," Lindsey said. "I feel responsible."

"You're not," Sully said. His voice was emphatic. "You have been nothing but patient, kind and helpful. What they do is on them."

"Do you think Barbara is lying?" she asked.

Sully shook his head. "I have no idea. If only there was some way to time travel back to that fateful night and figure out what happened."

Lindsey tapped her lips with her forefinger. "You've just given me a great idea."

Sully looked wary. "What's that?"

"I know what we need to do to figure out who murdered

Grace Little," she said. She held his gaze with hers and said, "We need to reenact that night."

W hy do I have to play William Dorchester?" Robbie asked. "The man punched me in the eye. I mean, look at it. It's still yellow."

"Quit complaining," Lindsey said. "You're supposed to be a professional. No part too small and all that."

"Says the woman playing the part of the dead body," he snapped.

Lindsey rolled her eyes at Sully, who laughed. They were standing outside the Blue Anchor. Parts had been assigned and Lindsey was playing Grace, Sully was Tim, Robbie reluctantly played William, Emma was Barbara, and Violet agreed to be Mrs. Dorchester.

Nancy had the final part, and she would portray Sarah Bessette, the observer of Tim and Grace's argument outside the Blue Anchor.

"Places, everyone," Violet called.

Nancy positioned herself in the parking lot right where Sarah had said she was at the time of the tiff. Lindsey had called Sarah and had her recount what she'd overheard and when so that they could craft a timeline of the events of the evening.

"Okay," Nancy called. She sent Sully and Lindsey a thumbs-up.

Sully and Lindsey looked at each other. They were standing on the pier beside the restaurant, and neither of them knew how to start the shouting match they were supposed to have.

"The thing is," Lindsey said, "I'm not really a yeller."

"Me neither," Sully said. "I prefer to just avoid the person I'm angry with until the bad feelings go away and we can talk more rationally."

"Exactly," Lindsey said. She studied him. "Have we ever yelled at each other?"

"Not that I can remember," he said.

"Same," she agreed. "So, how does one do this?"

"I suppose Tim was the outraged one here, over the flowers?"

Lindsey nodded.

"So, it stands to reason that he is the one who yells first," Sully said. He cleared his throat. His voice came out just as deep as usual but with a bit more force. "Who sent you those flowers?"

"I don't know," Lindsey said. She glanced at their audience and saw Robbie cup his ear to indicate that he couldn't hear her, so she yelled, "If they aren't from you, I don't care."

"But why is someone sending them to you?" Sully demanded. "What aren't you telling me?"

Lindsey thought about the creepy David Felder. Had Grace been keeping his inappropriate overtures from her husband because she was actually interested in Felder? Lindsey hated to even think it given how well liked Grace had been. Could it be that Grace was just a fraud? No, that didn't feel right. If anything, knowing her husband was the jealous type, Lindsey suspected that Grace didn't tell him about Felder because she didn't want him to go after her boss and wind up in trouble.

"There's nothing to tell!" Lindsey insisted. "I don't know who is sending me flowers. They never sign the notes."

"And who keeps calling the house and hanging up?" Sully demanded.

"I don't know," Lindsey said. She felt herself getting annoyed, as if she really were Grace and her new husband was being thick.

"I don't believe you," Sully said. He looked equally irritated.

"You don't believe me?" Lindsey gaped at him. "Look, I love you, but if you don't trust me, then I don't want to be with you anymore."

She turned and stomped away. She had no idea where she was going, but she was hurt and angry. She had no idea who would send her flowers or call the house . . . wait . . . Lindsey reminded herself that she was just playing a part. She wasn't actually Grace. Still, if she were Grace, where would she go?

Lindsey paused. She knew exactly where she'd go if it were her. She'd confront the person who she thought was sending her flowers and calling the house. If she ended up at the Dorchester mansion, then she must have suspected that the person responsible was her ex, William Dorchester.

"Fine! Good riddance!" Sully yelled after her, which only made Lindsey feel more determined to figure out who

was causing this rift between her and her husband . . .
er . . . Grace and Tim.

"Okay," Emma said. "So, Grace storms off and Tim
goes back into the bar to sulk, where he supposedly met up
with Barbara."

"Except Barbara now says she only chatted with him for
a minute before leaving him to his sorrows," Robbie said.
"How do we know who is telling the truth?"

"I think Grace went to the Dorchester mansion to confront William about the flowers," Lindsey said. "It's the
only thing that makes sense. How else would she end up
there? And Tim put the idea in her head that it was her ex.
I mean, if it were me, that's what I'd do."

"Excellent," Emma said. "I agree. Lindsey, we'll have
you go to the Dorchester mansion next, but first Sully and
I will go inside the bar and try to replicate what might have
happened between Tim and Barbara. Timeline keepers,
where was William Dorchester at this time that night?"

"According to his mother Marion's police interview at
the time, they were both having dinner at a neighbor's,"
Nancy said. She consulted her clipboard. "We can't confirm with the neighbors since they're both deceased."

"Right," Emma said. "They were out, but their housekeeper was home."

Nancy looked back at the paper. "But she is also deceased."

Emma heaved a heartfelt sigh. "This is why I hate cold
cases. Everyone is dead."

Robbie opened his arms, and Emma stepped into them for a quick hug.

"Chin up, love, we'll figure this out," Robbie said.

"I'm going to the mansion," Lindsey said. She was very much feeling Grace's need to confront William.

"Not by yourself, you're not," Sully argued. Lindsey frowned at him.

"Well, you have to stay here and see if you get any insights into the talk with Barbara," she said.

"We don't separate," Emma said. "If we do this as a group, someone may think of something that will bust the case wide open."

"She's right," Violet said. "Let's all go watch Sully and Emma be Tim and Barbara."

As one large group, they shuffled into the Blue Anchor. Sully took an open seat at the bar. Ian came over to pour him a drink, but Sully waved him off. Ian raised one eyebrow in question, but his wife Mary sidled up next to him and said, "They're staging a reenactment."

"Oh, yeah, you told me about this," Ian said. "I'm with you now." He pantomimed pouring Sully a beer and then pretended to slide it down the bar to him.

Sully grinned and shook his head. If the other patrons of the bar thought this was weird, no one seemed to notice. Possibly because the chief of police was there.

Emma sat down on the empty stool beside Sully and asked, "What's the matter, Tim?"

Sully shook his head. "Nothing."

"It's not nothing when you look like that," Emma said. "Come on, I've known you since elementary school, what's wrong?"

"I had an argument with Grace," he said. "It was stupid and I feel terrible, but I just feel like she'd rather be with someone else."

Emma put a comforting hand on his shoulder. Robbie's eyebrows went up at the gesture.

"She's married to you," Emma said. "Who else could she possibly be interested in?"

"William Dorchester," Sully said. He sounded morose.

Lindsey glanced at Violet and Nancy. They were watching the conversation intently as if looking for a clue. She focused back on Tim and Grace.

"But he refused to marry her when his mother said no," Emma said. "She can't possibly be interested in him when she has you. She'd be crazy not to be desperately in love with you."

Emma looked at Sully with a look of unrequited love that made Lindsey gasp. She felt Robbie stiffen beside her, and she knew he saw it, too.

"Oy!" Robbie protested but Violet shushed him. "Bleeding water boy gets all the girls, doesn't he?" he grumbled.

"You're very kind, Barbara," Sully said.

"No, I'm not," she said. She took her hand off his arm and stepped back. "I just think you deserve to be with someone who really loves you."

"Yeah." Sully pretended to take a drink. "You do, too. You're a wonderful woman."

Emma tipped her head as if she were embarrassed. Then she said, "Go home, Tim. Everything will be okay. You'll see."

She stepped back from the bar and turned to face the group. "Well, anything?"

"Barbara was already in love with him," Nancy said.

"That's how I played it," Emma said. "Lindsey, you said that the day they came to the library with their grandkids and you talked to Barbara, she said she'd loved Tim since she was six years old. It seems to me, if she married him with all of the scandal brewing and gave him an alibi, she never stopped loving him."

"Played it?" Robbie asked. "You mean that look you gave Barnacle Boy was fake?"

"Yes," Emma said. Her tone was thoroughly exasperated. "I was *acting*. I would think you of all people would recognize that."

"So, you're not in love with Sully?" he persisted.

"What?" Emma blinked. "Are you daft?"

"I think *jealous* is the word you're looking for," Sully said. He grinned at Robbie and said, "Might want to put a ring on it if you're feeling that territorial."

"Might want to punch you in the mouth, too," Robbie said.

"People." Violet clapped her hands. "Let's focus on the reenactment, shall we?"

"Of course," Robbie said. He brushed off his shirt as if he'd just taken a tumble, and said, "I'll show you some acting that will knock your socks off."

Emma rolled her eyes and said, "To the Dorchester mansion, everyone."

They all separated, piling into different cars to drive to the mansion. On the drive over in Sully's truck, Lindsey said, "Emma was acting, right?"

"Oh, no, not you, too," he said. "Robbie's just freaking out because he's realizing how much he cares about her."

"You're right, I know you're right, but I got kind of swept up in the drama during our pretend tiff," she said.

"I know what you mean," he said. "I felt Tim's frustration that someone was clearly making moves on his wife. I even had a flashback to your stalker."

"Ugh," she grunted. "You don't suppose that Grace had one, do you? Felder, her boss, certainly seemed obsessed with her."

"It's hard to say," he said. "Workplaces for women in the eighties were not as enlightened as they are now."

"As *most* of them are now," Lindsey said.

"We have a ways to go, for sure," he said. He turned onto the Dorchesters' street and parked in front of the mansion. Emma's car was already there, and Violet and Nancy parked behind him.

They all climbed out of their vehicles, and Emma waved them into a huddle. "I arranged for the Dorchesters to be out while we're here. I don't want any interference."

"Do they know what we're doing?" Lindsey asked.

"Yes," Emma said. "I thought it best to let them know this is an official part of the investigation."

"Should we start in the library?" Lindsey asked. "Somehow Grace ended up in there."

"Which means someone let her into the house," Emma said. "If we assume that Marion and William are telling the truth and they were out, it had to be the housekeeper."

"I can play her!" Nancy offered. She hurried up the steps, pausing while Emma opened the door using her key. Lindsey assumed that the Dorchesters had given her the key to help facilitate the investigation. Interesting.

Nancy went inside, and Lindsey stepped up and knocked on the door. After a beat, Nancy answered.

"Grace, how nice to see you," she said.

"Hi." Lindsey had no idea what sort of relationship Grace would have had with William's housekeeper, so she kept it neutral. "Is William home?"

"No, I'm afraid he's out, but you're welcome to wait for him inside," Nancy said. "I'm sure they won't be late."

"That would be lovely," Lindsey said. "Thank you."

"I'll show you to the library," Nancy said. "Can I get you anything? Coffee? Soda?"

"No, thank you," Lindsey said. She followed Nancy across the main room to the library. The rest of their group followed.

Lindsey stepped into the library and noticed the barren bookshelves, which made the room look empty of any warmth.

"Should I just wait in here?" she asked.

"Yes," Emma said. "Oh, hang on." She reached into her bag and pulled out a book. It was the actual volume that

Lindsey had discovered in the room with Grace Little's remains. "I thought I should bring it as a prop. Maybe it will spark a clue."

Lindsey took the book. It felt strange, or more accurately, creepy and weird, to hold the item Grace had had in the hidden room with her. She tried not to think about it, but took the book and crossed the room, standing near the entrance to the secret door.

The rest of the group went back into the main room. Emma instructed them on the next part, which was the arrival home of Marion and William. They said they'd come home late in the initial police report, but Emma wanted to play the scene out in a variety of ways.

The first one was Marion discovering Grace's presence in the house. It didn't go well. Nancy, now playing the housekeeper, was completely dressed down for letting Grace into the house. Meanwhile, William was eager to see Grace. He and his mother, played by Robbie and Violet, had an argument that Lindsey found riveting. This was to be expected, she supposed, as Robbie and Violet were the professionals in their group.

"Send her away!" Violet demanded. "I will not allow that trollop to try and win you back."

Lindsey wasn't sure she liked being called a trollop, and when she met Sully's amused gaze through the doorway to the library, she sent him a quelling glance that made him laugh.

Robbie made an impassioned plea as William about his love for Grace and demanded his mother approve of him running away with Grace, if she would have him. Violet as

Marion forbade it, of course, and she swept up the stairs from the great room.

"What would William do then?" Nancy asked. "He'd still go and talk to Grace, don't you think? Or would he have the housekeeper toss her out?"

Lindsey considered the book in her hands. Grace had this book in the secret room with her, so either she'd been reading it before she landed in the sealed room, or she'd found it inside after she was trapped. The thought sent a chill down Lindsey's spine. Grace's death was so very macabre; it was absolutely like something out of one of the Poe stories in the collection she was holding.

She opened the book to a random page. She knew the crime scene detectives had examined it for clues and found nothing. She leaned against the wall beside the secret room and perused the pages, pausing on "The Tell-Tale Heart." The story was published in eighteen forty-three and seemed weirdly appropriate for the mystery they were trying to solve. She wondered if Grace had read it.

As she skimmed, she noticed that certain letters had been underscored, not with a pen or a pencil but with a scratch, like someone had dug into the paper with their fingernail. She flipped back to the beginning of the book and began to scan every page. They were randomly placed, the marks, but they were definitely very obviously made throughout the book.

The air turned cold, and she felt the skin pucker on her arms and neck. She pulled her sweater more tightly about her and shivered. Then the lights went out.

CHAPTER

19

BRIAR CREEK
PUBLIC LIBRARY

No one move!" Emma ordered.

"Lindsey, are you all right?" Sully called into the library from the great room.

"I'm fine," she said. Her teeth chattered, and she wondered if the others were feeling the same frigid air that she was.

"It must be the circuit breaker again," Emma said. "William confirmed that they've been having problems. The electricity went out twice during our investigation."

"It did the same when Lindsey and I were here," Sully said.

"I'll go down to the basement and check," Robbie offered. He didn't sound happy about it.

"I'll help," Sully said.

"Violet is upstairs," Nancy said. "Violet, are you all right?"

"I'm on the landing, but I can't see anything," Violet answered.

"I'll go get her," Emma said.

"I'm coming with you," Nancy said. She sounded nervous.

"Lindsey? Will you be okay until we get back?" Sully asked.

"I'm not planning on moving," she answered. "I have my phone with me. I just need to get it out of my bag."

"We'll be right back," Sully said. "Yell if you need me and I'll come running."

A light shone into the library from the great room and landed on Lindsey. She saw Sully's face in the reflected light. She waved and he waved back. The light faded as he headed to the basement with Robbie.

She tucked the volume of Poe stories under her arm as she opened her shoulder bag and rifled through her belongings. She really needed to downsize. Either that, or stop buying everything in black—not that it mattered in this all-consuming darkness. She clutched the various objects, trying to determine which was her phone.

Distracted by her search, Lindsey jumped when the door to the library slammed shut.

"Sully?" she cried. But of course he was down in the basement and couldn't hear her. "Emma! Violet! Nancy!"

A shove hit her hard in her shoulder, and Lindsey stumbled sideways into the hidden room. She clutched her bag and the book in her hands to keep from dropping them while she fought to keep her balance. Another shove to her back sent her sprawling to the ground. She dropped the book and her shoulder bag, catching herself with her hands.

"Stop!" she cried.

The only response was that of heavy breathing and then the unmistakable sound of the bookcase door being slammed shut. Lindsey was trapped in the secret room just like Grace had been.

Her knees hurt. Her palms stung. And as dark as it had been in the library, it was as black as the inside of a tomb in the hidden room. She was panting with an adrenaline burst from the altercation and then remembered that the chamber was airless. She felt herself start to panic and breathe faster, but then shook her head.

The others were out there, and they knew she'd been in the library. They'd get the lights back on and realize where she was. Unless they were all murdered, because someone had shoved her in here, and it didn't take masterful detective skills to realize that it had to be whoever had murdered Grace all those years ago. The person would likely kill them all to keep their secret.

Stop it, she scolded herself. Panicking was not helping anything. She slowed her breathing and reached for her bag. Her phone was in there. She just needed to find it, and she could use her flashlight app or try to text Sully and tell him what happened. It was a long shot, as Violet's phone hadn't worked when they were trapped in here before. But someone—a person, not a ghost—had shoved her in here, and she was going to get out.

She knocked something with her fingers and realized it

was the book. The markings in the book! She felt around in her bag for her phone. Finally, her fingers grasped its hard case. She hit the flashlight button, and the room was illuminated in its glow. The small space was empty. The table, chairs and carpet had been taken out by the crime scene investigators. Without them, the cramped space felt more coffin-like than she wanted to acknowledge.

She tried to call Sully but the call wouldn't go through. She opened up her messages and tried to text him, but it wasn't deliverable. She wondered if the room was made of concrete or steel. Whatever it was, it was technologically impenetrable.

She glanced at the book. Well, that was one thing she could do. She turned the light on the book and opened it. Using the note-taking app on her phone, she started flipping through the pages, looking for the scratch marks. Some were fainter than others, but she typed in each letter that was marked until she had flipped through the final pages. There were no more scratches, but she looked at the string of letters, and they very clearly spelled out a message.

"Is this what happened to you, Grace?" she asked. There was no answer. No sudden coldness. No shift in the air. And the door to the secret room didn't magically open.

Engrossed in her puzzle, Lindsey had no idea how much time had passed. Surely, they had to have restored the lights by now.

Her phone's battery life was rapidly diminishing, so she put it on power-saving mode and then wrote a text to Emma spelling out Grace's final message. If Lindsey didn't make it out, she wanted the chief to know the answer to who murdered Grace Little was in the book. The thought made her shiver. She knew she was being a tad dramatic, but given the fate of the last person who'd resided in this room, she didn't think she was overreacting that much.

When she finished her note, she switched off the flashlight. She wanted to save her phone's battery life, for what, she didn't know, but if she was trapped in here and they couldn't get her out, she didn't want to die in the dark.

She wondered how much oxygen she had left before she would be breathing in her own carbon dioxide. What were the symptoms Emma had described? Light-headedness? A headache? She did feel a twinge behind her eyes, but she supposed it could be from the stress of the situation. She wondered if Grace had known she was dying. Lindsey suspected she had because she'd left the answer to who had killed her in the book.

Lindsey didn't want to go out that way. If the persons who'd shut Grace in the secret room were the same ones who shoved Lindsey inside, she had to wonder at their motive. What did they have to gain by murdering Lindsey? There was no way they could know she'd been about to find the message from Grace—even the crime scene investigators had missed it.

She remembered the night she and Violet and Nancy had gotten locked inside. Sully had heard them banging against the door. The noise had been faint but he'd heard it. She knew that was her last shot. She had to get someone's attention.

She crawled over to the door. She thought about knocking, but she knew her knuckles would take a beating pretty quickly against the steel-reinforced door. Instead, she slipped off her shoe and used the heel to bang on the door. She knew Morse code was a series of threes, but she had no idea if it was three long, three short and three long or the opposite. She figured it didn't matter since she couldn't make a heel tap last that long anyway.

She banged the heel of her shoe against the door. There was no noise from the other side. She didn't know if there was anyone in the library to hear her or if this was just an exercise in futility. Who knew what had happened to the others? She felt her stomach cramp at the thought that there might have been some sort of killing spree out there.

The cold started to seep into her bones, and she banged her shoe harder against the door. It was so dark in the room she almost felt as if there were no walls, no floor and no ceiling. It was as if she'd fallen into a black hole somewhere in space. She pressed her free hand to the door. She needed to ground herself as she suspected the complete sensory deprivation she was feeling was making her a bit wonky.

"Come on, someone, hear me," she whispered.

Was this how Grace had felt? Was she scared? Cold? Alone? Had she still had light in here, or had she died alone and cold in the dark? Lindsey felt empathy for the runaway bride deep in her soul. How could another human being have done this to Grace? And why had they done it to Lindsey? Someone had pushed her into the room and shut the door, but why?

Her fingers were getting stiff from the cold. She felt her

throat get tight. Fear started to spike through her. She dropped her shoe and curled up, wrapping her arms about her legs and resting her head on her knees. Someone would come. Someone would find her. She thought about Grace again and wondered if she'd had the same belief, that someone, maybe Tim, would help her, but the help never came.

Well, to heck with that! Lindsey lifted her head and let go of her knees. She was not going down without a fight. She picked up her shoe and began to bang on the door as hard as she could. She didn't know if it would work, but at least she was moving, and the motion was warming her up. She took off her other shoe and used both hands to slam the heels against the door. Just when she was getting a rhythm going, the door gave way and bright light blasted her eyes, making her squint. Two arms reached into the room and snatched her out. She couldn't see who it was, but she recognized the feel of her husband and the sea-soaked scent of him. Sully!

"Darling, you just scared five years off me," he said. He half carried, half dragged her into the library.

Lindsey clutched him close, absorbing his warmth. She realized her teeth were chattering, and trying to stop only made it worse. Her entire body was shivering, and Sully shrugged off his flannel shirt, wrapped it around her and hugged her close. His hands were rubbing her arms and her back, trying to warm her up.

Emma appeared behind Sully. Her forehead was creased in a frown and she asked, "Are you all right?"

"Yeah, I'm okay." Lindsey hugged Sully tight and then

stepped back. He kept his arm around her as though he didn't want to let her move too far away.

"What happened?" Emma asked.

Lindsey said, "I'm not sure. I was standing in the library in the dark, trying to find my phone in my purse, when someone shoved me from the side. Before I could get my balance, I was shoved again and I fell into the hidden room. Then I heard the bookcase door slam shut behind me."

"It was the ghost of Grace Little," Nancy said. They all turned to look at her. "Well, who else could it be?"

"It didn't feel like a ghost who shoved me," Lindsey said. "I could hear them breathing. I don't think ghosts do that."

"Hmm." Nancy looked unconvinced.

"Someone in this room trapped Lindsey in the hidden room," Emma said. "And no one is leaving until I figure out who it was."

Lindsey looked past Emma and saw that Tim and Barbara Little, as well as Marion and William Dorchester and Mrs. Sutcliff, were standing in the library. Lindsey felt her heart hammer hard in her chest at the sight of them.

"Grace?" Marion stared at Lindsey, and then a slow smile crept over her features. "You're here. Now William will forgive me."

"Mother, no," William said. "I've told you before, that's not Grace."

Marion looked confused. "But I thought . . ."

"That's Lindsey the librarian," he said. His face was grave. "Did you do something to her, Mother? Did you do something to her because you thought she was Grace?"

"No, I would never!" she protested. Then she looked confused. "Would I?"

Lindsey glanced at the faces in the room, watching the conversation between the mother and son. Nancy and Violet both looked horrified, while Robbie and Emma were intently watching the conversation. Tim and Barbara were standing apart. Tim looked the picture of misery, as if being in this space made his grief rise up to the surface again. Barbara, however, looked coldly furious.

"Why do we have to be here?" she hissed at her husband. "Hasn't your first wife caused enough trouble between us?"

"I'm sorry," he said. "I never wanted to hurt you."

"Too late for that, isn't it?" Barbara snapped. She turned to Emma. "There is no point in my being here. I'm leaving."

"Since you recanted your original statement that you were with Tim when Grace went missing, I'd say you're more than involved in this case," Emma said. "You'll stay."

She glanced at the doorway to the library, and Lindsey noticed that Officer Kirkland was standing there like a sentinel. No one was going to get around him. Good.

"It's time to tell the truth, Mother," William said. He looked ill at ease but determined. "You need to confess what you did."

"Tell the truth?" Marion looked frightened.

"Yes, Moth—" William began, but Lindsey had heard enough.

She stepped away from Sully and turned to Emma and asked, "Did you ask them to come here?"

"Yes, I asked them to meet us," Emma said. "I wanted to discuss our reenactment with them after we finished. I was hoping they could offer some insights. Of course, I didn't know the lights were going to go out and chaos would ensue. You sure you're all right? You look weird."

"Yeah, I'm good," Lindsey said. "Hang on, I just need to grab my things." She pivoted and reentered the secret room. She grabbed her bag and the book of collected works by Poe and then stepped back into the library. Sully moved with her as if worried she'd get trapped again.

"Lindsey, on behalf of the Dorchesters, I want to apologize," William said. "You've had quite a fright. I'm sure my mother is very sorry for pushing you. Isn't that right, Mother?"

"I . . ." Marion blinked at Lindsey, and her face crumpled in confusion. "I don't know."

William heaved a sigh. "I think it's clear what happened."

"Oh, really?" Emma asked. "Why don't you explain it, then, because I have no idea what's happening."

"My mother murdered Grace," William said. "It became obvious to me tonight when I found her in the library after she'd closed the door on Lindsey."

Lindsey glanced at Sully and asked, "Is that true? Was Mrs. Dorchester in the library?"

He nodded. "When the lights came on, both she and William were in the library, and Tim and Barbara were in the main room. In the confusion, we didn't notice that you were missing or that the bookcase had been shut, but as soon as we did, we knew you had to be trapped in there."

Lindsey nodded. "But the lights were out, so no one saw Mrs. Dorchester push me?"

"No," he said. He glanced at the others in inquiry. "No one saw anything, correct?"

"I didn't," Nancy said.

"Not me," Violet said.

"I was down in the basement with you, mate," Robbie said.

"And I was upstairs with Nancy and Violet," Emma said.

Lindsey turned to William. "Just to be clear, you're saying that your mother is the person who shut Grace Little up in the hidden room all those years ago?"

He lowered his head, looking devastated. "I'm horrified by it, more than I can say, but yes, I believe my mother is responsible for Grace's death, and I believe that she shoved you in there because she's been confusing you for Grace for weeks."

An anguished sound came out of Tim's throat, and Lindsey felt a moment of despair for him, because she knew it was only going to get worse.

"Well, you're wrong," Lindsey said.

"What?" William cried. "How can you say that? The evidence is right here. She keeps calling you Grace, and then at the first available opportunity, she tried to make you disappear just like she did Grace."

Marion's eyes were round and she stared wide-eyed at her son. It hurt Lindsey to see her look so vacant and confused. It was clear her dementia was making her ability to defend herself nearly impossible.

"That would be very neat and tidy, but life is seldom that accommodating," Lindsey said. She felt Sully's hand at her back, and she realized her voice had come out a bit shaky. She cleared her throat.

"What are you saying, Lindsey?" Emma asked.

Lindsey held up the book that Emma had given her. She showed it to everyone and then said, "While I was trapped, I had some time to study this book. It's the same one that was found in the room with Grace's remains."

She saw Nancy and Violet twitch, and she knew they were thinking about finding her skeleton and the book that had been sitting on the table beside her hand.

"What's that got to do with anything?" Barbara asked. It was then that Lindsey heard a quiver of uncertainty in Barbara's voice.

"Grace used this book to leave a message for whoever found her. Quite cleverly, she named the persons who sealed her in that room," Lindsey said. "I know who killed Grace Little, and it wasn't Mrs. Dorchester."

There was a collective gasp and then Emma said, "Who was it?"

"William and Barbara," Lindsey said.

William went pasty pale, and Barbara swayed on her feet. She rallied quickly and said, "That's the most ridiculous thing I've ever heard. How could you be so cruel as to say something like that?"

"I say it because Grace spelled out your names and what you did to her by marking individual letters in the book," Lindsey said. "I noticed the markings before the lights went out, but then I was shoved into the hidden room, where I didn't have much else to do but study the book, and I found the rest of the letters. It quite clearly says, 'William Dorchester and Barbara Peel left me in this room to die.'"

"You lie!" Barbara raged. Her husband was staring at her with a shocked expression, as if he didn't recognize the woman standing beside him.

"It's not a lie," Lindsey said. "It's all here. Peel is your maiden name, isn't it? It would have been your name at the time of Grace's murder."

"I demand to see it." Barbara charged forward and tried to snatch the book, but Lindsey tossed it to Sully, who caught it neatly and tucked it against his chest. Barbara would have better luck trying to wrestle a picnic basket from a bear.

Lindsey turned to Emma. "I also took pictures on my phone of every mark, and I messaged them to you." She opened the display on her phone and checked her messages. "It finally went through. You should have all the evidence you need." Then she turned to Barbara. "You're the one who shut me in there, aren't you?"

William opened his mouth to speak, but Barbara sent him a look of such fury that he sealed his lips together and stared down at his shoes.

"What a cold-blooded, hard-hearted thing to do. Grace must have been terrified," Nancy said.

"How could you do such a thing?" Violet added. "It's absolutely vile."

As if their condemnation broke down his barriers,

William's head shot up, and there was a look of pleading in his eyes.

"She wasn't supposed to die!" William cried. The words exploded out of him as if he couldn't hold them in any longer. "I never wanted her to die."

"Shut up, you imbecile," Barbara said. Her jaw was clenched, and she looked like she wanted to take a swing at him.

"A bit late for that," Robbie said. He glanced at William. "Out with it, then."

"Don't say a word," Barbara hissed.

"You were still in love with her, Dorchester, weren't you?" Tim asked. His face was pale. He looked like someone had stabbed him and left him to bleed out, but he continued. "You were the one sending her flowers and calling our house and hanging up, making me crazy. I thought she was still in love with you, too."

William shook his head. "That wasn't me." He pointed at Barbara. "It was her. All of it. Everything was her idea. She wanted Grace out of the picture so that she could be with you. I was still in love with Grace, so she convinced me that Grace loved me, too, and that I could convince Grace to leave you and come away with me to Florida."

Tim stared at his wife. "Is this true? Did you do this?"

"Lies!" Barbara cried, looking hysterical. "It's all lies. He did it. He's just trying to blame me."

"What happened, William?" Emma asked. "What happened that night?"

William looked slightly ill. He sagged against an empty

bookcase and said, "Barbara's plan worked. Tim thought Grace was cheating on him with me. She wasn't. She came to the mansion to talk to me. She wanted to know if I was behind the flowers and the phone calls. I wasn't, but I let her think I was in the hope that it would woo her back. But as I said, it was really Barbara."

"Stop lying!" Barbara cried.

"I told Grace that I loved her and that I wanted her to come away to Florida with me," he said. "But she said no."

"No?" Tim repeated. His gaze was intent upon William's face.

William held his gaze and said, "That's right. She rejected me. She said she was in love with you. That you were the best man she'd ever known since her father, and she wanted to stay with you and be your wife and have your children and live out her days in Briar Creek with the man she loved."

Tim clutched his chest and emitted a heart-wrenching sob. "She loved me. She didn't want to leave me."

"Don't listen to him," Barbara said. She grabbed her husband's shoulders and shook him. "He's lying. He's a bad man who did very bad things, and he's trying to blame me and tear us apart. Don't let him."

"For the first time in over thirty years, I'm telling the truth," William said. His face crumpled and he sobbed. "Oh, Grace, I'm sorry. I'm so very sorry."

"There, there." Marion Dorchester wrapped her skinny arms round her son's chest and held him as if he were a boy instead of a middle-aged man. She patted his chest with one hand and said, "You didn't mean to hurt her. I know that. That's why I sent you to Florida."

Emma and Lindsey glanced at each other. This seemed like a particularly lucid moment for Mrs. Dorchester.

"Marion," Emma said. "Do you remember what happened that night?"

Marion gazed at Emma and nodded. Her voice when she spoke was soft, as if she were delicately unwrapping the memory in her mind.

"William and I went to dinner at the neighbor's, but he left early," she said. "When I arrived home, he was entertaining a friend in the library. I never used the library much, but he seemed to be spending an inordinate amount of time in there with his friend. I was just happy that he seemed to have gotten over the Hartwell girl. She'd married someone else. As far as I was concerned, it was done."

"But it wasn't," Lindsey said.

"No," Marion agreed. "Three days later, he came and told me that he and Barbara, who was the friend he'd been entertaining, had shut Grace into the secret room. The plan was to get her to change her mind and go to Florida with William, but she didn't change her mind, and they didn't know that the room was designed to be airless, to preserve my husband's rare books and such. The poor thing suffocated to death. I sent William away so that he wouldn't have to face what he'd done every day." She looked at Lindsey and reached out to touch her hair. "But you're here now, so everything is okay. See, Willie? Mommy told you everything would be just fine, and it is."

William gazed down at his mother and wrapped his arms about her. It was the first display of affection Lindsey had ever seen him show his mother, and the look of pure joy on her face at being hugged by her son after all these years made Lindsey's throat tight.

"I'm sorry, Mommy," William said. He kissed her head. "I'm so sorry."

Tim turned to his wife. "Whose idea was it to put Grace in there?"

Barbara just stared at him. Not speaking.

"Whose, Barbara? Yours?" he asked.

Again, she said nothing. The tension between them felt stretched to the breaking point, and Lindsey noticed Robbie moving closer to Tim as if he thought he might have to intercept him.

"It was her idea," William said. He pointed to Barbara. "I wanted to call it off and let Grace out, but Barbara said we had to get her to change her mind; otherwise, we'd be arrested and go to jail for kidnapping. I pleaded with her every day through the back of the bookcase, but Grace wouldn't cooperate. I almost let her out on the second day. I wish I had, but I thought she'd come around. We'd stocked the room with food and water, but we didn't know it was airless. When I went to talk to Grace on the fourth night, she didn't answer me. I realized she was never going to give Tim up, and I went to let her out. That's when I discovered she had died. We caused her death, but it was an accident."

"An accident?" Tim roared. His face was mottled, and

tears were pouring down his cheeks. "She was the love of my life."

"She was the love of my life." Barbara made a singsong mockery of his words. "No she wasn't. I am the love of your life. I am your wife. I am the mother of your children. And I have given you an amazing life."

"An amazing life that you stole!" Tim roared. He clenched his fists. Robbie put his hand on his shoulder, and Tim took a steadying breath. He pointed at Barbara and said, "You are a murderer. You killed my wife, and everything we had was a lie. All of it."

"Pffft." Barbara made a dismissive sound. "You're being so dramatic. I did you a favor. Grace wasn't right for you." She pointed to her chest. "I was. She didn't love you the way I do. You belong to me."

Tim muttered an epithet and stumbled back from the woman he'd called his wife for over thirty years. "You're evil."

Barbara narrowed her eyes at him. "I'm not. You are my husband and you made vows to me. You will love, honor and cherish *me* all the days of your life. And no little accident is going to change that."

"Little accident?" Tim gaped at her. "You murdered *my wife.*"

"Stop saying that!" Barbara screeched. She clapped her hands over her ears. "It was an accident. You have to forgive me. For better or for worse. You promised."

Tim backed away from her, shaking his head. "No, I won't. I can't. I can't ever forgive you for this."

"And not just this," Robbie said. "You were going to let an old woman with dementia be charged with the murder you committed."

"Mind your own business," Barbara snapped. "This has nothing to do with you."

"When you put my friend at risk and drive my girlfriend crazy with your schemes and lies, you bet it's my business," he said.

"You tell her, Robbie," Violet said. "I'll bet she's the one making us think this house is haunted, too."

"Yeah, flicking the lights on and off, making doors and windows slam randomly," Nancy said. "That must have been huge laughs for you to make us all terrified."

"I never did any of that," Barbara said.

"Sure," Nancy said. "As if any of us are silly enough to believe those things were real."

The lights flickered and Nancy yelped. She hugged Violet, who clutched her close in return.

"I didn't do that," Barbara said. "Obviously."

"No, that was Grace," Marion said. They all turned to look at her. She was still standing with her son, their arms around each other as if making up for years lost. "She does that from time to time, but I think she'll feel better now that the truth is out." She glanced at Lindsey. "You feel better now, don't you?"

Lindsey thought about the cold spots in the house, the weird noises and even the cat that she'd adopted that looked just like the one the Dorchesters used to own. Her gaze met Sully's, and he shrugged as if to say, *Who knows?*

"I've heard enough," Emma said. "Barbara Little, you're under arrest for the murder of Grace Little."

"What about him?" Barbara cried and pointed at William.

"He's under arrest, too," Emma said. She nodded at Officer Kirkland, who stepped forward. Emma glanced at Marion. "And I'm sorry, but I'll need you to come to the station, as well."

"Am I being arrested?" Marion asked. Mrs. Sutcliff stepped forward as if to lend her employer some support.

"I'm afraid you obstructed justice by helping your son flee the scene of a crime, so yes," Emma said.

"Well, so long as I'm with William, that's all right with me," she said.

"Oh, Mommy." William started to cry. "I'll get you out of this mess. I promise."

Kirkland helped Emma take them all to the station.

Robbie sat quietly with Tim in the main room, talking him through his initial shock. His family as he'd known it had just been completely blown apart. Lindsey had no idea how he was going to come back from this. She knew it was cold comfort, but she wanted to share with him the other message she'd found in the book, which she'd given back to Emma as evidence.

She entered the living room, knelt next to Tim's chair and said, "There was one more message in the book, Tim."

He glanced up at her. His face was wet with tears, his skin blotchy and his nose red.

"What's that?" he asked.

Lindsey cleared her throat and said, "Grace underlined more letters that spelled out 'I love you, Tim, forever and always.'"

Tim blinked. A silent sob racked his frame, and he covered his face with his hands. Muffled but still audible, he said, "Thank you for telling me."

Lindsey glanced at Robbie, and he nodded. She knew he would take care of his friend. She rose and crossed the room to Sully. Her heart hurt for Tim and for his family. The devastating revelations of the day were going to take a long time to come to terms with.

"Come here," Sully said, and he pulled her close. Lindsey leaned her head on his shoulder, finding comfort in his arms. "Promise you'll never scare me like that again."

Lindsey leaned back and met his gaze. That was the thing about life, wasn't it? She could make that promise just like Grace had made her vows to Tim, but there was no way to know what could happen tomorrow, next week or a few years down the road. Still, she could tell that Sully needed some reassurance. She nodded.

"I promise I'll try not to scare you like that ever again," she said.

He sighed. "I suppose that'll have to do." He hugged her close, and Lindsey felt the air shift around them. It wasn't a cold spot as much as a feeling of something lifting, like a fog. The air seemed lighter somehow, and she thought that perhaps Grace was at peace now.

CHAPTER

20

BRIAR CREEK
PUBLIC LIBRARY

H ow are the Littles' kids taking the news?" Violet asked.
"I can't imagine what I'd do if I found out my mother
had murdered my father's first wife."

They were seated at the crafternoon table, discussing the
events of the past week while working on their latest craft.
Paula had brought in bags of dried leaves, and they were
making a garland out of them to use to decorate the displays at the front of the library. Surprising herself, even
Lindsey was able to manage to string the leaves on the
yarn, going right through the center of them with a needle.
The colors were amazing, and Paula finished them off with
a bow made out of buffalo plaid.

Mary had provided the food, which meant it was take-
out from the restaurant, a favorite of Lindsey's since it in-
cluded their clam chowder, which was the finest in all of

New England. Sully had shared the family recipe with Lindsey, but hers never came out like Mary's. Lindsey suspected the recipe Sully had given her had an ingredient missing, but she didn't want to cause any friction by saying as much. Mary's soup was the perfect antidote to the gloomy gray day outside, and for Lindsey that was good enough.

"It's not going well," Nancy said. "Britney, the mother of the twins, is closer to her dad, so she is standing by him and shunning her mother for being a murderer, but their son Steven, who is close to both parents, is having a really hard time seeing his mom go to prison."

"Even though she murdered someone?" Paula asked. She looked shocked.

"I expect it's complicated when it's your mom," Violet said.

"Is it?" Paula asked. "Because it would not be that complicated for me. I mean, she murdered a man's wife so that she could have him. Then she let him think that his first wife left him while also allowing him to be the prime suspect for over thirty years for a crime *she* committed. If I was her son, I'd be very nervous about getting too close to her. She's a sociopath or a psychopath, I'm never sure which is which."

"A psychopath is a genetic condition, whereas a sociopath is caused more by environment," Ms. Cole said. "Also, psychopaths are not impulsive, whereas sociopaths are. Both have a decided lack of morality, but sociopaths are less dangerous to others than psychopaths."

They all paused to look at her, and Ms. Cole shrugged. "I'm a politician now. I have to know these things."

"Fair point. By that description, Barbara is a psychopath," Violet concluded. "Because planning to lock a woman in a hidden room and removing the door handle on the inside so she couldn't get out took some serious forethought."

Lindsey shivered. Even though she'd survived the ordeal, she didn't think she'd ever get over the powerless feeling that had caused her to curl up into a ball of despair for those bleak moments in the airless room.

"Not to mention the fact that she managed to get William Dorchester to go along with her plan," Nancy said. "That is some high-level manipulation. To think that he could have let Grace out at any time during those first few days."

"He admitted he was terrified of going to jail for kidnapping at that point," Beth said. "Or he was afraid for his life because he knew if Tim learned what he'd done, he'd rip him apart."

"I feel for Britney and Steven. They have to reconcile the loving mother and grandmother they've known for thirty years with the woman who felt she was justified in taking the life of another so that she could have the man she wanted for her husband," Mary said. "That's a lot to take in."

"Maybe," Ms. Cole said. "But whether they accept it or not, the truth is that Barbara Little is a murderer and so is William Dorchester. They have to face the consequences of their actions."

"Agreed," Lindsey said. "Emma did tell me that because

of her age and fragile mental state, Mrs. Dorchester will likely be sent to a group home to live out her days under supervision for her actions after Grace's death."

"All this time, Marion Dorchester lived with the public perception that she and her son were estranged because she refused to let him marry Grace," Violet said. "When in reality, they were estranged because she sent him away from the scene of the crime he had committed. What did she think was going to happen when she died? Did she think no one would ever find the body?"

"I imagine she thought William would inherit the house and wouldn't do anything with it, letting the body be discovered after he died," Lindsey said.

"But he needed the money from the sale of the house to pay for his mother's assisted care," Nancy said. "Which changed everything."

"That must have sent Barbara into a tizzy, because she had to be terrified that the body would be discovered," Mary said.

"Apparently, it did terrify her, and when William came to town and told her he had to sell the house, she came up with the idea of framing Marion for the murder," Lindsey said. "I spoke to Emma yesterday, and she said that Marion repeatedly thinking I was Grace gave William and Barbara the idea to shove me into the hidden room and pretend it was Marion who had done it, thus making it look like she was confused and tried to kill Grace again. They were planning to frame her anyway, but our reenactment gave them the perfect opportunity to lock it down in front of the police chief."

"What if something had gone wrong?" Violet asked. "Lindsey, you could have died."

"Thankfully, I didn't," Lindsey said. "And at least we finally discovered what happened to the runaway bride."

"It's a very sad ending to a mystery that has plagued the village for decades," Beth said. She tied off the end of the yarn in her hands and glanced into the stroller at her side to see that baby Bee slept on even through the grim discussion.

"Is it just me or was this week's book extremely on the nose for what happened to Grace Little?" Mary asked.

"It's not you," Lindsey said. "When I was looking through *The Complete Works of Edgar Allan Poe*, the volume that Grace used to tell us what happened to her, I realized it had been years since I'd read Poe, and it just felt appropriate."

"'The Cask of Amontillado' had to be a tough read for you, what with all the deep, dark, enclosed spaces in the story," Violet said. She cast Lindsey a concerned look.

"It was unsettling, for sure," Lindsey agreed. "But then all of his stories are. Poe had a spectacular insight into the dark side of human beings."

"In his eighteen forty-nine letter to Maria Clemm, he wrote, 'I was never really insane except upon occasions when my heart was touched,'" Paula said. "After what was revealed at the Dorchester mansion, I'd have to say he wasn't the only one to suffer that affliction."

"What about the odd happenings at the mansion?" Beth asked. "Did Barbara or William ever confess to trying to scare everyone by pretending to be the ghost of Grace Little?"

The others exchanged a look. They hadn't talked openly

about the strange goings-on yet, and Lindsey wasn't sure they ever would. Had the Dorchester mansion been haunted? She only knew what she had felt when she was in the hidden room.

"Did I tell you all what happened yesterday between Zelda and Heathcliff?" she asked.

Nancy and Violet glanced at her in relief, and she suspected they didn't want to talk about it either.

"No, what happened?" Nancy asked. "Has Heathcliff accepted her?"

"When Sully and I came home from work, we found them curled up in Heathcliff's dog bed together," Lindsey said. "We thought something was horribly wrong because Heathcliff didn't meet us at the door like he always does, but when we found them, we realized he couldn't get up because the cat was asleep on top of him."

"The equivalent of not being able to do anything because a cat is on your lap," Paula said.

"And everyone knows you don't move a sleeping cat," Violet added.

They shared a laugh, and the talk moved on to other things. Just before the group adjourned, Mary asked, "Did you manage to get all of the books from the Dorchester mansion?"

"We did," Lindsey said. "They are safely tucked away in our storage room."

"And I hear the lone candidate for mayor is eager to approve the installation of specialty shelving in the room designated for the books," Ms. Cole said.

"It's good to have friends in high places," Nancy teased.

"About that collection," Lindsey said. She felt the collective gaze of the crafternooners upon her. She knew that she would have their support, but it was the first time she was going to say what she'd been thinking about for the past few days, and she was nervous.

"Is there something wrong with it?" Violet asked.

"No, it's just that donations of this caliber usually have a name, and it occurred to me that since we're housing the collection in its own space, we could call it the Grace Little Rare Book Room."

"Are we voting on this?" Beth asked. "Because it's a yes from me."

"And me," Nancy said.

"Me, too," Paula said.

"Me three," Violet and Mary said together. Mary laughed and said, "Okay, me four."

Lindsey turned to Ms. Cole, who was soon to be Mayor Cole. The final decision was ultimately hers.

Ms. Cole nodded. "I think it's an excellent suggestion. The Grace Little Rare Book Room it is."

Lindsey felt a pang in her chest. Dedicating the room to Grace wouldn't bring her back, it wouldn't give her the life that was stolen from her, but it would be a remembrance of her, and that felt good and right.

Crafternoon Guide

One of my favorite tasks when writing the Library Lover's Mysteries is putting together a guide so that readers can have a starting place for their own crafternoon. Here you'll find a readers guide to P. G. Wodehouses's *The Code of the Woosters* as well as some vegetarian snack ideas and instructions to make your very own autumn leaf garland. Have fun!

Readers Guide for
The Code of the Woosters

by P. G. Wodehouse

1. Bertie Wooster and his manservant Jeeves are the pro-
    tagonists of this mystery. What is their relationship
    like? Do you think Bertie could manage without Jeeves
    and vice versa?

2. Who are "Stiffy" and "Stinker" and what do their
    nicknames reveal about them?

3. What does the silver-cow creamer have to do with the
    story?

4. The book was released in 1938. Do you think the novel
    is an accurate portrayal of life in the upper classes of
    England at the time?

5. How do you think the events of the world at the time informed the novel, particularly in the character of Roderick Spode?

6. Would you like to have your own Jeeves? *I think this might be a rhetorical question!*

7. What is the code of the Woosters?

Craft
DIY Autumn Leaf Garland

**I love this one because it can be an activity
for the book club, too!**

Leaves—lots of them!
Twine or yarn or your string of choice
Sewing needle, large
Measuring tape
Scissors
Florist tape
Florist wire
Ribbon (buffalo plaid, or whatever suits your taste)

First, get outside and collect leaves—the more colorful, the
better!

Next, measure a length of twine/yarn the desired size of the garland.

Tie a length of ribbon on one end of the twine. Thread the needle on the opposite end.

Put the needle through the center of each leaf, like stringing beads, until the desired amount of leaves are on the garland.

Tie a decorative ribbon on each end and in the middle of the string. Drape on a mantel, hang over a doorway or wherever you like.

Alternatively, you can use florist wire to wrap the stems of five leaves together and then attach them to the twine with florist tape.

Tape the bunches all along the twine. This will make for a fuller-looking garland, if you want to get fancy.

Recipes for an Autumnal Book Club

RADISH CHIPS

1 pound fresh radishes, washed
2 Tablespoons olive oil
½ teaspoon sea salt
½ teaspoon cracked black pepper

Preheat oven to 400 degrees. Thinly slice radishes (a mandolin is best) and put in a medium bowl. Toss with olive oil and salt and pepper until well coated. Place a sheet of parchment paper on a large baking sheet. Spread the radish slices out in a layer with no overlap. Bake for 14–16 minutes.

FIGS IN A BLANKET

1 package puff pastry
6 Tablespoons fig jam
1 package dried figs, 24–30 count
8-ounce brie cheese wedge
1 egg, whisked

Preheat oven to 425 degrees. Slice figs into strips. Slice brie into 2-inch slices. Lay out the puff pastry and cut it into 4-inch squares, which should make 12 squares in all. Drop ½ teaspoon of fig jam in the lower right corner, then layer on a slice of brie and 2–3 fig slices. Coat the edges of the pastry square with the egg wash. Then fold the pastry, matching the upper left corner to the lower right corner. Seal the edges of the pastry with a fork. Place on a baking sheet and lightly brush top with more egg wash. Bake for 11–13 minutes until pastry is golden brown. Serve warm.

SWEET POTATO CASSEROLE WITH PECAN STREUSEL

3 pounds sweet potatoes (3 large), peeled and cut in
*   1-inch chunks*
¼ cup butter, melted
¾ teaspoon salt
½ cup brown sugar

¼ teaspoon nutmeg
2 large eggs, slightly beaten

Preheat oven to 350 degrees. Boil sweet potato chunks in a large pot of water until soft, about 25 minutes.

While potatoes are boiling, make the topping.

¼ cup butter, softened
1 cup packed brown sugar
⅓ cup flour
1 teaspoon cinnamon
1 cup chopped pecans

Mix the butter, sugar, flour and cinnamon until it appears crumbly. Add more flour if needed. Lastly, mix in the pecans and set aside.

In a large bowl, mash the cooled and drained potatoes with a potato masher until smooth. Then add the butter, salt, sugar and nutmeg. Mix well. Then add the eggs. Spread the mixture evenly in a 2-quart baking dish. Sprinkle topping across the top. Bake 40 minutes until topping is golden brown. Serve hot.

Acknowledgments

Writing a book is a team effort, and I have the very best team in the biz. Thank you to Kate Seaver, Mary Geren, Jessica Mangicaro, Natalie Sellers, Dache' Rogers and everyone at Berkley. I feel very fortunate to have you as my publishing house. Also, I do judge a book by its cover, so I am ever grateful for the art department and cover artist Julia Green for making these books stand out. I hope the story is worthy of the spectacular art.

Thank you to everyone at the Jane Rotrosen Agency, especially my fabulous agent Christina Hogrebe. You take care of the details so I can do the fun stuff, and I appreciate that more than I can say.

Much gratitude to my squad(s). My assistant, Christie Conlee, and the Facebook group McKinlay's Mavens. Always such a fun place to hang out. My plot group buddies Kate

Carlisle and Paige Shelton, just a text away when I need them. The Jungle Red Writers, who have welcomed me into their sisterhood of daily blog posts about writing, and whatever else catches our fancy. My life is infinitely richer for having all of you in it.

Special thanks to my frat house. I couldn't do what I do without my dudes. Much love and gratitude to the best men I know—Chris Hansen Orf, Beckett Orf and Wyatt Orf. You three are my whole world.

Keep reading for an excerpt from
Jenn McKinlay's new Hat Shop Mystery . . .

FATAL FASCINATOR

Available soon from Berkley Prime Crime!

Bella, sit. Sit, Bella." She didn't sit. "Want a treat? I'll give you a treat if you sit or just aim your bottom in the general direction of the ground." I swear she smiled at me as if this had been her ploy all along.

Bella was the corgi puppy that my fiancé Harrison Wentworth and I had adopted several months ago in a case of cute-puppy-induced delirium. She wiggled her heart-shaped bottom and cocked her head to the side. I was undone by the adorableness and tossed the treat in the air. She nabbed it before it completed its arc.

"Scarlett Parker, did you just give that dog a treat when she didn't even do what you asked?"

I turned and saw my friend and neighbor, Andre Eisel, strolling down Portobello Road toward me while shaking his head. A strikingly handsome Black man with diamond ear studs that winked at me in the morning light, he was wearing jeans, a white T-shirt under a black blazer with the collar turned up, and thickly soled combat boots. He was a professional photographer, and his impeccable sense of style was enough to make me feel dowdy in my brown ankle boots, cream colored midi dress, and loose-fitting navy cardigan.

Bella recognized him immediately and simply lost her puppy mind, barking and jumping as if she never saw any affection at all, and like I habitually left her outside in the cold, chained to the gate. The little conniver.

"Bella, my love!" Andre cried. He immediately dropped into a squat and gave her all the affection her doggy heart could hold.

"Encouraging her in her histrionics is not helpful," I said.

He glanced up at me, completely unrepentant. "Where's Harrison?"

"He had to go into the office early today," I said. "So, I'm bringing Bella to Mim's Whims with me."

"Viv is going to love that," Andre said, eyebrows raised.

"Meh, she'll get over it," I said. "She won't admit it, but she secretly loves Bella."

Andre rose to his feet and fell into step beside me. It was a glorious May morning. The sun was warm, the air was cool, the birds were—Bella stopped our walk to do her business. Again.

"Here." I handed Andre the leash. He made a face while

I took out a biodegradable bag and cleaned up after my girl. I tossed it into a nearby bin, and she glanced at me over her shoulder with her little tongue hanging out of her mouth. "Who's mama's good girl?"

She wiggled and I gave her another treat, bending over to pat her soft head.

"She's going to get fat," Andre observed. He squatted down beside me and pointed to Bella's soft tummy.

"Hush," I said. I clapped my hands over her ears. "She'll hear you and you'll scar her for life."

"I would never—"

"Andre! Yoo-hoo!" Andre glanced across the street where a tall, curvy brunette stood waving. She was dressed head to toe in designer clothes, from her pink Christian Louboutin heels, to her blue silk Stella McCartney dress, to her matching pink Chanel bag.

"*Ack!* Hide me," Andre said. I glanced at his face. He wasn't joking.

"Who is she?"

"Bridus horriblus," he muttered. "Piper May, about as posh as they come. Her wedding is next month. I've been dodging her for weeks."

"But you're a photographer," I said. "Aren't wedding gigs your bread and butter while you pursue your artsy photos on the side?"

"They are, but her wedding is in the country, and I hate the country." He shuddered, emphasizing his point. Bella took this as an invitation to offer comfort, and she hopped up and licked his chin. "Also, I loathe her fiancé."

"That is problematic," I sympathized.

"Do you think if I pretend not to see her, she'll go away?" he asked.

I glanced over his shoulder. Piper May was on the move, jogging on her tiptoes and dodging pedestrians, bicycles and moms with strollers . . . er . . . prams, as the locals say, to get to Andre.

"Not a chance," I said. "That is a woman on a mission, and if you try to escape, she'll run you to the ground."

"Blast!" Andre muttered beneath his breath.

We rose to our feet, resigning ourselves to the unavoidable meeting.

"Piper, how are you?" Andre greeted the woman as she hopped up onto the sidewalk. They air-kissed each other's cheeks, and then she stepped back and narrowed her eyes.

"You've been avoiding me," she said, accusingly. She had a long waterfall of dark brown hair and thick eyebrows that had been shaped into arched accent marks that highlighted her big, brown eyes; high cheekbones; and pointy chin. She was a very attractive woman, but I wondered how much of it was dependent upon the thick coating of makeup she wore.

"I would never," Andre declared in a flagrant fib. "Nick and I have just been so busy with his vineyard in France, I haven't had a minute to myself."

This was true. Nick Carroll, Andre's life partner, had recently invested in a friend's vineyard in Provence, and when he wasn't busy with his dental practice, Nick was off tending his vines, taking Andre with him. Nick had big dreams of retiring to the south of France to pursue a second career as a vintner. Andre was dubious but kept his reservations to himself and to me. Lucky me.

"Piper May, this is my friend and neighbor Scarlett Parker, one of the proprietors of Mim's Whims."

"Hi—" I began, but Piper interrupted.

"Mim's Whims?" she cried. "Then you know Vivian Tremont."

"She's my cousin," I confirmed. "We inherited the shop from our grandmother, Mim."

"That's right," she said. She looked me over from head to foot in an assessing glance, as if trying to place me on the social food chain. "You're the American who bagged Harrison Wentworth." Before I could confirm, she wagged a pointy acrylic nail at me and continued, "The one who went viral as the 'party crasher.'"

I sighed. It seemed that neither time nor distance would allow me to leave my sordid past in the past. I mean, you have one bad day when you stumble upon the anniversary party that your boyfriend, whom you thought was single, is throwing for his wife, so you inadvertently throw some cake at him and *BAM!*—you're labeled the party crasher for life. It wasn't fair. I blamed my red hair. If I was a cool brunette like the woman standing before me, I was quite certain the video would not have gotten the three-point-two million views it had.

"Yes, that's me," I said. At least the part about bagging Harrison Wentworth, although I would argue that it was him who bagged me.

"Well, you are just the person I need," Piper said. She slid her arm through mine as if we were old friends—pushy!—and then began to walk in the direction of the shop, leaving Andre and Bella to follow.

I noted that Bella did not jump on Piper. In fact, it appeared to me that she was giving her side-eye, as if jealous that Piper had managed to take the attention of the adults away from her canine self. I could sympathize. No one likes a limelight thief.

"With what do you need help?" I asked.

"My wedding," Piper said. "Specifically, the fascinators for the bridal party."

"Isn't your wedding next month?" I asked.

"Yes," she said. Her long legs ate up the sidewalk with determined efficiency. I had to scurry to keep up. Andre was behind us, looking relieved that I was the one who was presently the focus of Piper's attention. "I'm in a fizz as my original designer, Javier Sebastian, has been embroiled in a scandal."

"Scandal?" Andre piped up from behind us.

Piper waved her free hand dismissively. "He murdered his lover by putting cyanide in his food and then fled the country with my money, all because of his little drama. I need to get this sorted right away."

"Little drama," I repeated.

I glanced over my shoulder at Andre to see if he was getting this. He raised his eyebrows and made a face that told me he was equally horrified and yet not surprised.

"Where did he even get cyanide?" I asked. "I mean it's not like you can just pick it up at the Tesco in the 'how to lose a lover' section."

Piper turned her head to look at me. She examined me from head to toe again, and I was immediately as self-conscious as a middle schooler with a pimple on the end of their nose.

"You're funny," she said. But she didn't laugh. "Vivian probably enjoys that." She didn't say it, but I felt it was implied that she did not—enjoy it, that is.

"I read an article recently that poison is easily purchased off the internet," Andre said. "We're living in very scary times."

"Indeed," Piper agreed. "Which is why I need Viv to save my wedding."

"About Viv," I said. "She usually requires months to create custom designs for weddings, so I'm not sure she'll be able to—"

"Nonsense," Piper said. "With all of the royals married off, mine is the wedding of the year. Viv will want her stamp all over it."

"Viv?" I repeated. I glanced at Piper's pointy chin, which was level with my eyes. "It sounds as if you two know each other."

"Viv and I go way back," she confirmed. She didn't elaborate, but given that Viv had never mentioned Piper to me, I assumed they were acquaintances from university. Viv and I had been less close during those years.

"So, you're friends?" I asked. I felt the need to understand what I was getting into before we stepped into the hat shop.

"Not precisely," Piper said. She kept her gaze forward as the shop came into view.

The blue-and-white-striped awning was out, and the sign on the inside of the door was flipped to OPEN. This had to be because Fiona (Fee) Fenton, Viv's assistant, had arrived early today. Viv never bothered to unlock the doors or flip the sign to OPEN.

I suspected if Fee or I didn't show up, Viv would keep the awning tucked in and the door locked all day. Viv was not what I would call a people person, which was primarily why I was feeling nervous about walking into the shop arm in arm with Piper. If Viv didn't like her, the potential for a scene was high.

"Are you enemies, then?" I persisted. I tried to pull my arm out of her grip, but she tightened her fingers, not allowing my escape.

"Not exactly," she said. She paused in front of the door and turned to face me, releasing my arm. Thank goodness. She looked thoughtful and said, "Frenemies. Viv and I are definitely what I would call frenemies."

This did not sit well with me at all. Viv didn't have frenemies. She had friends or enemies. There was no gray area in between and definitely no mash-ups.

Before I could think to move, Piper grasped the door handle and yanked it open. She strode inside as if she owned the place, and I felt Andre step up behind me.

"Now you see why I was avoiding her," he muttered. "The woman is a force."

I glanced over my shoulder at him and lifted my right eyebrow. "So is Viv. This could get ugly."

"Do you think there will be actual bloodshed?" he asked.

"Doubtful," I said. "Probably just a delicious set down. Viv isn't the violent sort."

"I do love a tasty battle of wits." He grinned.

Together we entered the shop, anticipating the drama that was about to unfold. We were woefully disappointed.

"Vivian!" Piper called. She raised her arm and gave a little finger wave.

Viv was standing on the opposite side of the shop. She was fussing with a series of mannequin heads all sporting her latest creations. Viv had been on an organza bender last month, crafting luscious, frothy confections in brilliant shades of yellow and orange, magenta and purple. It had felt like having yards and yards of a sunset swallowing up the shop, which was rather delightful, actually.

Viv turned slowly to face us. Her long blond curls reached halfway down her back, and she was wearing a formfitting blue dress that perfectly matched her large eyes. Our eyes were the only feature we shared, inherited from Mim. Viv was all creamy skin and wicked curves, while I was pale freckles and stick-straight red hair with a figure to match. Honestly, if I didn't love her like a sister, I'd be consumed with jealousy. When Viv was in a room, everyone stopped and stared, and I do mean everyone. Except Piper, apparently.

"How are you, darling?" Piper strode across the room with her arms held wide.

Bella sat down, planting her rump on my toes. Her head cocked to the side as if she, too, could not comprehend the audacity of this person who thought she could cold call Vivian Tremont—acclaimed milliner, mild eccentric, and temperamental artist—and live to tell about it.

To my shock, Viv smiled a real, genuine, teeth-showing grin and cried, "Piper!"

As if this wasn't stunning enough, the two women hugged. Hugged! Well, technically, I suppose it was an air hug. They didn't actually touch each other but sort of leaned into each other's proximity and made kissing noises in the vicinity of each other's faces.

"I'm gobsmacked," Andre said.

"Ditto," I agreed. It felt as if the planet had shifted on its axis without warning. "Viv looks genuinely happy to see her."

"And Viv is never happy to see anyone," he said.

"It's alarming," I concluded.

"What brings you by, Piper?" Viv asked. She looked her friend over, clearly approving of her cheerful spring ensemble. I knew Viv well enough to know that she was already debating what hat would best complement Piper's outfit.

"Betrayal," Piper said. She dragged out the word for full dramatic effect.

Andre and I didn't even pretend not to be listening. Piper was building her case for Viv to step in and save her wedding. I couldn't help but wonder if it would work.

"Do tell," Viv said. She gestured to the deep blue love seat and two matching armchairs arranged in the corner of the shop in front of an old wardrobe of my grandmother's. I glanced at the antique cabinet, which sported a large carved bird on the top with its wings spread out. I had dubbed him Ferd the Bird when I moved in several years ago, and while I supposed it sounded overly imaginative, I truly thought he listened to everything that was said in the shop.

Piper dropped her purse at her feet and sank down onto one of the armchairs as if she were about to collapse. High points for dramatic effect. Then she heaved a sigh that sounded as if it had come all the way up from her feet.

Bella, of course, took this as an invitation to join Piper in her chair. Only Andre's quick reflexes managed to snatch her out of the air before the pup's diving leap landed her in Piper's lap. Andre met my gaze over the head of the wiggling puppy with a look that told me I owed him one and then turned to the others and said, "Shall I fix some tea?"

"That would be lovely, Andre, thank you," Piper said.

Viv pursed her lips as if she wasn't pleased with Piper making herself quite so at home. I wandered over to the main counter in the shop and started to busy myself with rearranging a pile of invoices for materials. It felt much like pushing my broccoli around on my plate as a kid and trying to convince my parents it was actually getting eaten when it was really just doing laps. Neither Viv nor Piper paid any attention to me, so I assumed it was working.

"Tell me what's happened," Viv said.

"Javier Sebastian happened. He fled the country with the money I paid him to make my bridesmaids' fascinators," Piper said.

"Oh, dear, that's awful," Viv said. She settled into the love seat, propping her elbow on the armrest and her chin in her hand as she considered Piper's tale of woe. "I thought Javier was the most sought-after hat designer in town, no?"

I was quite certain I was not imagining the note of satisfaction in Viv's voice, and suddenly her gracious welcome of Piper made perfect sense. She knew. She knew Javier had split town. She knew Piper was in a jam. And she was enjoying every bit of the grovel show. Huh.

"Just to be perfectly clear, *I* didn't want to hire him," Piper said. "My mother insisted. You know how she is, so concerned about what everyone will think all the time. Javier was the flavor of the week after he designed Hannah Waddingham's iconic hat in the last season of *Ted Lasso*. There was simply no talking her out of him."

"The cost of life in the society pages, I suppose," Viv said. She made a sympathetic noise in the back of her throat. She didn't have me fooled one little bit, however.

"You know you're my absolute favorite milliner in the whole wide world," Piper gushed. I thought she might be putting it on a little thick there, but Viv didn't seem to mind.

"Thank you," Viv said. "I imagine the loss of the bridesmaids' hats is quite a crushing blow."

"I'll say," Piper said. "They cost seven hundred pounds

each, and I have seven bridesmaids. My father about had a fit."

Viv nodded. She was used to the expense of custom-designed millinery, but I was not. Being an American, I didn't entirely grasp the whole hat thing. Even though I'd grown up in Mim's Whims during my school holidays and summer breaks, and I appreciated the artistry that went into each one, I was still frequently caught off guard by how much a single hat could cost.

"Such a shame," Viv said. "Perhaps you can find something suitable at Harrods?"

Piper made a pained face. "Off the rack? Really, Viv, there's no need to be cruel."

A small smile curved Viv's lips. Whatever she'd been about to say was interrupted by Andre with a tea tray. Bella was not with him, so I assumed he'd left her with Fee in the workroom. I knew I should probably go and check on my baby, but I wanted to know what was going to happen between Viv and Piper. I watched from my spot at the counter while Andre served them.

"Cuppa, Scarlett?" he asked me.

"Yes, please," I said. This was all the invitation I needed to join the ladies. I took the seat next to Viv on the love seat, leaving the other armchair for Andre.

He handed me a delicate china cup of tea prepared with milk and sugar exactly as I liked it, which was a true mark of friendship in my book. I took a cautious sip. Perfection.

"Viv." Piper paused to sip her tea. She beamed her thanks at Andre. "Are you really going to make me beg?"

"Of course not," Viv said. "I would never be so hateful, especially since there is no amount of begging that could change the circumstance."

"The circumstance?" Piper repeated. "I'm sorry. I don't think I'm following."

"The simple fact is that while I know you're hoping that I can help your situation, I just don't have enough time to design and produce hats for your wedding, which is in, what, six weeks?"

"Eight weeks, at the end of June. But Viv, you have to," Piper wailed. "My wedding will be ruined without you, absolutely ruined."

I glanced at Andre. He ignored me and blew delicately on the tea in his cup. Obviously, Piper's dramatics were nothing new to him.

"Dearest, so long as you and the groom show up, I sincerely doubt your wedding could be ruined by your bridesmaids' hats, or lack thereof," Viv said.

"Oh, it'll be ruined. Whatever would people say? My mother would have an absolute episode. No, it's completely unacceptable to have a hatless bridal party. I mean, we're not savages," Piper said. She glanced at me and said, "No offense."

I sipped my tea and shot my pinky out as if that proved I wasn't a barbarian from America.

"Viv, I'll do anything," Piper wheedled. "You know, with all of the royals now married off, my wedding is to be the wedding of the year. I can't have some second-rate milliner for the bridal party. It has to be you."

"I'm sure you'll find some resourceful up-and-coming milliner willing to fill the void," Viv said. She set her cup on its saucer and placed it on the low table in front of us, indicating that the discussion was over. She looked every inch the picture of millinery royalty that she was.

Piper's face became pinched, and she looked like she was considering having a tantrum. Her face cleared as she thought better of it. Good call. Tantrums never worked on Viv; they just got customers banned for life.

"How about? Why don't you come to the wedding as our guest of honor?" Piper asked. "You could stay the entire weekend. We're getting married at Waverly Castle in Sussex, you know. Lots of hills, fields, sheep and quaint little villages. You could use it as a holiday."

I saw Andre shudder. I wondered if it was the hills, fields or sheep to which he objected.

"Andre is our photographer, and he'll be there all weekend," Piper said.

"Right. Wait . . . what? Me? I'm your photographer?" Andre asked.

Piper turned her enormous brown eyes on him and blinked once, then twice and then added a lip tremble. Andre was a goner. I'd known him for years now, and he was useless with tears, anyone's tears—child, woman, man, didn't matter. Tears hit him like a wrecking ball.

"Yes, of course. Do not tell me you're backing out, too. I mean, you promised me, Andre," Piper said.

"I did?" He looked alarmed that he might have made a promise of which he had no recall.

"Yes," she said. "When you took our engagement photos, I asked you to do the wedding and you said 'yes.'"

Andre frowned. "I did? I don't remember. That was a rather stressful day."

"I know Dooney was late and not behaving his best," Piper said. "But you know he'll show up for the wedding, and he'll be on his best behavior, I promise."

"I—" Andre began, but she interrupted him.

"I'm counting on you, Andre." She said it with the firmness of a governess disciplining a student. Andre wasn't having it.

"When we took your engagement photos, Piper, I was under the impression that the wedding would be in town," he said.

"Maybe it was. That was months ago, after all." Piper nodded thoughtfully. "No matter. I've always dreamed of being married in a castle, and Waverly Castle is stunning. My father managed to convince them to rent the entire place to us for the big day. It's going to be the grandest wedding since Will and Kate. The main staircase is the stuff of fairy tales. You're going to love taking pictures of me when I make my grand entrance."

"It sounds amazing," I said. I wondered if this was something Harry and I should consider; a big, old castle in which to tie the knot.

Harrison was an investment wizard in the financial district, and I knew if I really wanted a castle for our ceremony, he'd be game. But was a castle really who we were? Then again, he had a new business with a lot of people to impress, so maybe it was. Hmm.

"You should come, too, Scarlett," Piper said. I turned to look at her. It was like she could read my mind. "After all, Waverly Castle is the hottest spot for a society wedding, and this would give you a chance to check it out while it's in use."

"That's a brilliant idea," I said.

"No." Viv smashed my hopes to bits without even a smidgeon of remorse. "We have too much happening in town. Ascot is in mid-June and it's one of our biggest events of the year. We have so much to do before then, we simply can't take on another wedding. I really am sorry, Piper."

Her voice was full of regret, and I thought it was actually genuine.

"But my wedding is two weeks after Ascot," Piper protested. "You will absolutely need a rest after that, and the castle has a spa."

"A spa," I said. Visions of massages, facials and mud baths danced in my head.

I glanced at Viv. She was the artist, and I wouldn't push, but oh, getting away for a weekend after the flurry of Ascot would be fabulous timing.

"Having the wedding after Ascot does change things a smidge," Viv said.

"We can go together," Andre said. "It'll be fun."

He didn't sound like he thought it would be fun. He sounded like he was trying to convince us that dancing on hot coals was a great idea.

"I think Fee can handle the shop for a couple of days," I said.

"And what about Bella?" Viv asked. "Are you just going to abandon your baby at the first chance you get to go play in a castle?"

"No," I said. *Yes.* "She'll be with Harry, and she can go visit Aunt Betty and Freddy, who'll be delighted to have her."

"That's true," Andre said. "Aunt Betty dotes on Bella, as does Freddy."

I turned and glanced at Andre. He had a look of desperation in his dark brown eyes that shouted louder than words that he absolutely didn't want to have to go out to the country by himself.

"Who is Aunt Betty?" Piper asked. Then she tipped her head to the side. "Never mind, I don't care. No dogs at the wedding. Dooney is allergic."

"Of course he is," Andre muttered.

I shot him a questioning glance, which he ignored.

Aunt Betty was Harrison's aunt. She had entered her Freddy, also a corgi, in a dog show last year. In a roundabout way, that was the entire reason Harry and I had adopted Bella, whom I loved as if she were my firstborn. But even new mamas needed a break every now and again, and a spa in a castle sounded like just the ticket.

"Oh, come on, Viv, we can do it," I said. "A castle. Just think how cool that will be. Plus, it's the wedding of the year. We don't want to miss out on that publicity."

Viv couldn't care less if it was the wedding of the year.

She was an artist first and a businessperson second, whereas I was a people person first and not a businessperson at all. This was why we needed Harrison so much, to help keep the money side of things in the black.

Viv pursed her lips, considering.

"And Andre will be there," I said. "The three of us can soak up the inspiration of a nice English spring and sip boba tea while wrapped in seaweed."

Viv frowned. She enjoyed the country about as much as Andre did. Neither one of them were completely comfortable unless there was a Tube stop within walking distance.

"Isn't there a famous hat maker in East Sussex?" Andre asked. "Dominick Falco. Does that name sound familiar?"

"Sound familiar?" Viv cried. "He's one of the best milliners in England. His designs were revolutionary in the seventies. When his wife died, he packed up his studio and left London. No one knew where he went, and he doesn't design professionally anymore. I'd heard he was a recluse, but I had no idea he lived in the country. I thought he'd taken off for France or Italy."

"Nope." Andre glanced up from his phone. "It says here that he lives in the village near Waverly Castle."

Andre met my gaze and winked. Well, color me impressed. How had he thought to look for hat designers in Sussex to leverage Viv into going? Brilliant!

"We have to visit him," I said. I sensed Viv's resistance was crumbling. We just needed to hammer it in the right spot. "I'm betting he'd be thrilled to talk shop with another milliner after so many years in seclusion."

Viv bit her lip as she considered. She glanced up at Piper. "With this little time, the hats won't be ready until the wedding and, quite possibly, the very day of the wedding. You're going to have to pay a rush fee, and I will have complete artistic control. What I design is what you get, no quibbling."

"Understood." Piper sat up straight. "I'm sure I'll adore whatever you create."

"Of course you will," Viv said. She sounded bored. She reached across the table and took Piper's cup out of her hands and set it down on the tray. She then gathered the rest of our cups. She lifted the tray and headed for the workroom. "Work out the details with Scarlett. I need to think."

"Don't you want to know the color and style of my bridesmaids' dresses?" Piper asked. Her eyes went wide in alarm.

"Not necessary," Viv said. She carried the tray on one hand and waved her other hand dismissively.

"Oh, goodness, what have I done?" Piper asked. I was certain she had visions of hats that clashed with her chosen colors or were an artistic statement of Viv's that would overshadow her, the bride, on her special day.

"You're not the first bride to ask that question," Andre said.

I shot him a quelling look. This was actually why I was needed at the hat shop. I was the customer pleaser, the client liaison, the person who convinced the patron that wearing an enormous peacock on her head really was the height of fashion. Thankfully, I'd only had to do that once, and a photo of the woman had made the society pages above the fold, and she was delighted with the notoriety.

"What colors have you chosen?" I asked Piper.

"Blush," she said. "Silk with high waists, mini length, and cap sleeves."

"Sounds lovely." I nodded, stifling a yawn.

This had been the chosen color for every bride we'd designed hats for all season. I had no doubt that Viv had walked away without asking because she knew exactly what color she was going to be dealing with. She was fashion savvy like that.

"I'll let Viv and Fee know," I said. "I am positive she will create something amazing."

Piper rose to her feet. Satisfaction curved her lips in a triumphant smile. "I'm sure she will."

She strode across the room to the door, where she paused and said, "I'll be in touch."

"Cheers," Andre said through gritted teeth.

"Looking forward to it," I called and waved until the door shut after her. Then I turned to Andre and hugged him. "This is going to be so great. A castle, Andre! An actual castle."

He turned to look at me. He wasn't smiling. "There are probably spiders and rats and an angry ghost residing in the old pile of stones."

"A ghost?" I asked. "Really?"

"Scarlett, this is England. You know every place has a ghost," he said. "It's like a point of pride."

I thought about the scent of lily of the valley that occasionally appeared in the shop. Both Viv and I had come across it at various times, and it was a scent we associated with Mim, as it had been her signature perfume when she was alive. Did I think she was still here in the hat shop?

Maybe.

"So what if there's a ghost?" I asked. I was trying to cheer him up. "You'll have me and Viv to scare away any mean spirits, squash any spiders or catch any rats." That was a lie. I wasn't catching any rats or squashing any spiders, but Andre didn't need to know that. "It's going to be a wonderful adventure. You'll see."

He didn't look like he believed me. Not one little bit.